# Hollyhocks, Lambs *and* Other Passions

# Hollyhocks, Lambs *and* Other Passions

## *A Memoir of Thornhill Farm*

*by* Dee Hardie

The Johns Hopkins University Press
*Baltimore and London*

*Printed in the United States of America on acid-free paper*

*Originally published in hardcover by Atheneum Publishers, 1985*
*Johns Hopkins Paperbacks edition, 1992,*
*reprinted by arrangement with Atheneum*
*Publishers, an imprint of Macmillan Publishing Company*

*The Johns Hopkins University Press*
*701 West 40th Street*
*Baltimore, Maryland 21211-2190*
*The Johns Hopkins Press, Ltd., London*

Library of Congress Cataloging-in-Publication Data

Hardie, Dee.
Hollyhocks, lambs, and other passions : a memoir of Thornhill Farm / by Dee Hardie.
p. cm.
Reprint. Originally published: New York : Atheneum, 1985.
ISBN 0-8018-4408-8
1. Hardie, Dee. 2. Baltimore Region (Md.)—Biography.
3. Farm life—Maryland—Baltimore Region. 4. Country life—Maryland—Baltimore Region. 5. Thornhill Farm (Md.)
I. Title.
F189.B153H374 1992
975.2′6–dc20 91-42725

*For* Tom,

*and* Todd, Louise, Tommy *and* Beth

# *Preface*

BEFORE I moved to Maryland when I was twenty-eight, my life, geographically, was a patchwork quilt. Born in Rhode Island, I spent my youth in other New England states—going to the Yale Bowl with my father when I was only nine to watch some funny fellows called the Bulldogs and, years later, eating, every Saturday night, Boston baked beans made by my mother.

I went to college in northern New York State, where the Saratoga Chip was unwittingly invented by a cook who sliced his potatoes too thin, and where horse racing and ballet are now the summer pastimes. My first job was in the Big Apple, followed by jobs in London and Paris. I didn't learn how to speak French very well, but I fell in love in English—with a Marylander.

We married and lived in Paris for a year. It was intoxicating, oui, but it wasn't home sweet home, and I wanted to go home again, especially to Maryland, where I had never been. My only reference was Tom Hardie, and that was good enough for me. Maryland was my target, and I was right: I scored a bull's eye.

I came determined to become a Marylander and forever keep my place and peace. Maryland wasn't the North, and it wasn't the South. Maryland is like the middle child in a family, sometimes overlooked, but in that benign neglect, always free. And that's what I wanted—freedom, but in one place.

It wasn't, it turned out, that simple. No matter where you settle, if you weren't born there, you're an outsider. Now this isn't true in a cityscape, and probably not true in Missouri, but, in Maryland, tracing family antecedents can often be the topic of an evening's entertainment. And why not? It's fun to find out who was on first way back then.

We moved to a special pocket of Maryland, the horse country. Our children rode ponies, but Tom and I raised sheep instead, which helped blend us into the flavor—and perhaps favor—of the countryside. Looking back now, I think that was our silent declaration of independence.

My mother-in-law, Agnes, who became my best friend, wasn't much help in those early days in Maryland when I was desperately trying to transplant myself and become part of the scenery. She invariably introduced me as "my *Yankee* daughter-in-law." As for Tom's school chums, friends he had made as early as the first grade, they always introduced me as "Tom Hardie's wife." I didn't mind that introduction—in fact, I liked it and still do. Very much.

But now I have my own name. I am of Maryland. That song from the First World War that asks, "How you gonna keep 'em down on the farm after they've seen Paree?" may have a catchy lyric, but the writer, I'm sure, must never have lived in the Maryland countryside. Tin Pan Alley is a far cry from the Worthington Valley.

I am now a senior citizen, by law and perhaps by looks. That gets me into the movies, one of my passions, at a lovely lower price, but that's not my true self. Who am I then? Well I'll tell you. I am a Marylander thirty-seven years young, still holding onto the state that made me feel at home, at ease, and happy. Maryland, My Maryland! With grateful thanks.

# Introduction

THIS book was written in a Maryland farmhouse built by Quakers who hid their accumulated wealth, two sturdy brown workhorses, in the backwoods when the Yankees came through. Built in 1843 with good intentions, but hardly any architectural design, it is a simple farmhouse, half fieldstone, half wood, where we have lived for the last three decades. And it has, over these years, become the most constant ribbon of my life.

That's what this book is all about. But it is a ribbon I never expected to unfurl, a life I never expected to live. No indeed. When I graduated from college, New York City, the Big Apple, was going to be my oyster. I wanted to be Dorothy Parker.

There was a certain glamour to my first job. I was a fashion copywriter with *Vogue* where all the senior editors wore hats—even at their desks. I saw plays, visited museums. I relished the rush of city life. A year later *Vogue* sent me to London and Paris, and it became quite a different tale of two cities. I was terrified. Growing up in New England, our only long-distance family excursion had been to Niagara Falls to see where the man had gone over in a barrel. Now I was sailing to England on a Cunard ship, the *Mauretania*.

London conquered all fears, became my cup of tea. I spoke

the language, kept time by Big Ben. I fell in love with every bowler hat, every regimental tie. Too soon, although it had been six months, it was time for France.

But without the ambiance and ease of the language—my only phrase remembered from school was "*Les affaires sont les affaires*" which means "business is business"—and with the privacy the French seem to treasure, especially when it comes to outsiders, Paris was very lonely.

The time had come to do a little research. I searched frantically for the list of names scribbled on an envelope by a gallant fellow I had met at a dinner party before I left New York. But I had lost it. The only name I could remember, and well I should as a college English major, was Thomas Hardie. And the address was easy—The American Embassy, Paris.

To this day I often wonder how I had the nerve to write to a man I had never met, but I must have been that desperate, that lonely. And it worked. He promptly invited me to lunch, and we saw each other for the next two weeks. Paris began to bubble like French champagne. There was a lot of whoopee, indeed, a wonderfully heady two weeks. I was smitten. Absolutely. Then, alas, it was the middle of April, time for me to return to the New York office of *Vogue*.

My emotions went up and down like a scale. It was time to go home again, but I was intrigued by Tom. He was tall, dark, and handsome and twenty-eight years old. Just right! Three years before, he had left the *Washington Post* to work in Paris publicizing the Marshall Plan, also known as the European Recovery Plan.

In a very short time he started promoting himself—much to my delight. A few days after I had returned to New York on the *Queen Mary*, there was a letter from Tom, the beginning of our courtship by mail. For six months we wrote to each other every single day. Those letters in the airmail envelopes bound in red, white, and blue were as potent as cupid's arrows.

Tom returned to New York for a week in October 1950, took me to a Princeton football game, and gave me his grandmother's engagement ring. It was that swift, but then everything had been said by mail. Two months later in December I followed him to Paris where we were married, twice in one day, two days before Christmas.

In the morning we walked to our first marriage in the *mairie* (town hall) of the 16th *arrondissement* and in the afternoon we drove our secondhand Citroën convertible to our wedding in the small chapel of the American Cathedral on Avenue George V. We were covering all flanks, both in the eyes of the State and the Lord.

After our honeymoon (it does sound more romantic in French, *lune de miel*) in southern France, Tom went on to work for the wire services, INS, and then UP, as a foreign correspondent, while I wrote free-lance fashion articles for American newspapers, from San Francisco to Boston. My office was in our third floor apartment, once the nursery of a private home. Marie Thérèse came Monday through Friday for the equivalent of ten dollars a week, shuffled around on rags to make sure the floors stayed polished, and taught me how to make carrot soup, how to iron a Brooks Brothers shirt. When we left the rue de la Pompe a year later, it was to live over the hardware store on Main Street, in a small New Jersey town. We were following Tom's dream, we were publishing a weekly newspaper, the *Netcong–Stanhope News*, in rural America.

It was a dream that lasted a year. After our son Todd was born, Tom, the new father, realized business *was* business, and left the penurious Fourth Estate to enter his father's textile firm in Maryland. We settled in a small cottage in Baltimore County, then in 1955 we bought this house that has been forever ours.

In the last six years I've had the time and the reason to write about our world. I wanted to reach out, to stretch again. But at the same time I wanted to capture a chronicle for our family. Originally it was a monthly column for *House & Garden* magazine, and now it is a "View from Thornhill Farm" in *House Beautiful*. And with this monthly column, my own world has widened. I receive mail from people I've never met!

I love it. I love hearing from readers in Scott Depot, West Virginia, from Choctaw, Oklahoma; Brooklyn, New York; Topeka, Kansas; Bath, Maine. It amazes me, it pleases me. One woman from San Marcos, Texas, told me the last time she had written a fan letter was when she was in high school, and it was to Charlton Heston after she had seen *The Ten Commandments*. Another, from Seattle, Washington, compared me to her faithful old sweater! "Comforting," she wrote, "and warm."

It sometimes makes you wonder if you can live up to their image. But more than fans, these readers have become friends. I answer every letter, and they respond with photographs of their dogs, birth announcements, Christmas cards, recipes, and presents for our grandchildren. Bobby Dyson of Lakeside, Oregon, writes me a poem a month. When I once wrote about herbs, she answered with a lengthy epic, this the last stanza:

> *And I'll never* Rue *this verse*
> *for you,*
> *Because for me*
> *Twas some* Fennel *to do.*

These letters still surprise me, always make me happy. As I seem to touch my readers, they have touched me. More than they realize. And they ask questions—"Have you written any books?" "What are the titles of your books?" "Are you out of print? I can't find you." "*Why* don't you write a book?"

Well, here it is. And I hope they discover even more about Thornhill. By writing this book, I certainly have learned more about myself. Maybe it shows.

This is for Tom, as well. To thank him for all the ups and downs. And for our children. Without them and Thornhill, there would be no story to tell.

DEE HARDIE

*Thornhill Farm*
*September 1984*

# *Illustrations*

*Illustrations*

# Hollyhocks, Lambs *and* Other Passions

# *Chapter* One

As we came to the rise of the hill, we saw the house, a house that seemed to have been forgotten, a country remnant, a house with a past, but certainly no presence. When, I wondered, was it last loved?

It had survived, as country houses have a way of doing, but without any architectural grace to tease or invite the eye. No elegant fan of pleated wood over the front door, as I had seen in other mid-nineteenth-century houses, no touch of whimsy that could have been added by later Victorians. There were no fine bones, not even any fun.

The shingles were a sad faded gray, once probably white, and the windows, like solemn eyes, stared out at me with as much suspicion as I felt. And the roof of the small front porch sloped like the shoulders of a man who had almost, but not quite given up. It seemed a house without an ego, yet somehow there was that faint trace of pride, that occasional glimpse of honor one often finds in a derelict. Would it, I wondered, ever again have a heart?

Not that I was *that* house-proud. And I certainly wasn't accustomed to grandeur. I had grown up in modest houses, houses without vanity, without age. But they were tidy and immaculate, thanks to a Swedish mother, and they knew their place, did their job. My mother would never have understood what we were doing standing on a hill, in front of a house so frankly forlorn.

Tom hardly noticed. All he saw, and it is quite an eyeful even to this day, was a sweeping view of a wide green valley, and tucked into a hill, a small house. He made a decision. This was where he wanted to raise his family.

There must have been, as well, thoughts of that first Hardie who left Scotland in 1817 to plant his seed in Alabama, and of his son, Tom's great-grandfather, whose Mississippi River boats, sternwheelers, carried his cotton crop, and of the following generation when it all floated away down river. Everything lost. Standing on that hill, Tom saw a new family seat, surrounded by land, while I, with my peasant stock, saw only work.

The size of the property (the deed reads "59.6 acres more or less") frightened me as much as the condition of the house. How in the world do you think we can handle all that, I asked Tom, already the Grand Seigneur looking over the fields, if we can barely manage to cut the lawn on three? He never really answered, just counted his chickens, which at that point numbered two—one boy, one girl.

That Saturday morning he had been insistent. We *had* to drive out into even deeper country to see a house with acres and acres of land which Frank, best man at our wedding, had told him about over lunch. Frank had learned of the property from a law partner who lived in the country and who felt the land was in jeopardy. Rather than remain in one parcel, there were threats to divide the land four ways. To the fox hunters, this was treason. And so I, who had never mounted a horse, piled into a car with Todd, then aged two, and Louise, a babe in arms, to drive to an unknown province.

I was against it. I thought we should have stayed home and cut the grass we already owned. I thought we had a perfect nest, a Gothic cottage where we had been living a year, a house restored by someone *else.* And I liked our country life on a miniature scale, I was content. We owned three acres of America, three sheep, and we were proud of ourselves. Paris had been exotic, indeed, but it wasn't home, and certainly that New Jersey apartment over the hardware store, and growing a garden on the fire escape, was still camping out. I figured we had at last planted the flag.

Our parents were pleased that we were settled in the cottage after our gypsy beginnings, but they wondered about what they considered a remote location. Theirs was a generation, and a background, that enjoyed the sociability of a neighborhood, the everyday contact and cozy ambiance of a house next door. We simply preferred another route, as children often do.

We even hid behind the pages of *Walden* and the frock coat of Thoreau, trying to explain ourselves. We called our cottage Pumpkin Hill simply because Thoreau once wrote that he would rather be all by himself on a pumpkin than be crowded on a velvet cushion. And we thought we were clever, instantly relating to our chosen leader. Like so many of the young, we thought Thoreau could write no wrong.

I later learned that our noble Thoreau was only human. Although he liked to rough it, and wrote about it beautifully— "I had three chairs in my house; one for solitude, two for friendship, three for society"—he spent just as many afternoons sitting in a tufted armchair drinking tea in the civilized parlor of the Emersons in the close, cultural community of Concord, Massachusetts. Mrs. Emerson, I suspect, was the lure. And perhaps he would have liked our parlor as well.

Newly restored, the cottage was ready-made. The old window sills recessed wide enough in every room to hold books; there was a fireplace in our living room, dining room, even our bedroom. Outside an immense, inherited garden held row after row of pink peonies, mature enough to let me cut them every

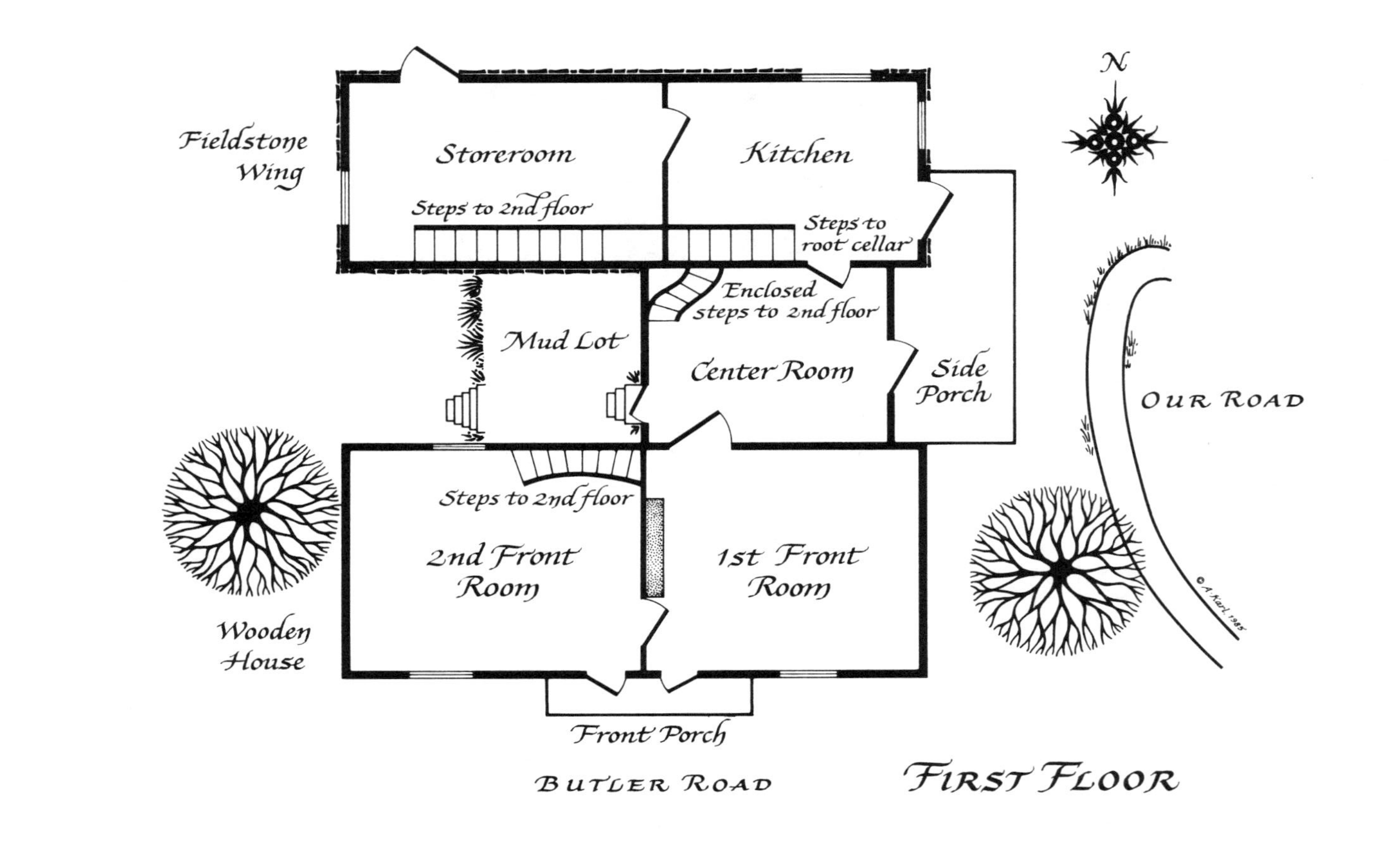
N
Fieldstone Wing
Storeroom
Kitchen
Steps to 2nd floor
Steps to root cellar
Enclosed steps to 2nd floor
Mud Lot
Center Room
Side Porch
Our Road
Steps to 2nd floor
2nd Front Room
1st Front Room
Wooden House
© A. Karl 1985
Front Porch
Butler Road
First Floor

day in June. We weren't really trying to be all that different from our parents, we just wanted to be on our own. But that spring day as Tom drove us to this old house, into deep, deep country, up a hill road rough with neglect, I began to think that he was carrying this quiet declaration of independence a bit too far. I was sure of it when I saw the house.

The face of the house, the front, was traditional. Made of shingles with lines of a simple mid-nineteenth-century farmhouse, its small front porch shaded two front doors, often a feature, strangely enough, in Maryland country architecture, with a first floor window on each side of each door. Overhead there were four second floor windows and a slanted tin roof. It looked like the kind of house you might find under the Christmas tree near the toy train. Then there was a surprise. The back half of the house was of fieldstone, the top perfectly flat without the trim of a roof line, giving the look of an early Norman tower. A low, long side porch, facing the road, tried with some courage, but not much style, to make the two halves seem as one.

We learned later that after the fieldstone wing was built in the 1930s, two brothers lived in the house, and with great animosity. Never speaking to each other, one lived in the wooden front half of the house, the other in the back stone section. And as long as this sad sibling alliance existed, the house served as a duplex.

Yet as we walked around we could see the house as a whole. Starting in the front half and walking around to the back, the house was in the shape of a backwards C—two rooms, side by side, in the front, then a center room the only middle section of the house, followed by two rooms, again side by side in the back stone wing.

The first front room we entered, the room on the right, was painted the darkest of greens. It was a color I had seen in New York apartments, late 1940s chic, and it must have made some sort of impression as it is the only color I can remember from the first floor of the house. Yet in a small boxlike room the forest green, as it was then called, made everything seem that much darker. Even the woodwork was green. (This color, I think, is in style again as I notice my younger friends using it for *their* living rooms. But now it is called Windsor green and their woodwork is white.) In that entire room, there was only the one front door, and by its side, one low window. There were treasures, however, in darkness. Surrounding the fireplace was an old pine mantelpiece, handsome and stern, almost as tall as I was. And the floor of the room was laid with random-width pine boards, certain to be the originals from the 1843 birth date.

The second front room, except for the same white pine floor, had almost nothing to say for itself. It did boast its own front door, a window next to it, a window on the opposite wall, and a very narrow enclosed stairway, perhaps more fitting for those very narrow people of the past. I have since seen an identical staircase in a painting by Charles Willson Peale, with his son Raphaelle peeking around the corner of the curve, and another son, Titian, mounting the steps, but that first day it had no such credentials or class.

After examining the two front rooms, we walked to the middle room, the hyphen between the front of the house and the back. Here we found a second stairwell to the second floor, even more hidden than the front stairway. And the only way we discovered it was by opening what we thought was a closet door. It was an enclosed staircase.

The east and west walls, facing each other, had a door each in the center. One door led to the side porch, facing the road, while the door on the opposite wall opened onto an outside platform of mud. Perhaps it had been built up with a terrace in mind, but right now it was just a vacant lot.

I suddenly saw a small walled garden. To think that perhaps I could create *something* gave me a ray of hope, stirred my dormant imagination. Protected by three outside walls of the house, the open view looked out on a meadow, trimmed by a far horizon of trees, and to the right was a huge red barn.

I must admit I felt the pangs of birth. There would be sun at least half the day, even drainage, a perfect place for a raised garden. That I had never created any kind of garden, except those well-behaved window boxes on the fire escape in New Jersey, didn't seem to enter my mind. Nor had I yet heard of Vita Sackville-West, an English author, who created in the Kent countryside room after room of gardens from an old Tudor ruin.

Good thing too as there was no comparison. I simply saw a patch of soil that was empty and asking. I saw a way to embroider some sort of charm around that old house. It could be a surprise garden, I told myself, if not a secret one, in the center of a house. It would be like a cloister with ivy and roses climbing the fieldstone wall, a very private place for private thoughts.

It was strange the way my mind was working, a flight of fancy. A small enclosed garden, completely imaginary, was certainly a peculiar way to start thinking about unraveling the more major problems and puzzles this house could present. Why didn't I add peacocks perched on the wall? Still the thought of this garden was the very *first* spark, a sudden awareness that making a house live again might be the joy of our lives. It was, without my knowing it, the beginning of a long-time seduction.

I even found myself reaching back, as if for support, from families I never knew. After all, I had a Swedish grandfather who had come to this country as a designer, not of houses, but of fabrics. Still, he must have had some sort of discerning eye, some artistic bent that might have been passed on to a hopeful descendant. And behind both of us were generations of Scandinavian farmers. Why was I so afraid of testing my heritage?

Was it because I was tired? Being a mother, quite unexpectedly, twice in two years was exciting and rewarding, but absolutely exhausting. I liked the family circle as it was—two parents, two children. And this old house, although ringed with age, was, if I ever saw one, a foundling—not even in swaddling clothes.

Even the back fieldstone wing, the later addition, had only the bare essentials. There was first the kitchen, then next to it a storeroom, both the same size. From a corner in the kitchen, steps reached down to the root cellar with a dirt floor. On the wall were shelf after shelf of empty, dusty preserve jars of every size. It was as if a family had, some time ago, given up all the pleasures received from country chores—jams and jellies, green tomato pickle, and sugared plums. It was an almost ghostly collection from the past. And I thought very sad. In the country shelves of preserves should be full and rich and juicy, winter treats after a lush, but never lazy summer.

Up again in the storeroom we discovered the fourth stairway of the house. It hugged the inner wall, and marched straight up to the second floor. Following its steps we found two second floor bedrooms with a bathroom in between. But that was it, the end of the line. We were captured in the stone tower. There was no way, on the second floor, to pass from the stone wing to the wooden house, probably the way one brother closed off his second-story life from his brother's. And so we went down the back stairs, crossed over the first floor of the house, up the narrow front stairwell to see how the other half of the house lived on the second floor.

Not much better, but far more colorfully. There were three bedrooms, and one was purple.

And that was the star of the second floor show. Who had

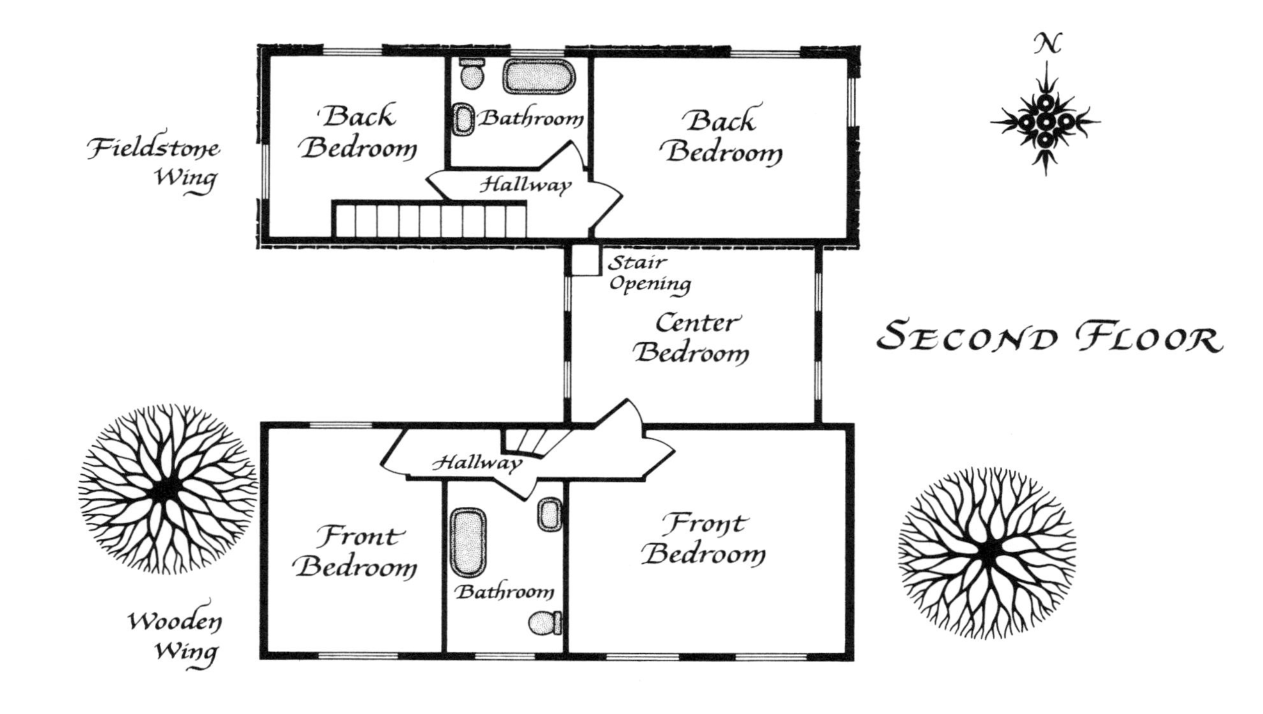
N
Second Floor
Fieldstone Wing
Back Bedroom
Bathroom
Back Bedroom
Hallway
Stair Opening
Center Bedroom
Hallway
Front Bedroom
Bathroom
Front Bedroom
Wooden Wing
Butler Road

ever seen, in 1955, a bedroom painted purple? Certainly not the Hardie family. We were much more accustomed to pansies and forget-me-nots on flowered wallpaper. I later learned that in the 1930s bedrooms *were* painted eggplant, or aubergine, as it was called by the more sophisticated, but this small front bedroom on the second floor was as vivid as a child's Easter egg.

Next to it was a bathroom with a wonderful old tub, its feet the claws of eagles. And the second front bedroom was the color of chocolate mousse. I passed quickly through. The third bedroom, the center upstairs room, was more rewarding, even more surprising. In a corner, coming up from the floor, was the stairway from below, as perky and unexpected as a chorus girl popping up from a birthday cake.

This room had the extravagance, the open delight of four windows, two facing east, two facing west. It was the only room in the house, upstairs or down, that allowed the country to come in to stay on both sides. If there were a bed in that room, I figured, every morning one would wake surrounded by the countryside—summer sheets of green, winter blankets of snow. It would be like living in a tree house, with running water just around the corner. And when the sun set early in the fall, there would be pink skies against the silhouette of trees on the ridge.

All three bedrooms opened onto a small upstairs hall. And in the ceiling of the hallway was a square opening which announced that there was indeed an attic for the inquisitive. While Tom hoisted me by the knees, I was able to pull myself into the opening. It was unfurnished, as was expected, and it had been made for midgets or squirrels, because that's where the squirrels lived. They darted frantically for cover as my head rose through the opening. And their companions in the attic, it would seem, were snakes. There wasn't any reptile action, thank heaven, while I was peeking, but there was evidence. Everywhere there were the long threads of discarded skins showing that the snakes had disrobed for the new spring season. Quite a beautiful design of nature, but I quickly asked to be let down.

We had now, I felt, completed a tour of the house. And I made sure to tell Tom of its resident population. He only laughed and said, "That's God's way," or some equally inappropriate remark to a woman terrified of snakes. He told me to rise above it, think about the house, not the inhabitants. And I did. Here we were in a ten-room house with strained relations on the second floor, that wall separating the wooden house from the stone addition. As for the attic, I just removed it from my mind. This house *was* larger than our present one, Pumpkin Hill, but its inventory was practically zero, and its itinerary was wild. If you wanted to go from the front of the second floor to the back, you had to go down and up and all around. There was no direct route. This house was a handful, I told Tom, trying to make him see the light, even without anything in it.

Two-year-old Todd thought it was just another adventure. He loved running around empty rooms, the speed of freedom in space. But then he wanted to see the Indians and their horses. Since there was a barn, there must be horses. It was that simple. And since there were woods there were, Todd told me, Indians. I'm not sure it was a complete sentence, but I got the point: an unknown tribe hiding behind the trees, watching our every move. Louise was oblivious, asleep in her father's arms.

And so we trekked down to the barn which was about ten covered wagons away. I could almost hear the neigh of the horses, the beat of the drums. I was feeling more and more like a pioneer. I felt I was going back in time. There wasn't a house in sight, just fields fenced by multiflora hedges, hills, and trees.

Once we stepped into the barn, I *knew* I was in another century. Nothing, I was convinced, had changed since it was built. And if there's anything at all to that architectural adage that less is more, this was it. It was bare and beautiful. And it had as much nobility in its simple lines as the rococo castles we had seen in France. I felt a certain peace. It was as if the Quakers were saying, if you do it right the first time around, it may go on forever. Not that they really knew, but they did know that a house didn't need to be fancy, but a barn *must* work.

*Here* were the good bones, defined lines. The ceiling was vaulted, supported by long logs, hewn by hand, one after another. And through the small slatted windows the sun flirted, making patterns of striped squares on the worn but still sturdy, heavy floor of rough beams. Like anything classic, the barn seams were well sewn, and all, everything, made by hand.

It was a Maryland bank barn, painted a proper red. Only the lightning rods were askew, like a tiara on an elderly duchess after too much champagne. The base was of stone, built into a bank of the hill, and housed the ground floor with all the animal stalls. And of course there were no horses, much to Todd's disappointment, but I was already counting sheep. The second floor, the entire huge main barn, hung over this base, a style natural to Maryland, and a tribute to country architecture.

Next we walked to the woods, but only made cursory passes because I wanted to get back to that house. Things were looking better and my native instincts were questioning my first impressions. The woods, ten acres of them, didn't have Indians either, but it was a forest of white oak, hemlock, beech, mountain laurel, and trees whose leaves were familiar from early Girl Scout days when I spent hours spattering paint around leaves tacked on white paper, small murals for proud parents. We also discovered a deep scar, a fieldstone quarry obviously the source of the stone wing.

When we came back, we stood on the front lawn again. I faced the house, Tom faced the view. I saw surgery, I saw intensive care, maybe even a heart transplant. Perhaps I was being too medical, too dramatic, perhaps my diagnosis was wrong. I needed another opinion, but I certainly wasn't going to get it from Tom. He had practically signed on the dotted line.

He was right about one thing: the view was spectacular. But even the location of the house made me wonder. It was right in the middle of a triangle, the land shaped like a piece of pie with the wedge of woods the widest spread at top. Here was this little farmhouse high on a hill. Why? Since farmers had lived here, why hadn't they built on the lower land, nearer to Butler Road, an easier access to market? Why had they made it more difficult to feed their livestock, plow out in the winter? Was it a marriage of convenience, tucking a house into a hill, the back slope giving shelter? Or was it an even earlier independence, a passion for privacy? Did we, after all, have something in common with this house?

A quick appraisal showed me there were some legacies left from the past. There were apple trees scattered about as if Johnny Appleseed had passed through on his way to Ohio. And nearer the house was an elegant pear tree, as tall as the apple trees were round. There was a chestnut tree, spreading in legendary fashion, and a majestic black locust which, I somehow knew, perhaps from those Girl Scout days, was George Washington's favorite tree. And in what must have once been a front garden, there were two forlorn rosebushes.

That, at least, was a beginning. The house had beginnings too, those simple, honest Quaker lines, and I liked the roof. It was pleated tin, painted green. The inside of the house hadn't committed any *real* sins, it just hadn't committed anything. I was beginning to sound like a mother trying to explain her child's deficiencies to a doubting teacher. All it needed was some color in its cheeks, someone to pretty it up, someone to plump up the rooms with love.

I realized too that it wasn't the house's fault, this abandoned state. It simply had been left alone for too long, its owners having moved on to another location, another job. Houses, I've since discovered, like children and the very old, and most all of us, need company, some life and love, an affectionate pat on the back every once in a while.

And as for the stone wing, there was hope. Maybe we could put a slant to the roof, soften the fieldstone walls with wisteria, hang shutters at the windows. Make it think it really belonged. I had already moved in, and I didn't even know it. Suddenly the house was becoming real to me. Perhaps I *was* beginning to think of it as another child—demanding, surprising, rewarding, sometimes disappointing. But it was going to get in shape, we were going to be proud. This foundling was going to grow up, or I was going to know why. What I didn't know was that we were going to grow with it.

# *Chapter* Two

ONCE I accepted the house, the house accepted me. It opened its arms, the rooms looked larger, it stretched my imagination. We seemed to make a bargain, a hopeful blend of my innocence and its age. Tom and I now owned two houses, and my almost daily commute was between our small cottage and our new annex, Thornhill Farm.

"*Don't* call it Thornhill," pleaded Charlie Rogers, the real estate agent. "It sounds prickly. Names like that don't sell." I wonder what he would have thought if I told him that when the land was surveyed in 1789 it was called Black Patch? I like to think it meant that everywhere there were patches of wild country blackberries. Charlie would have preferred, I'm sure, Cole Castle, certainly presumptuous but the original title given on a letter patent from the Crown in 1749, the same year George Washington was a seventeen-year-old surveyor in nearby Virginia. The day before I had spent the afternoon searching the deed books in Towson at the county courthouse. If this was to be my future, I wanted to know its past, and study the lineage of this house built in 1843.

Since 1955 it has been called Thornhill Farm. There was never any naming contest, no disputes, hardly a discussion. It was predestined. Tom's great-great-grandfather came from Thorn Hill, Scotland, and that was that.

Our neighbors to our east, fields away, call their place Northwest Farms, a name with direction, while on the other side of us sits a baronial mansion we can't see for the trees, christened God's Acres. But then to each his own. Our farm's name was Tom's tribute to a sturdy Scot, and I liked it, it meant something.

In 1816, John Hardie, then nineteen years old, left his family home, Thorn Hill on Loch Leven in Kinross Shire, and walked the twenty miles to Edinburgh. A year later he sailed to America, a voyage of nine weeks. While on board the brig he sold his only possession of worth at auction, his gold watch. By the time he was forty he was master of a cotton plantation in Alabama which he named Thornhill, perhaps out of affection, more probably out of pride. He had proven himself. Now four generations later, on a hill in Maryland, we were rebuilding a third generation Thornhill.

My mother-in-law, Mamoo, as she was known by her grandchildren, merely called it "*The* Farm," and with gusto, as if it were the only farm in the world, as if she had been invited to Mr. Jefferson's Monticello. It surprised me that she condoned our passage into deeper country, although she never truly approved of Pumpkin Hill. To her, I later discovered, it simply had no social grace. But here in a woebegone house she saw hope for her only son, her only child, and his wife, whom she always introduced as her "Yankee" daughter-in-law. What she really saw, I suspect, was land. Just like Tom. Just like Scarlett. It must have something to do with being a southerner, a hidden side of their psyche, Civil War revenge.

Agnes, as I called her ("After all I'm not your mother"), was raised in New Orleans, relished being Queen of Atlanteans at the 1910 Mardi Gras, spent endless weekends as a girl on plantations in the bayou. And although we were practically homesteading, she loved our farm.

Agnes means *lamb*, but this one was a lion. She would roar out from Baltimore in her ancient Mercedes to "*The* Farm" in twenty-eight minutes flat, while it took her more conservative husband, my father-in-law Harry, almost an hour to cover the same route. Not quite five feet tall, she became my tower of strength. While we were working on the house, she would bring us homemade vegetable soup, take Todd and Louise off for a toot at the zoo. And the first tree planted at Thornhill, perhaps the first in fifty years, was her gift, a white birch, to remind me of my native New England.

We had our times, our differences. She had supreme southern self-confidence. My sense of color startled her. She liked the conventional, the traditional, the accepted. But in six months she would be proclaiming my colors the best idea of all. And she was constantly telling me that the minute you walked into a house you knew if a lady lived there. I couldn't have cared less. "I hate oriental rugs," I told her. "You'll learn," she said. I suspect another reason Tom moved to the country was to keep us apart. Little did he know. Although our backgrounds were even more opposed than North and South, she became my best friend. And together we made the first garden at Thornhill, a long line of peonies I had transplanted from Pumpkin Hill.

The peonies were about all I *could* transplant. Charlie didn't want us to leave our Gothic cottage until it was sold. "Without the furniture, this house loses its charm," he told us. I thought he was wrong. I thought prospective buyers would like to imagine their own furniture in the rooms, cleared of our personality. But we stayed, and it turned out to be a convenience as Thornhill had a long way to go. It took us almost a year to empty one house and to rehabilitate another.

In quick order Tom found an architect, a construction crew, and Cornelius Jackson who, as the previous owners told us, "comes with the house for a dollar an hour." Neal, an elderly handyman, didn't make his fortune at Thornhill, but he did make a terrace, transforming that muddy square outside the hyphen of the house into an outdoor room.

Every day he would rattle up in his old truck, held together by great expectations and blind hope, the back loaded with fieldstone from a nearby quarry. He made the steps down from the dining room door to the terrace which he had laid with assorted sizes of flat fieldstone, fitting them all together like a jigsaw puzzle. On the open side, facing the barn, he built a stone wall to bank the terrace as well as reach three feet higher to enclose it, giving a border, a trim. On top of the wall, together we cemented flat rectangular pieces of slate, one after another, like dominoes laid in a line.

The day he finished I put pots of geraniums on the slate shelf, and a sundial. Although the interior of our house was in shambles, we had a terrace with flowers and the passing of time. Neal had given us our first complete room. A day later he returned, handing me a dozen brown eggs. It was a gift I'll never forget. I felt accepted. For many years now, the Tommy Elders have lived in Neal's house and their two Guernsey cows named Florence and Fancy supply our luxurious milk. Neal, I'm sure, would approve. In a way, his gifts have been continued.

The rest of Thornhill didn't come as easily as Neal's terrace. Our architect, Dicky Jackson, no way related to Neal, did draw a preliminary blueprint that made our ugly Maryland duckling look like a New England swan. He removed the front porch, made the second front door into a matching window, and added an exterior molding across the façade, between the first and second story, giving an amazing but modest face lift. To me it looked like the houses I knew in Massachusetts. It was far more cosmetic than structural, and it fit us fine. It was like one of those old movies I saw as a teenager when the secretary took off her glasses, undid her bun, shook her hair loose, and became a beauty.

But Agnes, our overseer, wasn't satisfied with the blueprints. And this was a woman who, moving to Baltimore thirty years earlier, discovered *her* architect when she saw him wheeling a handsome baby in a carriage. Outgoing as always, she knew nothing of reticence, Agnes started talking to the young man, discovered his profession. "Well," she said, "if you make babies like that, your houses must be all right." Rather risqué, if you ask me, for 1926. But the next Sunday when she met him at church, she knew she was going in the right direction. After seeing a few of his houses, Agnes commissioned Howard Baldwin to build 1017 Winding Way, Tom's home address from the time he was six until the day he married in Paris.

"The living room is about the size of a closet," said Agnes, scanning our blueprint. She was arranging, I'm sure, the furniture for our first dinner party. She solved it all by opening her purse, as well as her thoughts, financing twelve extra feet to the length of the living room. This made the living room twice its original size, giving an extra small room overhead. Dicky was as thrilled as we were, and went back to the drawing board. With revision, the front of the house now continued along as if it always had such a generous length, while the back roof of the new addition had that steep slant of an eighteenth-century salt-box.

Dicky, who lived even more up country in a contemporary house of his own design, saw a chance, at last, to apply some modern ways to the face of an old house. In the front of the new addition facing the view, he proposed three tall windows, ceiling to floor, each a long single pane of glass. He called them "the garden doors." Tom thought they were out of character, and drew instead a bow front with three traditional windows, twelve over twelve. Dicky's version would probably have given us a much better view, but Tom's decision gave us a window seat in the living room where we would read to our children when they were young, and a chest below that hides, even to this day, early Christmas surprises.

The only other exterior construction was to continue the side porch roof from the back door of the new addition to the existing kitchen door. This porch still shelters our woodpile and a 1930s child's kitchen cupboard, about as tall as a five year old, where I keep my garden tools. Nailed on the side of the house, under the porch roof, is a country montage of herb wreaths and relics we've found in digs around the house. The most intriguing is an angle iron. In the open space of the right angle, connecting one end to the other, is a lovely naked lady, as on a bow of a ship, her skirt the curve of a cornucopia. We often wonder *what* she supported in this house long ago.

By that first early fall, although the interior was far from finished, we could paint the outside of the house. "I'd like it to be beige," I said to Tom taking a bold stand. "Beige!" said Tom, "what kind of color is that?" I told him to look around, forget the green of summer, think of wheat fields, cornstalk in autumn. "It's the color of mushrooms," I said in desperation.

I knew beige would make the house look more of a whole, rather than in halves. Beige, after all, was the color of the fieldstone wing. And we could borrow other colors from the old stone—gray for the shutters and roof, white for the trim. But as Tom had grown up in a white house, he didn't know houses came in any other color. And so the first time we painted Thornhill it became a white house.

The only departure from tradition was the door. I insisted on red. Not a bright red, I assured Tom, but perhaps a deep ruby, or a lesser garnet. *That* was another whim from a woman's world of color, but he acquiesced. The shutters, all fifty-two of them, were painted as black as the Angus cattle in the

neighbor's field. Nor did they all match. Some we found
barn, and we paired them off. The stone wing, probably
the first time, had paneled shutters, while the wooden half h
louvered ones. They gave the windows, no longer solemn, a certain sparkle, like a woman's eyes after she's feathered her lashes with mascara. Our house was slowly putting on its Sunday clothes while we were weekend painters in overalls.

Tom did the roof, where he could see even more of the view, while Neal painted the second floor, quoting the Bible as he climbed the ladder. I was in charge of trim and easy reaches. By the time we had finished, two months later, hair prematurely streaked with White 103, we swore never to try to paint a house again. But it *was* the most beautiful white house we had ever seen, a house again with honor. I bought the largest American flag I could find at the five-and-ten and hung it from a second floor bedroom window. Flying over the red front door, it was our badge of courage, even the house seemed to stand taller, and we knew which way the wind blew.

Skirmishes in the interior went on forever. Dicky wanted to do away with the narrow stairway in the other front room which we now called the library simply because bookcases had been built along the walls. "A stairway should make an entrance into a living room," said Dicky, "like Carole Lombard," which dated us both. As for those random-width boards in the living room, he felt they should be covered up. We should start all over again, he said, and put down an entirely new floor, a floor that would be the same, even for the new growth of the living room.

I can't remember whether I ever cried in battle. Maybe tears are an older woman's weapons. I'm sure I was difficult and I do remember being very upset when a missing hammer was found plastered in a new wall. But money does talk, which immediately finished the conversation about the stairway. We simply couldn't afford to change the stairway from the library to the living room. Moreover nothing would induce me to give up those old pine floors. With Mr. Baublitz, the contractor, I drove to one lumber yard after another, finally finding enough old white Georgia pine boards to continue the floor of the living room. They may not have matched, and I admit they sometimes undulated as you walked on them, but I wanted patina more than perfection.

I saw more of Jesse Baublitz than I did of Tom. I knew more about his hobby, homing pigeons, than I did of my husband's business, textile machinery. I was living by day in one house, by night in another. One morning Mr. Baublitz found me sitting in our car, my head resting on my arms crossed on the wheel, a position I often see young farmers take on their tractors after a long day of making hay. Jesse was alarmed, he thought I had taken gas. I was merely sleeping. Two houses, two children, too much. I finally admitted that we not only were going to have a new house, we were going to have a new Hardie. And the gestation period was about the same length of time. As the house bloomed, so did I.

After hearing the news, Calvin and Paul, the carpenters, seemed to work faster. They took away the stairway in the dining room, gave us more space, added a corner cupboard. They insulated the storeroom next to the kitchen, and suddenly Todd and Louise had a playroom. Upstairs they carved a door through the stone wall so we could now walk from one end of the house to the other on the second floor. This was a major invasion as the stone wall was two feet thick. The middle bedroom, high with debris as if a bomb had fallen, now had the freedom of a second door.

Tom and I chose the larger front bedroom as ours, and here Calvin and Paul made tall cupboards, the paneled doors once the pale pine walls of a country church. Billy Elder, a neighbor, and once curator for Jacqueline Kennedy at the White House, found them for me. And we recycled more than church walls.

On the first floor in the library we fitted the windows with indoor shutters we had bought from a tobacco auctioneer in southern Maryland. Once the dark brown paint was stripped from the shutters, we discovered the wood was the color of tobacco. It was a mellow color, "taupe," I told Tom, "not beige," and we left them that way.

More shutters were hung in an opening between the living room and dining room. These were tall and elegant and might have known the sound of a butler's voice and a dinner gong. We won them at an auction in Saratoga Springs, New York, back in our newspaper days, but had never known what to do with them. They were from the ballroom of the Grand Union, a palatial resort hotel at the turn of the century, where Victor Herbert led his orchestra in the waltz, and the actress Lillian Russell led Diamond Jim Brady in other steps. The shutters that had once screened such an opulent life were now enjoying sedate retirement in a Quaker farmhouse.

Tom and I sanded the old floors ourselves, and the night before our third child, Tommy, was born we were sanding until midnight. The next morning I was in town with Agnes at the Baltimore Gas and Electric Company choosing sconces for the dining room wall. Suddenly lights began to flicker, and I knew. She called Tom, then rushed me to Johns Hopkins Hospital. Tom came in fast pursuit from his office, so fast that he was arrested for speeding. When he explained to the officer the imminent birth of a child, the officer radioed a fellow member of the force, and Tom was escorted to the hospital with a motorcade, arriving in style. So did Tommy, an hour later.

Although we hadn't even moved into Thornhill, we now had a full house. A week before we were a concise family of four, now we were a parade of six. Bringing up the rear was Mabel Cook who arrived five days after Tommy was born. From that day forward she was part Master, part Mammy, in the most affectionate sense of this southern word from the past. We had a partnership that worked. While she diapered Tommy, I papered walls.

A woman of generous size, her lap was our children's hammock. And they were thrilled that she had one brown eye, one blue one. That was magic. She was special. Around her head she wore a white turban to disguise, I'm sure, her age, her head of gray. But on her days off it was a wig of curls, church curls because that was her day to "rejoice with the Lord." During the week she sought other protection, wearing a clove of garlic, sewn in a tiny pocket of cheesecloth, around her neck to ward off evil spirits. Mabel did everything, had her Sabbath off, and a half day Thursday, and for that she was paid thirty dollars a week, the going salary thirty years ago in the country.

Tommy, *her* baby, could do no wrong. But Todd was occasionally flung a homespun epigram, "If you don't eat those prunes, you'll be as tight as Dick's hatband." Mabel continued her reign of love, and a little necessary terror, for a decade. She was with us until she admitted, "I feel right poorly," her legs giving out. I suspect she knew that her Tommy could stand on his own, although he was only ten when she left.

But that April day we moved into Thornhill, she was in full control. She looked like a huge Hawaiian queen, the kitchen her realm, the playroom her protectorate. And she refused to allow a clothes dryer to enter the house, even though there were three small children, the oldest one three years old, to keep laundered. "*My* wash faces the sun, feels the wind," she'd say. She had a point. Nothing smelled better than a big basket of her country-aired laundry—except perhaps a loaf of her homemade bread. Nor did I object at all to this domestic autonomy. We both knew our place. Mine was polishing floors.

Most of them were shiny by the time we moved in. I had discovered music to wax by. There is something very satisfying about waxing an old pine floor while listening to Frank Sinatra all by oneself. I was doing a solo on stage, I was getting in shape again.

The house was in even better shape after a long winter of work. The walls on the first floor were all painted white except for the living room which was still half forest green, half new white plaster. And all the bedrooms were embraced with the small, safe provincial patterns of colonial wallpaper. Even Dicky, our modern architect, approved my choice, and said so. I felt as if I had won a gold star. Tommy's room, one of the bedrooms in the stone wing, was more fun. Babar the Elephant pranced around the walls.

It was time to sit back and relax. We had sold Pumpkin Hill at a loss, but we had gained Thornhill Farm. By blood, sweat, and family donations, we had made a house live again. Any slight differences of point of view that may have passed between Dicky and me soon faded, healed by our evident pleasure with our work. After he finished the house, we became even better friends. And whenever we met at a country party, we always had a dance.

There still wasn't a proper lawn, the front of the house looked neat but naked without any landscaping. But it was June and the peonies we had transplanted were already established, giving baskets of old-fashioned blooms, and the two resident rosebushes were showing off. Even a hollyhock or two had volunteered to join the garden. Our tribe had increased in every possible way. Our empty house, our hollow crown, had been fulfilled.

Within two weeks we had an unexpected celebration. We were jubilant, Thornhill Farm was going to have a wedding. Our house was starting a new life, and so were Bettina and Henry, both Americans in Paris. When they cabled us to ask if Elkton, Maryland, was still *the* place for quick marriages, we wired back, "Why not Thornhill?" We found a minister, and our friend Elmo, a local lawyer, quickened the paperwork,

Mabel wore her wig, Mamoo made crab salad. And the day before the wedding I painted the entire living room oyster white, removing the dark green forever. Bettina and Henry were married at noon on June 2, 1956, in front of an old English desk at Thornhill Farm. And after lunch we threw grass seed along with pale pink rose petals.

# *Chapter* Three

LIVING on a hill suddenly went to my head, gave me lofty ideas. I was proud of Thornhill. I wanted to show off, just like the pink roses. I wanted to drop the gauntlet, challenge that old woman I had met at tea, the one who had said, when she heard we had moved in, "So you're the ones who bought that lemon." Instead I thought we had pulled out a plum, and I wanted everyone to taste the proof of Tom's pudding.

Maybe it was the country air that gave me this new courage, but more likely it was Mabel's cooking. She never once turned to what she called a receipt book, and the memory of her apple pies—always a little lemon balm tucked in—still lingers on. As for her chitlings and greens, to us they were haute cuisine. I wish now I could thank her again for those early years.

Mabel cared and gave me a certain freedom I never thought I was to have, once we moved to deep country. She gave me the chance to create, although it was usually all her idea.

"Why not give Mr. Tom a birthday party?" she said one morning. "After all, we've done in a wedding." Then she shuffled off to the kitchen to let me think, smiling all the way.

I leapt to the bait. And as three weeks after the McNulty wedding was Tom's fete day, I swung into action, sending out invitations tied with pale blue ribbons, "Announcing the birth day of Thomas G. Hardie, 35 years, 175 lbs., 6 ft. long." It was to be a surprise and I asked everyone to come as someone or something from the year 1921. I must have been going in full gear. We had only been in the house for two months, there was a new baby, and here I was giving another party. And I wasn't even from an entertaining family.

In my youth I do remember my father's clambakes when, wearing a long white butcher's apron, he gathered all of summer's delicacies in one big pot, the clams especially succulent as a friend was a clam inspector. And I still miss my mother's Saturday night baked-bean suppers. And *only* on Saturdays. Yet my father managed to start his Sunday mornings with cold bean sandwiches. But there were never any grown-up sit-down dinner parties. That wasn't their style. We lived as a small family unit and the best meal of all was Sunday night when my sister Robin and I were allowed to sit around the radio in the living room listening to Fred Allen, eating cold chicken sandwiches and my mother's homemade maple walnut ice cream.

Tom never shared my enthusiasm for baked beans, having spent three years in the Army eating K-rations. For his birthday party we went south. For days Mabel concocted Creole gumbo and other mysteries, dishes I had never known. Spoon bread was one of her specialties. We were busy. But it was a good time. Our three children were young enough to be content within their perimeters. The house, although relatively bare, was in reasonable attire.

Even the grass on the front lawn, the old and the new, rose to the occasion. It needed cutting. Tom didn't think so, he *never* thinks grass needs cutting, and I didn't want to push the issue *or* the lawn mower. The morning of the party, however, I felt something should be done. I managed to carve out, with the reluctant mower, the year of his birth—1921—right in the center of the lawn.

# *Chapter Three*

It must have been a provocative year. At least our cast of characters, our guests, made it seem so. Along with cropped heads in tidy cloches and baroque pearls languishing to the knee, we had Edith Wharton carrying her latest book, *Age of Innocence.* Edith, in real life, was a proper gent named Charles who was chairman of the English department at Johns Hopkins University. He won the prize, but he certainly had competition. One guest arrived as Vitamin D, discovered, we were told, in 1921. Then there was President Harding, even Al Jolson singing his latest hit, "April Showers." And throughout the evening lovely chiffoned Zeldas danced on the lawn.

Tom *was* surprised, a bit embarrassed by the fuss, and I, just another flapper, felt immodestly triumphant. Thornhill Farm had announced its intentions. We were going to have a good time, here on this hill. Thornhill was becoming our centerpiece. And with a little help from some friends, we proved that after all, it did indeed have a heart.

What it didn't have was much furniture. When we were married in Paris, Tom was convinced that the Russians were coming. That was 1950, and the Cold War was still chilly. He said I could buy anything as long as *I* could carry it away. You cannot flee Paris, he kept telling me, on a bicycle carrying a Louis Quatorze chair. He was sure the taxis, all driven at that time by White Russians, would be going the other way. Maybe to the Front—as they did in 1918.

Perhaps it was his way of keeping me on a newlywed's budget. Perhaps he thought he knew something I didn't know. Maybe he was a spy. Whatever his reason, his method worked and I only made one purchase—a small Empire table with delicate fluted legs and a marble top about the size of a large pizza, edged with a crown of woven brass. And when I look at it now at Thornhill, I think of Paris when we were young.

After a year we came home with what I thought was quite a bit of savoir faire, but with few worldly possessions—that one small table, a wicker trunk packed with a nest of copper pots and blue-and-white checkered china I had bought at the Marché aux Puces, plus a canvas trunk filled with our clothes. On the top of the canvas trunk I had painted, just for the fun of it, "The Dancing Hardies." It didn't turn out to be so amusing. The customs officers gave us a hard time when we tried to re-enter America, thinking we were either smugglers or just plain foolish.

As we weren't a dancing troupe, although Tom does a fine fox trot with an occasional dip, and we couldn't sit or sleep on savoir faire, our families came to our rescue. Our parents gave us additional furniture, as their own parents had done. It wasn't new furniture, just good old family retainers: a dining room table that started housekeeping with Tom's grandparents, some beds, a sofa that looks like Queen Victoria lying down, the curves of her era.

It all worked, and sat comfortably in our New Jersey apartment, and later in the small Gothic cottage. But Thornhill was stretching our inventory as well as our pocketbooks. You cannot, we found, turn a sow's ear into a silk purse without spending money. Our house was growing, and so were we. To help fill out the rooms, we attended auctions, the summer socials of the country. We ate endless hot dogs wrapped in white sandwich bread, drank homemade corn soup out of damp paper cups. By the end of August all we had to show for our attempt to translate the peal of the country auctioneers was one gold-painted ballroom chair and one rusty manure spreader.

Next I haunted Howard Street, then and still the antiques row of Baltimore. I was thrilled when I found an Italian dressing table for Louise (she was then all of two years old), a bentwood settee, and a sofa that thought it was Sheraton. I also brought home six well-shaped dining room chairs, fifteen dollars each.

I was ready, as the interior decorators say, to make a statement. The living room at Thornhill would be red, white, and blue. But when I tossed off my idea to Francophile Tom, I said the room would be "*bleu, blanc, rouge.*" When we lived in France, I felt very American, and when in Maryland, very French. Paris had such style, such elegance. Paris opened my eyes, my palate, awakened my senses. Any travel is an education, but a year in Paris is like getting a masters in the Arts. And as I had lived in France, our country neighbors thought I was different from the other girls. I *had* to play the part.

Paris conjures up all sorts of exotic ideas. Little did my country neighbors know that I cried by the Seine because I was homesick for America. I think now, at this age, I could have handled Paris with more aplomb. But then it was *I* who wanted to come home and strike up the band. At Thornhill, I decided to do just that.

I certainly didn't want to turn a Quaker farmhouse into a French *manoir*, but neither did I want ducks and geese flying across the fabrics and lampshades, a scene familiar in many Maryland homes. Nor did I want pastel portraits of each child in the dining room watching us eat. We had lived in France, after all, where paintings were of oil. Again I was showing off. Eventually we did have portraits painted of each child. And I always figured that in case of fire, after the children, the portraits would be rescued next.

I'm not sure how I came up with the color scheme for the living room. I think it started with a bolt of material I found, a red-and-white toile de Jouy. This is a French linen that is always printed with a pastoral scene, or a commemorative issue, such as Lafayette arriving in America. Ours was of a shepherdess with her flock. Since the walls were white from the wedding and I had the red-and-white toile, I decided I might as well bring in some blue.

For months I had been watching a handsome wing chair in the window of one of Baltimore's decorating firms. After six months, I became bold, decided to strike. I asked them if they didn't think it was time the chair was retired and reduced. They agreed, and I could finally afford to buy it. I covered it in dark blue with a white trim, and when our second son, Tommy, was much older, he always said the chair looked like it was wearing a sailor suit.

It was the only red, white, and blue living room around. There wasn't even one at the Flag House in Baltimore where Mary Pickersgill in 1813 made the flag that inspired our national anthem, made it so big she had to finish it in a brewery. Made it so big that everyone saw it by the dawn's early light.

Francis Scott Key may not have wanted to write a song about our living room, but I thought it was pretty grand. It made me feel particularly patriotic, although I'm sure no one else even noticed it was a tricolored room. There was a time I even asked a visiting French artist friend from New York to paint *Washington Crossing the Delaware* over the fireplace. Dinner wine goes to my head, and fortunately my friend never got his palette together.

That living room set off sparks for me. I thought I was daring using red, white, and blue, when all around me neighbors' rooms blended politely with Williamsburg creams and greens. Now when I look back on it, even with its red glare of color, that room was a safe room, even a traditional one, but I didn't realize it. Maybe I was unconsciously trying to have a ladylike living room to please my mother-in-law. I thought I was being *so* different, while I was just being *so* young. And it stayed that way until I blossomed into an extravagant English chintz when I became older and wiser, and wilder.

My mother took care of the kitchen designs, finishing brown-and-white gingham curtains while gathering gossip from Mabel. My mother and father came down from Boston often. And while my mother sewed, my father planted hundreds of tulip bulbs, helped Tom put up a white fence behind the front garden and chased, with frequency, the neighbor's wayward cattle. Those stampedes remained among his favorite stories of Thornhill.

He loved it on the farm because it reminded him of his youth. As a boy, his father had a small weekend farm on the outskirts of Fall River, Massachusetts, his hometown. And when our children were older, he gave them all sorts of ideas. One was how he collected dry manure from his father's farm to put at the bottom of his teacher's May basket that he hung on her doorknob, early in the morning, every first of May.

The best part was that all the grandparents enjoyed each other, actually liked each other's company. And when my parents drove from Boston there would be a big family reunion over the dinner table at Thornhill. And inevitably my father would quote Longfellow's "Listen, my children, and you shall hear, of the midnight ride of Paul Revere," or the one about "The boy stood on the burning deck, whence all but him had fled." These were my father's party tricks, poems learned when boys were taught to recite for their elders.

Then my father-in-law, a southern gentleman from his gentle blue eyes to the tip of his polished shoes, would bring forth, once again, his *one* northern ancestor (far off on his mother's side), who had fought at the Battle of Bunker Hill. The musket, encased with silver and brass, would be handed around. It now stands, still at attention, by the fireplace at Thornhill. Those were wonderful days.

Agnes didn't have any Yankee lore to contribute. She was completely southern, with Georgia, Kentucky, and Mississippi blood running through her veins. And her contribution to the greening and growing of Thornhill was a fringe of boxwood bushes she planted in front of the house because she *insisted* every southern farmhouse needed boxwood. "Miss Agnes," as her husband called her, had strong roots. Although she had lived in Maryland since her mid-thirties, her greatest treasure was her Georgia grandfather's calling card which not only gave his address, but a complete list of his Civil War battles. For her the South rose again when she planted those boxwood bushes at Thornhill Farm.

The boxwood survived their first winter because we covered them with burlap bags to keep them warm. And as a family we nested together. Successfully so. Even before the first thaw we realized I was pregnant again.

I was fully unprepared for our first child, and now I was on the second month of the fourth edition. But peasant that I was, I didn't see why I couldn't trip the light fantastic at a spring dance. In the middle of the party there were medical signs, physical signals that I wasn't quite right, that our family might stay the same size. Tom immediately went to the telephone to call my doctor, dear old Eppie Harrison who never remembered any of his patients' names, just called them all Mother. He simply said to Tom, "If you want another child, take her to the hospital. If you don't take her home."

Without consulting me, or telling me what Dr. Harrison had said, Tom drove me straight to Johns Hopkins Hospital where I stayed the week of Easter, while Mabel dyed the eggs, made the coconut cake shaped like a lamb. Tom always did seem to make the big decisions in our lives—first Thornhill and now the safe birth of our fourth child in months to come.

I don't think he actually began to think about boiling water, getting white sheets ready for a sudden birth, but he did decide that our primitive road, our slender thread to civilization, needed improvement. Just in case. The half-mile road up our hill was passable if you had a strong constitution and quick reflexes. It had caused comment, well deserved. And so we bowed to progress, and to the bank. Our country pebbled lane, our uneven mosaic, became a direct route, a gray macadam road.

It was such an occasion that we had our third Thornhill

party—we christened the road. We invited all those who had braved it before—the milkman, the postman, our laundry man, and other friends. One even brought a present, his broken axle.

We strung ribbons across, put up pseudo Burma Shave signs that were so clever I can't remember a one. Our most prominent lawyer, Frank, who first introduced us to Thornhill, wore a top hat. Sitting high on the back of an open convertible, he cut away at the ribbons, making a speech at every clip. And the barn, for the very first time, served as a banquet hall.

Since we had christened a road, Agnes didn't see why we couldn't get around to christening her third grandchild, Tommy. "Surely," said Agnes who never missed a Sunday of church, "you *should* have Tommy baptized before the next baby is born." Everyone, it seems, was getting nervous.

Todd and Louise had been christened as babes in arms, but Tommy was seventeen months old, walking around with abandon where angels feared to tread. And still not blessed. But then he was always different. While the other two children were towheaded blonds, his hair was shiny dark brown. His dimple, the only one in the family, was deep and irresistible.

We talked a young minister into performing the rites on the front lawn of Thornhill. I wanted, even then, continuity. Agnes, with some grace, accepted the site, but gave the service some substance, she thought, by producing a small bottle of water from the River Jordan. She and Harry had visited the Holy Land during the winter. This water was a special prize she had carried home for her grandson's christening. Moments before the service she and Mabel thought we should boil the water to insure against impurities. After all it had been a long trip, and how many wash their laundry in the River Jordan? So boil it we did—completely away. And so little Tommy, in a white suit and bare feet, was christened, quite in order, with water from the stream at Thornhill, where the watercress grows.

# *Chapter* Four

If it hadn't been for Mabel's cousin John, a quiet man with a serious hoe, our first vegetable garden would probably have been a very small plot—a patch of Bibb lettuce, a side spurt of radishes, easily sown and grown by our children, and some kale just to please my father. But even in the winter, Mabel started planting seeds in the garden of our minds. Sometimes I suspected voodoo. She didn't stick in any pins, but she certainly made her point.

"Hmmm, I wish I had put up beets last summer, even store-bought," she'd murmur while cooking dinner. And "I *miss* my cucumber relish!" Then one spring Sunday when her cousin was picking her up on her day off, she introduced us to John, a man of ancient years, but in her eyes, a likely candidate as gardener, one day a week, to Thornhill Farm. "But Miss Dee," she wanted me to know, "he doesn't fuss with flowers."

We thought it was a fine idea. We needed all the help we could get. Naturally we wanted a vegetable garden, wanted our children to see how a garden grows, wanted them to watch the magic of tiny seeds become the lacy fringe of carrot tops. But that first summer at Thornhill it wasn't possible. We were overwhelmed. We were so busy working the topsoil, we didn't have time to think of digging our roots deeper in a vegetable garden.

That second spring our vegetables came in line. With John by our side, we planted an empire on impulse, a vast agricultural spread from rutabagas to melons. Tom and I didn't know a tuber from a root, but John's garden, and it was really his, was as precise as any garden I had ever seen. Still there was a flow, a grace—the pole beans trellising over the wire fence, the flowers of the snow peas, the tender leaves of early spinach. And I'll never forget, and it has never happened again, that first melon—a slice of sweetness, a product of Thornhill Farm.

The garden, stretching like an open accordian with row after row of vegetables, was adjacent to the front lawn, and the same length. We could have been greengrocers. At either end I planted nasturtiums which grew fat and fast, giving a short chubby hedge of round green leaves and yellow blossoms. At each corner of the garden I planted columns of raspberry-colored hollyhocks, their tribe increasing as hollyhocks do, volunteering more stalks of color the following year. John, indeed, kept the larder full, but I wanted the garden to be pretty as well. And nasturtium petals are delicious in a summer salad.

Since our children were spending so much time in the vegetable garden discovering small miracles—especially the birth of that first radish, those tasty green pearls they found in pea pods and ate immediately—we decided to add even more magic. We planted a butterfly bush. More properly called buddleia, our butterfly bush by the vegetable garden was a mecca for butterflies.

And we wanted our children to be able to watch, at close hand, the butterflies and their ballet, their dance around the long, lavender flowers of this willowy bush. Not having grown up in the country ourselves, we didn't want them to take the country for granted—which we found was becoming easier to do when it was right out the door, the windows, everywhere.

They were thrilled with the butterflies. Even Tommy, hardly a year and a half, was fascinated by their flight, his little head rising in wonder at the flutter of their wings. Mabel, believing that child labor was also important, taught them how to snap beans. And for a short while, they thought it was as much fun as trying to catch butterflies.

Scattered around the outside of the wire fence, we occasionally found small carrots that the children had left to feed the wild young rabbits. I could hardly blame them. These almond-eyed rabbits were as appealing as any found in Beatrix Potter's children's books. And many a morning I'd see one sitting by the fence gazing at the lettuce the same way I look at jewelry store windows—absolutely out of reach, but oh such pleasure.

Not so pleasurable was the weeding which we shared with John. We each had our own style. John seemed to weed standing up, cultivating with a hoe, while Tom, quite erect, trimmed row after row with the tip of his shovel. I'm not sure he felt this was his role in life. But they looked like a Millet painting, while I looked like a Muslim praying—on my knees, back doubled over, head down. I was able to attack better at close range. And although pregnant, it kept me agile. We did learn to mulch more and more. We fed our family, John fed legions of country cousins, and Mabel canned up a storm, her pressure cooker never stopped hissing. It was her kitchen symphony.

The following spring our garden became smaller as John grew older. And every year it diminished, but never disappeared. We found we had to try to size up the garden, perhaps outwit it, rather than have the garden outsize us. When John finally retired, in his mid-eighties, Tom and I went into shock. Without John there was no way we could have such a generous bouquet. We gave up corn because it took up too much room, added more asparagus. The pride is still there, the joy of going out into the garden for dinner and coming back with a basket of acorn squash, soon to be baked, the center filled with sautéed spring onions, is still as rewarding. But that very first garden with John, which gave us such summer feasts and such winter banquets, has never been repeated. And its extravagance and accomplishments amaze me now. He was old, and we were young, and it worked.

## FLORENCE'S STUFFED ACORN SQUASH

- 2 whole acorn squash
- 2 cups dry whole-wheat bread cubes
- 3 tablespoons Parmesan cheese, grated
- 3 tablespoons fresh parsley, chopped
- 1 teaspoon poultry seasoning
- 6 tablespoons spring onion, chopped
- 4 tablespoons celery, chopped
- 3 tablespoons butter
- 2 eggs, beaten
- 4 tablespoons water, if needed
- Salt and pepper

Bake whole squash for 45 minutes in a 400° F. oven, or until soft. While the squash is baking, combine bread cubes, Parmesan, parsley, and seasonings. Cook onion and celery in the butter until soft. Add the eggs to bread mixture and toss lightly. Combine with the vegetables, adding water for moistness if needed. Cut squash in half and scoop out seeds. Fill squash halves with stuffing mixture. Bake stuffed squash for 20 minutes.
Serves 4

The white fence, put up by my father and Tom, divided the vegetables from the flowers. And while John cultivated our taste in eggplant, it was Mrs. Hughes who led me down the garden path, *fussed* with my flowers. "Here in the front garden, Dee, put columbine, delphinium, phlox, Shasta daisies, and a border of pansies every year. But iris, lots of sturdy iris, is what you need on that bank by the kitchen porch. And weave in some myrtle. Otherwise it will all flood away. Alongside the peonies, why not Anthony Waterer, and everyone should have a snowball bush!"

When I first met Janet, as I learned to call her, she was probably the age I am now, but I thought she was an older woman. Actually she was ageless. She was a blithe spirit who would swoop into dance if something pleased her, a wiry fighter who would banish fox hunters if she thought they were riding too near her garden. She was a woman of no nonsense who was enormous fun. And any afternoon there was the best cup of tea by her fire.

She created a world of her own in the country, different from any world I had ever met, certainly different from any other around. And I realize now she probably influenced the way I live more than anyone I know. Although not born a country woman, she was a woman of the country. I'd like to think I could sit in the same pew. But there has never again been anyone quite like Mrs. Hughes.

Her daughter Jane introduced us, and the first time I ever saw Jane was the day I was married in Paris. She and her husband Frank had taken the overnight train from Frankfurt, Germany, where he was a U.S. government official, so Frank could be Tom's best man at our wedding. Before I realized what was happening, Jane was boiling kettles of water so I could take a bath (the hot water heater was as temperamental as the French landlady) and sewing a rip she had discovered in my wedding veil. This was only an hour before I was meant to walk down an aisle. And once I met Jane's mother, a few years later in Maryland, she took just as good care of me as Jane did that memorable day in Paris. Living only about five minutes from Thornhill, she became my country docent.

She herself lived Country English, walking her dog Bogus, a Scotty, every day, knowing the right mushrooms to pick to make the best soup of all, planting the most beautiful gardens. But she was always an American Original, her primrose-yellow house as many sided as she, eight to be exact, and she called it the Octagon House, built in 1840. On the third floor, where her grandchildren slept, she had painted the ceiling in red and white stripes like a circus tent. And in other bedrooms, she managed to camouflage the thin light cords from the wall lamps by painting them the same flowered pattern as the wallpaper. Her ingenuity constantly amazed me. She wrote children's books, painted portraits of our children, thought all little boys smelled like goats, and I still read only *English* mysteries because those are the ones she preferred.

A fierce independent, she convinced her father, a Washington lawyer, when she was only fourteen that she no longer needed any formal education at Miss Madiera's. But then there were those Sunday dinners at the White House when her uncle by marriage, William Howard Taft, was in residence, which must have contributed to her many-faceted, wonderful character. And throughout her life she studied art.

When I couldn't grow hollyhocks by the top side of our red barn, after two seasons of planting seed after seed, it was Janet who agreed to help me with a mural. "A little trompe l'oeil never hurt any girl," she said as she climbed to the top of our farm wagon with her broad brush and a bucket of paint.

With leftover paint we had scavenged from her house and ours, we spent the day painting giant hollyhocks of yellow, pink, and white, with green leaves flush against the red barn. In the center of this glorious, ever-blooming garden we painted two sheep facing each other—a ram and a ewe.

Countless generations of sheep have rubbed their sides against this pair, yet they remain there still, faded but faithful. The hollyhocks as well. The barn itself has been painted at least twice again, but *never* over our mural. This one side, not protected with new layers of paint as is the rest of the barn, might some day simply fall down. But somehow I don't think Janet, wherever she is, will let it.

She may have even hastened the birth of Beth. The weekend before Beth was born we went to a party at Janet's studio, which was built over her garage. We were asked to come costumed as a painting, any masterpiece would do. Great with child I went as El Greco's *Cardinal Richelieu* in full, flowing red. Tom went as a portrait of his grandfather in his father's tail coat. And although I didn't try to keep up with the Toulouse-Lautrec dancing girls, I had a hard time maneuvering in my ecclesiastical garb. Someone suggested that I should have come as an expectant Mona Lisa which I didn't think was at all funny. At that point I didn't think anything was funny.

The following Thursday, while most of America had just finished their Thanksgiving dinner, Beth was born in time for tea at Johns Hopkins Hospital. It was November 26, 1957, and she was perfect. My sojourn in the hospital the Easter before had done the trick. Beth was our fourth child, but our first child born of Thornhill.

When Beth, or Elizabeth as she was later christened, came home from the hospital, Todd, our oldest child, was still only four. That day in Paris we never dreamed we would have four children. During our entire courtship we never even discussed children. But that day in Paris we signed a French marriage certificate with spaces to register a family of nine children. And although Tom's great-grandfather, the cotton merchant, had twelve children and adopted two more, Tom and I, with our nest of four, were very proud of ourselves. A bit unconscious perhaps, but proud. It wasn't exactly as if we had found them in the cabbage patch, but almost. Our parents, however, informed us, with some tact, that it was time to think of other things. And they personally thought they had just enough grandchildren, thank you very much.

It *was* close quarters. The highchair was a hot ticket, no one ever lingered long in the crib, and you had to learn to hold tight to your teddy bear. There was never enough time to pass one down. We had conveniently produced built-in playmates in a countryside sparse with other children. We gave each sister a brother, and gave our family an assortment of beautiful eyes. Beth's eyes stayed blue, the boys' were brown, and Louise's a lovely green. We also produced the best years of our lives.

Those years were tested, often. There was the Big Storm of '58 that blew in soon after Valentine's Day, Beth's first winter at Thornhill. I remember being thrilled that we could at last christen the Christmas toboggan. It snowed and it snowed, and sitting at Thornhill was like living in the middle of a slowly rising giant soufflé.

Once the wind stopped I matched mittens from our collection, bundled up the three older children, and Tom and I pulled them around the farm. It was good exercise for us, and exhilarating for them—their first toboggan ride. They even found a dragon. It was really our woodpile completely covered in snow, which had graduated into steps as logs had been taken to use for the fire. But to the children there was a white dragon in the garden, and winter was rosy cheeks and hot chocolate and days of white surprises.

It snowed again, blew harder. One minute the snow piles were like beaten egg whites, the next moment white waves rolled in. And the bowed branches of the elm trees with their ice-caked leaves looked like country chandeliers. It was instant theater watching changing white topiary grow around the house.

For Tom the scene was far more serious. With a snowplow attached to his tractor, he had spent endless hours trying to keep the road open. Most of it, hedged by bushes and trees, stayed reasonably clear. But at the very end, the lowest portion which is flat and unprotected, the drifts kept coming back, higher and higher. He finally had to give in to the whims and winds of winter. He came up the hill like a vanquished, exhausted warrior and announced that we were snowbound.

"Daddy's home, Daddy's home," the children cried, and then went back to making sugar cookies with Mabel. I was especially thrilled, a husband home in the afternoon, an unexpected treat. Those next two days were a pleasant interlude—cut off from the world, snug in our cocoon on Thornhill. We erased with ease the timetables of a day. Moments became civilized—sherry before lunch, time to read out loud to the children. We soon began to know each other even better.

But the moment the " 'lectric," as it is called in the country, went out on the third day, we began to know each other almost too well. We had no heat, no water, plumbing became positively primitive. Since our domestic life was ruled by electricity, we didn't even have a stove to cook on. We became a one-room family, all seven of us moving into the living room, the only room warmed by a fireplace. We slept there on couches and mattresses, cooked hot dogs in a heavy pot over the logs, consumed a great deal of peanut butter, even boiled snow over the fire for Beth's formula. She was rolled like a sausage in blankets, snug in her bassinet. And the pile of diapers grew higher and higher.

We could have escaped, evacuated by foot to the bottom of the hill, then met by a car. It could have all been planned as our telephone was miraculously still working. But Tom, laird of our lodge, and with generations of Scottish will behind him, said, "We live in the country, we stay in the country!" He was trying to prove, again, our independence, showing the world, I guess, that Thornhill could stand alone on its own snowy hill.

There were some lighter moments, however, trying to teach the children to play backgammon by candlelight, telling ghost stories by the fire. But somehow camping out inside loses its allure after the fourth day. As the electric lines sagged, so did my spirits. I can't understand why I didn't *demand* a reprieve, but as a young wife, I was a much more trusting one. And I still have to admire Tom's tenacity, if not his sense.

We were rescued, finally, by Frances, a level-headed friend who lives on level land. She had trudged up our hill through high snowdrifts to announce that the authorities had insisted that all families with children under five must leave a house if the electricity had failed, if there was no source of heat. She hadn't even telephoned, she delivered the message in person. Tom, who is as law-abiding as he is stubborn, consented to the exodus. We struggled down the hill looking like Siberian peasants, carrying the children, even the pile of diapers. (This was before paper diapers called "Pampers" and "Luvs" were conveniently found boxed in supermarkets.)

Frances drove us to the heavenly warmth of Tom's parents' home in Baltimore where life was wrapped in the white of snow, but still working. I have never been so glad to see my mother-in-law, my father-in-law, and a washing machine. I felt the exhilaration that must have throbbed through Paris when it was liberated by the Americans near the end of World War II. Only later when we were safe in the arms of suburbia did we find out that the "authorities" had been Tom's parents and our level-headed Frances. Agnes and Harry had deputized her to get us out of the house no matter what. And that she did. She told a lovely white lie, pure white as the driven snow.

We had been headstrong and foolish. We should never have stayed at Thornhill, snowbound, especially with such a young baby. And Mabel claimed she never felt warm, *really* warm, again. That was a week of youthful error which our children now think of as one of the most courageous pockets of their past. Not that they remember, but it is a family story many times told. And Beth, to this day, loves cold weather.

The children heard more stories in the winter than in the spring or the summer, or even the fall. Reading to a child on my lap not only kept me warm, it was love, a wonderful moment of close contact. And we could hug a lot. There were always Winnie the Pooh books, and every one of Beatrix Potter's. Todd especially liked *The Tale of Mr. Tod*, a fox he thought was his own.

As they grew older they collected more favorites. Todd was intrigued by any horse book and Dr. Seuss. His enjoyment of clever Dr. Seuss lasted quite some time. When he was a senior in high school he even wrote a term paper for a literary club on Dr. Seuss himself. Tommy turned more to bears, especially Paddington, who was named after a London train station, and the adventures of Otto, a world-famous giant dog, beautifully written and illustrated by our friend William Pène Du Bois who had attended our weddings in Paris. Louise soared on to *Mary Poppins*, while Beth adored *Harriet the Spy*, a charming book, a modern classic about a little girl who spies on everyone—very much like Beth at a young age.

Reading in winter was warm comfort, but if we had thought about being bound by snow, or caught, as we later were, in a web of car pools, we might not have moved to the country. I wonder. But when we decided on Thornhill, it never entered our heads to think about where our children would go to school. Tom saw country, I saw house, and neither one of us saw the ABCs, the writing on the wall. Both of us had managed to graduate from college, but somehow we had forgotten about kindergarten. Nowadays young people, when buying a house, often choose a particular location because the schools are better. We never charted such a course, or curriculum. We just followed Tom's determination. But it was I who drove those car pools, at least in the early years.

Those car pools were sometimes dictators, telling me how to divide my day, aften delightful intermissions, battlefields, or back-seat playgrounds, open books of family affairs. One year we had four children going to three schools, all emptying at three different times. But every year was different, like vintage wine. And it also depended on the blend of the children. Like other country codes, it was often a survival of the fit-

An early photo of our 1843 Quaker farmhouse, showing two front doors but not much welcome.

Thornhill today—with one red door, the house painted beige, the boxwood bushes grown so full I can't even put my arms around them anymore. But I still pat them with thanks every year that I prune them for Christmas wreaths.

Pre-Thornhill—a Sunday morning in Paris, 1951. Bettina Coffin, who was later married to Henry McNulty at Thornhill, and the new bride Hardie, directing traffic in a gendarme's kiosk on the Left Bank. While gendarmes wear capes, we were wearing identical black wool coats that we had bought for $50 apiece when we worked together at *Vogue*. We thought we were so chic!

Some of the cast from the surprise party at Thornhill celebrating Tom's birthday in 1921. There's Ned Daniels suggesting he swam the English Channel, flapper Genie Anderson, and her husband, Charles, posing as the French boxer Georges Carpentier.

An early Christmas card of Louise and Todd, a practice we try to continue to this day. Family photos. As they grew older there was often protest, and it was harder to get the group together, but *sometimes* mothers know better. And friends seem to enjoy seeing a family grow.

Love in bloom in the kitchen. Mabel with *her* baby, one-year-old Tommy, in 1957. BELOW: Mutual Admiration Society: three-year-old Beth and Mother.

As Tom says, "A horse is uncomfortable in the middle, and dangerous at both ends." But that doesn't seem to bother the Hardie family—here, in 1958, thrilled with the arrival of a gift horse, Hammersmith.

A pyramid of Hardies, circa 1963. The house is now beige, about the same color as our Welsh pony, Kelly (shown nibbling on the lawn). At one end Tommy holds his favorite pal, and at the other, the girls, in their rush to get ready for the photographer, seem to have put on each other's gingham dresses.

Our proud young shepherds with their sheep during winter lambing, our cottage industry, at Thornhill in February 1962.

test. A mother not only had to be a chauffeur, she had to be a negotiator.

Catherine, one of my first friends in the country, introduced me to the mothers of my first car pool, most of them from old country families, and for some reason I was terrified. But getting a car pool together broke down *any* barrier. And to this day, Catherine and Kitty, who became master of the hunt, are still best pals. Car pools make a bond.

Eventually I was the one to organize the schedules. I wanted to make sure our children got to school, and besides I was the only one who knew how to type. A typed schedule with telephone numbers helps, but is no guarantee. One sympathetic father once said that to organize a country car pool, you needed a General Patton with the faith of Mary Baker Eddy. But I didn't see *him* giving us any space in his Volvo. There *was* always a certain pattern—telephone calls, hurt feelings, hedging tactics, or mothers who simply vanished when the going got hot. I was prime time, as I didn't hunt. And since we lived in fox hunting country, most mothers preferred to be on a horse the days of the hunt, Tuesdays and Thursdays. Needless to say, those were my days on the road.

Every school morning at eight o'clock a small herd of station wagons would gather at a forlorn, dilapidated drummer's hotel (now a commune of shops) where salesmen of the past once took rest, or at Sam Adams's grocery store across the way. These car pools, besides being our children's chariots to education, were a common denominator, a mafia of mothers. Some mothers, having combed all their children's hair, forgot to comb their own. And at least one mother was still in her bathrobe. I plead guilty. And if a mother was really well-dressed you knew not to call her if your car broke down because she was off for the day.

My initiation to the big time was my readiness car pool. This was the interim year in school between a mother's arms and first grade. Mine was a joyous, spontaneous, swinging group of five year olds. So much so that I finally had to tape a large chart to the ceiling of the car. The chart listed their names, followed by categories—"Yelling," "Teasing," "Not Listening to Nice Mrs. Hardie," "Biting," "Misc." Those with the fewest check marks were rewarded in June.

I also kept them quiet by feeding them black or red licorice sticks. The black, I explained, I made from old tires, and the red ones came from pigs' blood. All made at midnight and hung from our four-poster bed to dry. (After all, "Rock-A-Bye Baby" is just as grim.) They loved it. The care and feeding of car pools, I discovered, could be an important factor, but bribery only got me as far as the food lasted. Then they started throwing their apple cores at stop signs. Julian always got a bull's eye.

For a few harrowing months two rambunctious young men combed the back of my head, while I was driving, for a penny each. *Anything* to keep them occupied. Wicksie and John loved describing its country texture, like "hay," they'd say, "or maybe straw." They weren't far off. I had just started streaking my mouse-brown hair. This hair care scheme worked just fine until a visiting school psychologist asked Louise what her mother did, and she said, "She has little boys combing her hair in car pools."

One particular afternoon the calm was unusual, the quiet supreme. Only when we stopped did I discover that one member of the carpool had been gagged and bound by the others. And it was *his* mother who was picking up the group for the next leg of the journey.

They all sound like ruffians, but they have grown up very well indeed. From those car pools I learned to be more tolerant of my own children and more sensitive to others. I miss those car pools, I miss the cargo.

# *Chapter* Five

THERE was already an animal kingdom in residence when we moved to Thornhill. It is the nature of the land. Fat ground hogs waddle across the road in furry balls, tiny chipmunks are cliff dwellers in the stone wall by the kitchen garden. And harmless black garden snakes keep warm in the winter in the attic, leaving for greener pastures in the spring. The squirrels live there too. We can hear them scampering about. Sometimes I see them capturing chestnuts from the front lawn. Pleased with their prizes they stand on their hind legs, arms crossed in satisfaction, their plume tails curved around little feet like the trains of operatic divas.

And every fall, as constant as the season, a doe, followed by her fawn, will cross the west field, making her way with her young to the winter cover of our ten acres of woodland. Our farmhouse also becomes a refuge. Once the wind blows cold, families of field mice spend their winter season with us. After midnight they cavort in our kitchen and feast on our crumbs.

From the very beginning of our life at Thornhill, we had enough of a menagerie, the call of the wild. And every spring the lawn was alive with rabbits. When they heard us they would freeze in position, like bookends or the childhood game of statues. We even had a barn owl who would hoot its identity long into the night. But friends thought we needed more plumage. And as house gifts, Frances and Jerry gave us two gray-and-white Toulouse geese, while Merrall, a sporting gent, presented us with a black fighting cock with tail feathers of glistening green.

With the geese Thornhill received a touch of the French countryside, a Gallic accent, but the fighting cock was definitely an old English print. Here we were novices in the country, faced with old pros. Grounded by clipped wings, the geese preened and stretched their necks, looking as if they didn't approve of us at all, and the fighting cock strutted around the barnyard as if he were a Spanish grandee being presented at court.

Tom, now considering himself a farmer, decided we should go into the more domesticated, more peaceful realm of animals. He went out and bought one purebred Hampshire ram and six grade ewes. We became, quite suddenly, shepherds of the fields, and we learned as well, *never* turn your back on a ram. Head down, that first ram would zero in on those strange animals standing tall on two feet. With a powerful whack, you knew immediately who thought he was in charge of the barnyard.

Rams are like that, completely chauvinistic. And who can blame them? They are usually surrounded by a harem. One ram can "service," as they say in the country, forty ewes. That's power, and I do hope pleasure as well. That first ram proved his "kettle," another country colloquialism, when one of the ewes gave birth to triplets—a feat that was never repeated, and one we never forgot—three little black lambs all in a row. During the first lambing season, two sets of twins were dropped, as well as two single lambs.

We were fast learning the facts of sheep life. Hampshire lambs are always born black, in time turning white, or really more gray as they grow older and their wool increases. We learned to dock their tails by putting rubber bands tightly around the tails near as possible to their small bottoms. Other shepherds used a sharp ax for this operation, but we weren't that courageous, and the rubber bands did the trick, if not as quickly. The male lambs also had to be castrated, but I left that up to Tom. None of these physical intrusions seemed to bother them. In the springtime they would all gambol in the barnyard. It was a wonderful sight, little lambs playing leap-frog, or as Tommy once said, "leap-sheep." But they were never far from their mothers, and every morning the sheep would travel in single file down to the lower pasture, one after the other. In the evening they would return in exactly the same parade.

By June an itinerant shearer would arrive to shear the older sheep before it became too hot. At a dollar a head it was a bargain, and if he were really skillful, the entire fleece would come off in one piece, like peeling an apple. The barnyard was never noisier. The sheep would baa in protest, complain, understandably so, of being nicked. Once released from the grip of the shearer, a sheep would spring up like a jack-in-the-box, then wander around slightly dazed, bleating mournfully as if disgraced by its newly naked state. The whole flock looked like collaborators, shaven and shamed, in postwar France.

I almost became part of this June ritual. When we received a notice from the University of Maryland Agricultural School that a course in sheep shearing was to be offered on four consecutive Saturdays, I could hardly wait to enroll. Tom thought it was a good idea. We were never *quite* sure when the sheep shearer was going to arrive. This would give us another freedom, the choice to shear our sheep on time.

It surprises me now that I thought I could even corral a sheep in the barnyard, much less capture it long enough to hold firm while shearing. But enroll I did. I even talked Frances, whose husband also raised sheep, into joining me in this very adult education course. I was young and confident and wanted to contribute to our country life. But I never had to find out if I could have succeeded in this task because before the first Saturday class I learned I was pregnant with Beth. I decided, for the sake of further Hardie generations, to take maternity leave from sheep shearing. Frances seemed *very* relieved.

We continued with the same sheep shearer, and we continued having the wool woven into blankets for the beds of Thornhill. All of these blankets, most of them in natural wool color, are still warming our toes. But there is one blue one because Louise asked for blue, and a bright red one just for a little spice. The rest of the wool we sold at market.

This was the same route of the lambs. Boy lambs went to market on the hoof, girl lambs stayed at home for breeding. That one ram didn't need any younger male troops around for competition. Every spring a truck would come and take them away. It was all rather traumatic. We were not raising pets, we kept telling ourselves, but a product. The farm books had to show *something*, gain or loss. Some of our flock also went the way of the local butcher. There were many more lamb patties than there were chops, but we ate well. This was reason enough to avoid becoming attached to little lambs, beguiling little lambs. It wasn't always easy.

Todd and Tommy were the shepherds, giving daily bales of hay, buckets of grain, and boyish love. The girls, Louise and Beth, weren't quite as involved yet, but always joined in the chase when the sheep decided the grass was greener on the other side of our fences, which was a frequent exercise. Later, Louise went into pigs, and Beth followed the boys into chores.

For the annual dip-in when the sheep had to be dunked in a vat of lime sulfur or nicotine sulfate to protect them from parasites found in the fields, especially summer fields, Tom and our two sons somehow managed this. But I was the one who gave them the needle. *Someone* had to do it. And I seemed the only candidate able to inject the needle when necessary. "Pass the penicillin" was my one medical phrase. Without any training I became the vet-in-residence of Thornhill Farm.

Of course we had an established veterinarian, Dr. Rosenberger, but he was often busy with more important clients, like horses, and wasn't always on call. I was *always* on call. I'd hold the needle up to the light, just as I had seen Lew Ayres do in Dr. Kildare movies, slowly drawing in the antibiotic from the tiny vial. (We kept a supply of penicillin in the refrigerator.) Then I'd rub the rump of the lamb with the palm of my hand and inject with faith and force.

It usually worked, but sheep are not all that stoic. In fact they are dumb. I've seen an old ewe scratch a leg, and proceed to sit down to die from it. It's havoc when a band of wild dogs comes through. The sheep panic. Usually these dogs are neighborhood pets who become savage when running together. After one raid, we almost gave up sheep. The county will reimburse you if the losses are reported within a certain amount of time, but dogs were always a threat. In the middle of many a night, we would hear the howl of dogs and rush to the barnyard to make sure our flock was safe.

There was nothing Dr. Hardie could do about the vicious dogs. I was better one-to-one. And the second winter our fattest ewe lamb came down with tetanus. It's a lost cause, warned our honest-to-goodness vet, but if she lives a week you've got it made, he said.

It became my mission. The lamb lay in a horse stall on a bed of hay covered with an old blanket, and every day I nursed her, talked to her. Lambs, even sick lambs, have the most beautiful brown eyes. And those eyes looked up at me with such trust. I should have known better, I was getting too involved. When it got on to the sixth day I was proud, jubilant. I thought I was making medical history in animal husbandry. I told the children, or anyone who would listen, that they were looking at the Florence Nightingale of the barnyard, the lady with the lamp and some modern penicillin. The next day the lamb died.

It was very hard to take. We had made it through more than half of the week, but I couldn't save her. There and then I took down my shingle. It was all too emotional. I obviously wasn't made of the right stuff when it came to losing little lambs. I made a decision. If a lamb couldn't stand on its own four legs, I was not going to get down on my knees to try to save a life. Somewhat heartless, perhaps, but practical.

During the winter I did help Tom and the children carry hay on the toboggan to the snowy depths of our woods. There were five lost sheep stranded there, and our portable meals were the only way they could survive. We also threw bales of hay from the barn for the deer we had seen wandering with great dignity, but obvious dismay around the snow-crusted cornfield, foraging without hope. But that is about as close as I came to the barnyard for some time. That is until Mary Sue arrived.

Mary Sue, named by the children after a popular Baltimore candy Easter egg, was born brave, although late. Ideally lambs should be dropped in January or February in Maryland and planned parenthood is indeed part of sheep breeding. Born in those early winter months, they are considered well started, and therefore strong enough to resist summer parasites. Mary Sue arrived at the end of March.

You don't have to have a mother's ears to hear the plaintive cry of a newborn lamb alone in the world. Mary Sue's mother, we soon discovered, had died in the night. But not before she had done her duty. Somehow in her weakened state she had torn the sac from her lamb and licked the phlegm from her young's nostrils. The mother died, the lamb lived, and Mary Sue became another one of our orphans.

We had raised many a motherless lamb, taking them into the kitchen, giving them bottles every three hours. Tom, in fact, had probably given more formulas in the night to lambs than he ever had to his own children. But Mary Sue was not interested in being interned in the kitchen, or demand feeding in nocturnal hours.

She liked her freedom. She also liked her bottles. Whenever. The minute she saw a human approach with a bottle she would scoot under the barnyard fence and practically knock down the bearer of protein. That's if she was ever in the barnyard. She much preferred to sit on the side porch. And our children were her delighted accomplices. When Tom and I went to bed, they would slip her into the house and give her a sheep rug, a pelt from one of her ancestors, to sleep on.

Talk about discipline—there was none. But since she was on some vague sort of feeding schedule, I had to take her with me when I left the house. She rode in many a car pool to the utter joy of the children. And once we had given up our young passengers to school, Mary Sue and I alone in the car, the expression on the faces of other motorists at stoplights was worth all the trouble.

As she grew older we tried to introduce her to the flock, her family, her *real* family. We had to cut the silver cord. She'd follow us down to the barnyard, and then we would stand on the sidelines. Soon we would turn our backs, hoping to go unnoticed, and try slowly, step by step, to sneak back to the house. Usually Mary Sue was at the back door before us.

It wasn't her fault. The flock rejected her. She would nuzzle up to the others, knowing instinctively which were the ewes and where her next meal could come from, but they kicked her away. Sheep, for all their nursery rhyme charm, are not the most altruistic of animals. Some new mothers even refuse their lambs, and if a lamb loses its mother, it is almost impossible to have another ewe adopt the foundling. Mother sheep do not have the fierce maternal love of a lioness with her cubs, or even a cat with her kittens.

The only animal on the farm who paid any attention to Mary Sue was Horatio, our Sussex spaniel, who thought she was another dog. But Mary Sue knew better. She thought she was human. She wasn't at all interested in grass, grazing was the furthest thought from her mind. Instead she preferred willow leaves and potato chips and pink rose petals. Then she discovered red tulips.

The diet obviously agreed with her, and nature does work in wondrous ways. Soon she was so fat that she couldn't crawl out from under the fence, once we managed to inveigle her into the barnyard. Unable to get out, she finally discovered grass, and someone obviously discovered her. The next spring she gave birth to a lamb. Mary Sue had gone home again.

We named the lamb Patrick. We weren't in the habit of naming our new lambs, our flock having now grown to about thirty-five, but Patrick was born in March, as was his mother, and on the saint's day. We felt like grandparents. After all, *we* had raised Mary Sue. She was going to have the responsibilities, we would have the pleasures. She then promptly reversed roles again, as she always had. She merely walked away and left us holding the babe. Try as we did to introduce her to the joys of motherhood, she rejected us all, and without any feelings of guilt, gamboled with the group in the lower pasture.

And so we had Patrick to have and to hold until he finally learned how to be sheepy. We had Patrick to rub and to love, constantly to bottle feed, and occasionally to wonder why we had ever gotten into sheep in the first place. We couldn't really blame Mary Sue for our burden. She didn't know any better. *She* had never had a mother, a model to follow. But Patrick was certainly his mother's son. He never showed any interest in the barnyard, or joining his fellow sheep. Nor was there ever any thought of sending him to market. He had become our children's friend.

# *Chapter Five*

Endearing as he was, the pattern was beginning to wear a little thin. And when I read in the newspaper that wild dogs had recently devastated the flock of sheep at the Baltimore Zoo, I saw a solution. With one telephone call, Patrick went public, the zoo had accepted our ward.

Patrick's new home was a beautifully appointed playground in the children's zoo with bins of barley and a roommate named Lambchops. Later on in the summer we saw a newspaper photograph of Mayor McKeldin and his granddaughter petting a lamb in the zoo. The last part of the caption read, ". . . and the little lamb is Patrick." I immediately went out and bought four copies of the newspaper, and pasted the photograph in each of the children's scrapbooks.

Although we have that newspaper photo to remind us of Patrick's debut into public life, we have a much more decorative souvenir of Mary Sue. We have her portrait, right on the living room wall next to Tom's great-great-grandfather who looks a bit surprised by the company he keeps. I was surprised too. "Paint a portrait of Mary Sue?" I said in amazement. But Tom was determined to establish the fact that he was "sheepy rather than horsey," as he put it. He was not going to have a series of thoroughbreds prancing or hunting around the rooms of Thornhill, those handsome paintings so often found in the houses of our neighbors. Nor could we ever have afforded them. He was going to start collecting sheep paintings, and Mary Sue was the first, painted by our neighbor Meena Rogers.

Our collection has grown. Over the pine mantelpiece is a portrait of a fine English ram dated 1774. In the corner of the painting, faint with age, are the dimensions of this prize sheep—his height, length, width across his hips, his ribs. Another of Tom's acquisitions is a primitive of a hillside of sheep, the shepherd standing woodenly in the center holding his staff. The painting, Tom was told by the gallery in Brussels, was done by a woman who was *folle*, or in English, crazy. Tom particularly likes this story and usually tells it over dinner to guests as the painting now lives in the dining room.

But you can't always trust art galleries, at least small commercial ones in Montreal. After one business trip Tom came home with a painting which he proudly announced as the work of Charles Jacque, a member of the Barbizon School in France. And it only cost $200. I was furious. I didn't even like the painting. It was too slick, too much, I thought, like calendar art—a posed barnyard of sheep.

I finally talked him into offering it to the Walters Art Gallery in Baltimore as a tax deduction. After six months of investigation and a lunch, perhaps to soften the blow, the museum director, our friend Dick Randall, told Tom his Charles Jacque was a fake. Thus ended the career of Tom Hardie, connoisseur of sheep paintings. But while it lasted, he certainly did give the walls of Thornhill some classy country art. But our favorite still is Mary Sue standing in front of our farmhouse, looking as if she has just won the best in show at the county fair.

# *Chapter* Six

OUR flock of sheep was only part of the potpourri of animal life at Thornhill. Tom wanted to try everything. Next he went into chickens. From Cornelius Jackson, the builder of our terrace, he bought twelve brown hens. With Neal's help we erected a wire enclosure attached to the barn with a ramp leading down to the interior through an open window. If the chickens had had any sense, they would have walked down the ramp to find nests of hay we had carefully prepared for them. *That's* where they should have laid their eggs, but they preferred another egg route. And collecting them was like going on an Easter-egg hunt.

There would be some brown eggs in an old tree stump, a few by the stream, occasionally one or two in the barn where they were meant to be. I don't remember ever collecting six eggs for breakfast, one for each of us. More often it was scrambled eggs with the three we felt fortunate enough to find. It was obvious we were not to be chicken farmers, and I found this a relief. I didn't like the chickens at all. The fighting cock had style, was an independent creature, but the chickens were a nuisance, always escaping from their enclosure and pawing the new ivy I was trying to plant by the stone side of the house, leaving sloppy trails of droppings everywhere. We happily gave them away. Now our brown eggs are delivered to us by Cynthia who lives down the road.

Although we didn't succeed with hens, Tom was always ready to try another experiment in country living. Pigs will be better, said Tom. Pigs are smart. And they *are* smart, according to our farm book, smarter than sheep, which wasn't much of a challenge, smarter than horses which I found surprising. (Our "farm book" is the World Book, the encyclopedia we bought for our children and where I still find answers to all my questions from A to Z.) Tom proceeded to come home with two enormous Yorkshire hogs he called the Dolly Sisters.

The Dolly Sisters, as I remember from an early movie, were blond and bouncy, American entertainers who danced across Europe. (Movies played a big part in my young education. After all, a Saturday matinee was only a dime with a Tom Mix serial included.) *Our* Dolly Sisters were white and bulbous. And they were given to Louise. As the boys were in charge of the sheep, and as Louise had shown an early interest in A. A. Milne's Piglet, she was given two of her own. Beth, because of her extreme youth, was as yet not on the farm payroll.

Our Dolly Sisters ate royally, as their predecessors did in that movie. Every night on his way home from work Tom stopped at a local restaurant to collect garbage. This was supplemented with field corn we pilfered from neighbors' fields. Those sows should have realized they were in hog heaven. And they wore rings in their noses. It wasn't to embellish their beauty, which was questionable, but to keep them from rooting, or digging, in the barnyard. They too had a strong wire enclosure to call home, but they still managed to grunt and dig their way out from under the fence. They were incorrigible, always finding an underground route.

After their last escape, I gave up. I had four children to raise, a house to restore, a life to live. My patience with the pigs was finished. I called Tom long distance in Mexico City where he was at an important business meeting. He told me later everyone was impressed with his receiving a call from his home office. What they didn't know was I called to tell him, quite simply, that the pigs had gotten out. Again! It was a strange conversation as I remember it. On my end I was talking about pigs, two bad, fat pigs, and on his end he disguised my wrath by telling me about the elasticity of rubber on waistbands of pajamas. It was comical. It was also childish, impetuous of me to even call him, but I wanted to complain at once, announce my indignation, make a protest. When Tom arrived home, the Dolly Sisters disappeared. And for months afterwards we had the luxury of home-grown bacon or scrapple for breakfast every Sunday.

Louise, who was probably about eight, was upset by our new weekend menu, and never, never ate any of it. We had tried not to become attached to our farm animals, as their fate was inevitable. But it was much easier to become close to two pigs, rather than to a flock of sheep, and the Dolly Sisters had become part of Louise's life after school. She soon discarded all animal care, not going near the barn for a while, and Mamoo, wise Mamoo, took her, instead, to afternoon ice-skating lessons at a nearby indoor rink.

One of the only animals we didn't end up eating was someone else's goat. By the light of a new moon, a goat was unloaded in our lower pasture. Of course we granted him asylum. Thornhill Farm was becoming known as the home for wayward animals. Tom named him Lagniappe, Cajun patois for "something extra," like thirteen oysters when you order a dozen in his native New Orleans.

Although smelly, definitely a male goat tendency, Lagniappe had class. He looked oriental, the ancient mandarin of the barnyard with a long beard and curved horns. A mystery character for quite some time, we eventually learned that Lagniappe had been discarded because he was thought too old for his job.

Before dropping in on us, he was kept in a field with the hunters, the high-bred horses boarding at the Upper Club. Goats, we were told, are calming influences on equine aristocrats. But someone felt Lagniappe had passed his prime. Rather than "put him down," as they say, a benevolent worker in the stables gave us that goat who lived in peace for many a year at Thornhill, his golden eyes watching the lambs come and go.

We were even given a horse, Hammersmith, named after a bus stop in outer London. He was a bay, seventeen hands high, reddish brown, and big. Tom rode him around from time to time, thinking, I'm sure, that he was leading the cavalry. He wasn't a complete novice, having ridden in the ROTC in college. But he wasn't that keen on riding, and agreed with Ian Fleming, the English writer, who once complained that "a horse is uncomfortable in the middle, and dangerous at both ends." The children, however, were thrilled to have a horse on the place. We have vintage photographs in black and white of four children joyously astride one patient horse.

When Hammersmith started eating his bridle as if it were spaghetti, we thought something must be wrong with his diet. But quite soon he leaned against a post in the barnyard and quietly slid to his death of old age. We never replaced Hammersmith, and we've never replaced the post.

But this touch, although brief, of equestrian life made me realize even more that the children should have a pony. Four children, one pony, wasn't much of a ration, but it was better than nothing. And nothing was what we had. No pony! What kind of farm were we? It was now 1962 and we had been on Thornhill for seven years. It was time. These were the little "discussions" I would have with Tom as he was trying to go to sleep at night.

"Okay, you win," said Tom. "*You* buy the pony." And I did. I had been writing a weekly column for a local newspaper on interesting Maryland women. And although the pay was lowly indeed, I had accumulated $200. I called John Merryman who always knew what was coming up at the fairground auctions. Every spring we bought heifers from him which we fattened up over the summer, then sold in the fall. "Next Friday there's a horse and pony auction," he told me, "why don't you start there?"

Tom and I went to the auction, sitting in the stands filled with experts who knew what they were doing. This was a lot different from that country auction where we bought a manure spreader. These people meant business. They'd raise a finger, then scratch their ear, and pronto they owned a horse worth thousands of dollars. After the horses came the ponies, and since I didn't really know the sign language, I lost out on the first few. Then this fat, slow, beige pony came into the ring, and John Merryman, the auctioneer for the night, looked straight at me. I felt this was it, he was giving me a signal. I started bidding nervously, and rather than raising my arm casually, I shot up from my seat as if from a cannon every time I made another bid. For $165, I became the proud owner of a Welsh pony named Kelly. Shaking with excitement, I ran to a telephone to call our children to tell them the good news.

Kelly was a joint project, although Todd, who was nine and an older and more experienced rider, probably enjoyed him the most. Welsh and wide, Kelly was fat enough to carry two children at one time, and docile enough not to know the difference. Our special adventures on Sunday afternoons were pony picnics. Some would ride, others walk to a far field where our destination was a small stone ruin we called the Indian fort. It was probably an abandoned still, but that never crossed our minds. To us it held corners of secrets, and it was spring.

With spring and summer came Kelly's own particular picnics, lots of green grass. He would often overeat, which was our fault, and then he would founder, become lame. We'd supervise his feeding a little more wisely, and Todd would hold him by the reins while he soaked his swollen feet in the stream, trying to keep Gulliver-size boots on his hooves. Kelly always recovered and our children rode him until he seemed to grow smaller and their legs grew longer, trailing along on the ground as they'd take a little trot on their old, old friend. Hanging still on pegs in the kitchen hallway are four faded-to-brown velvet riding hats which, when new, were as black and beautiful as Kelly's mane.

All these animals, visually, framed an appealing farmscape. Even more they were a vital part of the pulse of Thornhill, of growing up. They gave lessons in responsibility, lessons in love. We grieved with them, played with them. Yet they had their own world, the barnyard was their neighborhood, the fields were their boulevards.

More constant companions were our dogs, irrevocably, wonderfully intertwined with our life at Thornhill. And they came in various sizes over the years. There was Lily, an English sheepdog, who should have been called Peony because her white woolly face looked like an open blossom in June. We bought Lily from an ad in the newspaper, and we trusted her heritage. But rather than guard our sheep, she eventually began chasing them. She also invaded a neighbor's sheep pasture, an unpardonable sin. She could have been shot, the farmer had the right. And so Lily had to go—and go she did to the large, free acres of a friend's farm, without a lamb in sight. I waited for the children's tears, but they were braver than I was. They didn't want Lily to be tied, caged, or bound. They understood. I still feel that there must have been a few tears when I wasn't looking—Todd the oldest was only ten. But they also knew that another dog was on the way.

Horatio, a copper-colored Sussex spaniel, came next, right from a pet-store window as I had to find a quick replacement for Lily. Maybe public exhibition, the suspense of waiting to be wanted, might make a puppy high-strung. And spaniels, I learned, do have a reputation for being a bit nippy. Whatever, Horatio was never very friendly, which our children overlooked, and he particularly relished biting visiting blond children which I found hard explaining to terrified mothers.

Tom was especially fond of Horatio and named him after Lord Nelson and a remote, very distant kinship with British naval history. Lord Horatio Nelson's first fleet captain was Thomas Hardy, and when fatally wounded by the French, Nelson's last words were "Kiss me, Hardy." That was a lot of background for a small dog. And maybe one of the reasons he was so disagreeable. More likely it was the entrance into his established domain of two balls of fur which grew bigger every day, Tuffy and Rosie.

For pure, unadulterated, giant-sized puppy love, these two Saint Bernards plummeted into our lives. When they licked my face it was like the Pacific rolling in. If we had a chance to relax in the sun, a large furry overcast would land on our stomachs. They just wanted to be near us, always. They even thought they were lap dogs. When Tom and I sat down to read the newspaper, so did they. They covered the news. They never climbed the Matterhorn, as did their ancestors, but they tried climbing everything else. Mostly people.

It was reciprocal. We thought we were buying our children two dogs, but it was more like two furry chaises longues. The children nestled into their shoulders while reading books, stretched on them while watching television. They were our children's pillows, their pals when no one else understood, their playmates, their rugs of fur. And on a winter night, if it was especially cold, they just pulled up Rosie or Tuffy a little bit closer. I can't remember why Tuffy was called Tuffy. I guess it was as good a dog name as any, but Rosie was because, as Beth said, she had such a pink nose.

Horatio tolerated, but never joined in the fun with the Saint Bernards. They didn't care. They just flopped. And they did it magnificently—paws in front, big sad faces in between, and enormous plaintive brown eyes watching everything, waiting, longing for their pals to come home from school. The afternoon reunions were delirious joy, plumes of tails wagging ecstatically. In the evening they would sit erect by the fireplace in the living room, as regal as the lions in Trafalgar Square, happy to be at home with their family at Thornhill.

It took them awhile to conquer the second floor. Although their ancestors had been climbing the Great Saint Bernard Pass, 8,100 feet high in the Alps, since A.D. 1081 (Tommy had a book, *The New Complete Saint Bernard*, which told us everything we ever wanted to know about our dogs, past and present), they couldn't make the fifteen steps to our children's bedrooms.

Tuffy had some of the instinct for Alpine ascent. First his chin would reach up and rest on a step, then the body followed gradually. Rosie needed help. But Beth was determined that Rosie would sleep in *her* bedroom. Tuffy had already chosen Tommy's, as had Horatio, and they all slept in the same double bed. When I looked in early in the morning I'd see one boy and two dogs all fitting together like a circular jigsaw puzzle.

Beth commandeered Rosie by picking her up at bedtime, and somehow managed to struggle up those fifteen steps. She was about eight and sturdy, while Rosie was the same age in months, and limp. Every morning Beth would come down with Rosie in her arms, staggering as if she were a Scot balancing one of those gigantic poles at the Scottish Highland games.

As the dogs grew older, and steadier on their own four feet, we thought we should put them to work. We couldn't use them as sheepdogs, the traditional jobs of Border collies, because we didn't really want them to become too acquainted with the barnyard. We knew it might be dangerous. But they could, we figured, become watchdogs, guardians of Thornhill. We had never had any threats of intruders, we didn't even lock our doors, but the Saint Bernards could pose as protection. Often delivery men would drive up, see the dogs, then honk away in fear until I came to their trucks to pick up the packages. And all Tuffy and Rosie wanted to do was give them a kiss.

We had to toughen them up, and so we enrolled the Saint Bernards in an obedience class at the local armory. The instructor was an ex-Marine with the same haircut he had in boot camp twenty-five years before. And the German shepherds were the stars. They stood at attention, they followed orders. When they were told to walk in a circle, they walked in a circle. Tuffy and Rosie would merely sit or flop and watch the canine world go by. "Up, up," we pleaded, and they looked at us from the depths of their deep eyes and remained absolutely motionless. It was humiliating. Even nine-year-old Tommy, who went with me to this evening class, was embarrassed. After three weeks we gave up. We became dropouts. The Saint Bernards never did learn much discipline, but they never really misbehaved.

Louise, our most languid child, concentrated on cats. What Sister Theresa is to the poor of India, Louise was to the cats of Thornhill. She is still rather feline with those wonderful green eyes. And sometimes secretive, you don't always know what she's thinking. But when she walks, it is with grace. She has that *je ne sais quoi* which I've always admired. The cats recognized it right away.

They were meant to stay in the barn, do away with those long-tailed rodents who bore holes in the bags of feed, scattering the grain around like it was confetti. But eventually the cats all swarmed at the house and into Louise's welcoming arms. She had legions of them. One season they were all black and when we tried to count them we didn't know whether or not we were repeating ourselves. If I left my desk drawer open, I usually found a cat sleeping in for the afternoon.

We also had yellow cats, beige ones, gray and white, tiger striped. And they all had kittens. Sometimes we were surprised. Sometimes our old fathers, or so we thought, became new mothers. Henry was really Henrietta, Emile was truly Emily. Louise took it all in stride, with a regiment of white saucers filled with milk. The large wicker laundry basket was their bassinet, and when they were older, a discarded tractor tire was their playpen. Louise put it on the side porch near the kitchen, and the kittens would run the inner circle as if they were on the spiral ramp of the Guggenheim Museum.

Even I, not a cat fancier, enjoyed watching the kittens playing tag with their mothers' tails, or shadow boxing with sprigs of ivy against the stone wall. But enough is enough, I told Louise, we must share the wealth. Going out on that side porch was like going on a safari!

Since we were going on vacation, Louise did find homes for most of her kittens. But three cats and two Saint Bernards joined us on our ride to Woods Hole, Massachusetts, to catch the ferry for the island of Nantucket. This was our first big holiday together away from Thornhill.

We thought we deserved a reward. It was late August 1968 and we had spent most of the month bringing in the hay. First there was the cutting, then the raking. And once raked the fields with lines of flat hay looked like enormous louvered screens. To finish the job a monstrous green baler rumbled in, gathered up the hay, spitting it out in neat bales.

With the help of two college students, we piled the bales of hay onto our old farm wagon, pulled to the barn by Tom on his tractor. Then we filled the ground floor of the barn with the bales of hay, blocks of it. It was heavy-duty work, and we were as proud of ourselves as if we had moved the great temples of Abu Simbel. It was time to go to the beach.

We left Horatio with a neighbor, and at 6:00 A.M. we gave Tuffy and Rosie their tranquilizers, prescribed by the vet to ease the long drive. At every gas stop we were quite a hit—all those children, all the animals. Tuffy and Rosie basked in the attention, not once closing an eye.

Nine hours later as we boarded the ferry, we actually carried the dogs. The tranquilizers had at last done their job. We were told the dogs must go on an outside deck, so we all trooped to what Tom called the "pup deck," a veranda filled with dogs.

Every owner had a story, and we were all exhausted. One man from Connecticut had taken his dog's tranquilizer in the morning by mistake, and had given his dog *his* thyroid pill. What were we doing here, I wondered, discussing tall tales? I was to blame, I was the tour director. I was the ambitious mother who wanted our children to see summer in my native New England. And I must admit I was looking forward to the extravagance of lobster and the peace of the sea.

The waves came mostly from Tuffy and Rosie. They kept running away. The picket fence of the rented house was higher than any locust post on the farm, and they could clear it by a foot. And Tuffy took to leaping out the front window at three in the morning. Then they proceeded to chew up a wing chair in the living room, something they had never done at Thornhill. They were as lost and confused as I was. I realized I didn't live too well in other people's houses. I kept cleaning the house, more than I ever did at home, because it was somebody else's. Todd still has a note I put on his door. "This is a broom. This is a dust pan. This is your bedroom, not a sand pile. Clean it up immediately. The Management."

Suddenly I was tired and homesick. I missed Thornhill and its familiar ways. The house I could walk through in the dark of night and never stumble. The only place I've ever been where I knew exactly where I was, and cared to stay. I thought a holiday in New England would be wings to my past, but it made me realize, even more, that Thornhill was my heart.

# *Chapter* Seven

THE main valve of Thornhill, without question, is our kitchen. Like the head of the River Nile, it's where life starts flowing. At Christmas it explodes with excitement. When Tom cooks, it is delirious. It's our active verb, where I cook, concoct, create. It's center stage.

Even though there are tables in almost every room of the house, the kitchen table is where I wrap presents, tie bows on the baskets I've made to give with my raspberry jam, where I type during the day when I want to be alone, yet not be lonely.

When the calm of the New Year comes, I'm still in the kitchen. It's time to catch up. And that's when I take the past year of our children's lives and paste it into their scrapbooks. I have a scrapbook for each child and one for Thornhill. I tell myself I should stop, our children have come of age. But I keep on recording. Now it's mostly photographs, but these scrapbooks hold priceless documents—Todd's first blond lock from his first haircut, Beth's first-grade drawing of her parents with a caption that reads, "My mother tells me what to do and sits in the sun. My father cooks eggs, and Mabel does everything."

Along with scissors and safety pins, I think rubber cement is one of the great inventions of the world. Maybe that's why I go on pasting. I think it is more that I don't want to lose any memories. I want *everyone* to remember. And I do get a lot of satisfaction when I see our children, home on a holiday, showing themselves off to a visiting friend. Page after page of their childhood. Sometimes, some things work, even though it doesn't seem very important at the time. Like pasting on a lonely kitchen table your family all back together again.

I also weave baskets in the kitchen whenever my world gets particularly hectic. It gives a certain peace, takes a certain patience. It slows me down. I make Nantucket Lightship baskets of the smallest size, as the wooden mold for this basket, called an egg or penny basket, is the only one I own. And the finished basket just happens to fit around a jam jar.

While I weave I hear the sound of our old Seth Thomas clock. It goes like a nursery rhyme clock, tick tock, tick tock. And it is as old as a nursery rhyme as it once hung in the Cotton Exchange in New Orleans, the same cotton market Degas painted when he visited his Louisiana family in 1873. Our clock was always in my in-laws' kitchen which they never much inhabited except for breakfast and Sunday night with shredded wheat. I admired it for years, and so does our son Todd. When he looks at it with longing, I see primogeniture. But he has to wait, as we did.

Roman-numeraled, this clock has a faithful pendulum, a steady beat. And if Tom were Fred Astaire he'd probably dance to it. The clock has that kind of rhythm. But Tom's routine, rather than tapping his toes, is to wind the kitchen clock every Sunday, as his father did before him. It's one way we start our week, one way we continue our life with traditions. It gives a certain continuity, but every once in a while you have to bring in some new spice. Never get in a rut, is what Tom remembers his mother telling him most.

He seems to follow her dictum. When he told me that he was going to have a portrait painted of our Mary Sue, our adopted lamb, I thought at first he was foolish, carrying his sheep herding a bit too far. But when I told him, more recently, that I was going to have a watercolor done of our kitchen, he never questioned me.

I really wanted the rooms of Thornhill done as a series, a portfolio we would always have. I had seen the work of a young neighbor, David Brewster, who had been painting the countryside of Maryland with clarity and grace, and a touch of Wyeth. Others had asked him to paint the facades of their farmhouses, but I wanted interiors. David was enthusiastic, but as he had so many commissions, he only had time to paint one room before leaving to study in France. I chose, above all other rooms of Thornhill, the kitchen. And now on a wall of the kitchen is a charming watercolor which David titled *Mrs. Hardie's Tea Cup*.

Others on the farm often choose the kitchen as well. In years gone by, whenever it rained our kitchen looked more like a primitive painting by Henri Rousseau with animals coming out of everywhere—the Saint Bernards, Horatio, a few cats, a fleeing field mouse, a frog or two. One spring afternoon, a shiny black garden snake, at least six feet long, joined the company, coiling itself neatly around the center leg of the kitchen table. At first I thought it was another one of the children's inner tubes. Then it moved. And so did we, with lightning speed.

These days, however, *nothing*, unless I really care about it or unless it is Christmas, sits too long in our kitchen. Dogs have diplomatic immunity. It is still the keeping room, a name I like from the eighteenth century, a room where our family gathers, a room of collections. But I try to collect rather than accumulate. And as the kitchen has become, for me, the most personal room at Thornhill, I choose to edit what it contains. I couldn't always do this when our children were younger, nor did I want to, but as they have grown up, so has the kitchen.

I keep the house and the house keeps me, and the kitchen must be tidy before I can go on with the day. This often drives

Tom crazy. "Where is the book I left here last night?" he asks when he comes home from the office, "or those newspaper clippings?" I then show him his pile carefully placed on a lower step of the stairway going to the second floor. These steps are handy indeed. I use them as a filing cabinet for Tom's assortments which he often leaves around like Hansel and Gretel crumbs. He has a much more laissez-faire attitude toward housekeeping than I do, but as I am the charwoman, as well as the chatelaine of the kitchen, I assume certain rights.

I often use these steps to cache my own books, papers, the usual miscellany of daily life. And it's often the first step to getting clothes to their rightful place on the second floor. Looking at one of the steps now, I see a box of preserve jars waiting to be filled with homemade marmalade, a pair of gold earrings, and my Last Will and Testament, which Tom just brought home for me to sign. I can't quite face that last document. It seems so final, and I feel too filled with life. And so I'll just move it up to another step until tomorrow.

The kitchen is brimming with life as well, our life. Hanging high on the wall is a border of working baskets, the summer pink geraniums crowd the deep recessed window sills, waiting out winter, growing taller, trellising the small window panes, and photographs of our family stride across the white walls. I have surrounded myself with ourselves, and it gives comfort.

I should really put up more cupboards, be more practical. We need storage to house the inherited pots and pans of Mamoo, which I never use but someday think I might. Her lifestyle was so different from ours, large dinner parties, her feasts finished off with tortes and tarts, and what in the world did she do with twelve identical tin molds, all in the shape of a fish? Down to the basement they go, and I keep the walls clear. We need that space for a tree at Christmas.

The kitchen is the back wing of the house, banked against the hill. Its outside walls are the lower portion of the stone wing. This fieldstone overcoat helps retain the heat from our wood stove in the winter, and in the summer the kitchen is the coolest room in the house. The side door, which faces east, is the door *everyone* enters. Often to my dismay. Sometimes I think I should put out arrows pointing to the front door. If visitors are coming, especially if they have never been before, I am delighted when they chance to come in by the front door. It's easier for me to show off Thornhill with a view of the valley. But instead they usually stumble in from the back and I have to rescue them from the swinging doors between the kitchen and the dining room which really don't do their job very well. Rather than swing, they clutch.

That side door, I must admit, is the most convenient entrance, the door nearer the top of the road. The other kitchen door stands in the corner of the north wall, and leads down to the barn. And both doors have a frame of window panes on the top half which allows one to monitor the outside world.

When we first moved to Thornhill, the kitchen was ample. There was a stove, a refrigerator, a sink, and a wall of shelves that was second-class Sunday carpentry. The linoleum covering the floor looked as if it had been in battle, or at least someone had cut himself seriously—a background of gray with little red spots everywhere, a speckled bloody pattern. It turned out to be not such a bad choice. Almost anything spilled on it became invisible, and with young children and a menagerie that was definitely a housekeeping plus.

Later we exchanged the spotted floor for a grander covering of Vermeerlike black-and-white twelve-inch-square tiles of linoleum. It's still here and I have spent a large portion of my life trying to keep it clean. *Everything* shows. I have one friend who insists that guests take their shoes off when they enter her house, and she isn't even Japanese. But I would never get away with that. I chose the black and white, I live with the black and white, and as often happens with style, and this floor has lots of it, you have to work a little harder.

Next to the original kitchen was a bare room where the former owners kept their deep freeze and their hunting boots. We made it into a playroom, the stairway leading to the second floor. I remember one birthday party we gave in the playroom for Tommy when he was sailor-suit age. I turned the room into the *Queen Elizabeth II.* There were cardboard portholes on the walls, paper streamers of every color, floating down from the stairway as if from the deck of a ship, even a captain's table with Tommy at the head. It was the last night on board ship with horns and balloons. It was the gala evening except it was two o'clock in the afternoon.

It took a much longer time to give ourselves a party in the kitchen by giving it a new look. It was well deserved, long awaited. We changed its proportions, but not its intent. The kitchen has always been, as Noah Webster defines it, our cookery, but longing for more of a sweep for living, we removed the wall between the two rooms to spread the largesse.

That first night after the wall had been torn down the kitchen was in shambles and I was thrilled. I saw open space, I saw the new kitchen although the cupboards were bare. It was a phoenix rising from the ashes of the old dry wall. And like the mythical bird, the kitchen was going to have a new life. But not, we discovered, without considerable growing pains.

We even hired a kitchen consulting company for direction. And in turn they supplied us with an efficiency expert. Experts, I thought, were meant to guide, but I often found myself arguing for my own way in my own house. And he was *much* younger than I was, which is often the way with experts these days. So much so that I hardly seek advice anymore. Besides I know Thornhill, its ways and means, better than anyone else in the world. It *is* my world.

Tom, on the other hand, likes to take surveys. He'll ask dinner guests, "Do you think that sofa really goes there?" pointing to a genuine leather (it smells delicious) Chesterfield I bought with my own paycheck, a sofa he secretly hates. It drives me wild. I don't like to have my taste questioned, debated about, especially before dinner. And whenever he starts going into interior decorating, I slip into the kitchen to fiddle with the hors d'oeuvres, putting more curry on the stuffed eggs, testing the toast for the paté. If Tom doesn't like a sofa, I wish he would tell me about it in the privacy of our bedroom, rather than in the open forum of a dinner party.

Our efficiency expert was just as maddening, a bit like a mixed platter of hors d'oeuvres himself—giving a selection of little ideas, some hot, some cold. He enclosed the washer and dryer behind shuttered doors which I approved, but at the same time we lost the light from a window. He built a broom closet where I still hang my aprons, and he lined two walls with cabinets which we needed. But no, I did not want an island in the middle of the kitchen floor, topped with a thick butcher's block. He wanted to add, I wanted to subtract. I wanted those spaces for other things. Like Louise's piano, an upright I had bought off the bulletin board at Sam Adams's grocery store for thirty-five dollars.

The thought of an old piano in his pristine kitchen almost made the expert cry. He begged us to think twice. Why the kitchen? Why not any other room? It was quite simple. Louise's piano didn't fit anywhere else. There was no room in the inn except in the kitchen. I didn't think it was so unusual. I had already known a piano in a kitchen. It was in a Chinese restaurant in Saratoga Springs, New York. And when I was at Skidmore College, Katey and Sally, my two roommates, and I would go there to listen to the owner, a large black woman from New Orleans, play the blues.

In time our concerts were over, the restaurant became restricted. It turned out that more than an eating place with music, it was a *maison de rendezvous*, a playground for ladies of the evening. The news titillated our young ears, and I've never forgotten that Madam, her warmth, her piano, or her spicy kitchen. It was our first introduction to so-called unsavory ingredients, and we relished what we thought was our escape, or our near plunge into the demimonde. We felt, as nineteen year olds, that we had learned even more than our college curriculum had offered. We felt wonderfully jaded, and the boys from Dartmouth and Williams thought we were worldly.

Louise's piano was more like a schoolgirl in a flowered dress. I had upholstered it. I didn't want to paint over the mahogany, although it didn't blend with the pine furniture. I didn't want to strip it, so I clothed it. With a heavy cotton of orange and pink flowers and four packages of thumbtacks, I revamped the piano. My efficiency expert merely put his head in his hands. His plumber, with the most appropriate name of Mr. Fawcett, was more broadminded. He admired my ingenuity, he said, and never in his entire career had he ever been a plumber in a music room.

The music room, as he called it, was the old playroom, now the second half of the long, new, revised kitchen. Separating the room, briefly like a dash attached to the wall, is a white vinyl counter. The children loved it because when they sat there on stools they felt as if they were eating in a diner. It's where Tom eats breakfast every morning. And I do feel like a short order cook with the stove by the top of the counter. But I can only handle two or three customers at a time as the counter isn't very long.

The old kitchen has always been the working half of the kitchen, and when first finished by the expert it looked military with chrome and lights, buttons and switches, all standing at attention. Over the years its posture has toned down a bit by my additional fancies. It has more warmth now, I think, even with the oven turned off. It still has all the same equipment—the same stove, the same double sink, the same refrigerator. Somehow we've lasted together, waiting for old age and the first breaking down of limbs and parts. The refrigerator is definitely getting gray hair. Icicles form every day in the freezer at the bottom of the refrigerator. That lower door just doesn't close properly. I solve this by stabbing the icicles away with a carving knife, kicking the door shut, then mopping up the puddles.

The second half of the kitchen was where we relaxed, all eating together around a long rectangular country table surrounded by pine chairs bought from Bloomingdale's, but really born somewhere in Spain. Other foreign elements absorbed themselves as easily in this room, especially "The Irish Washerwoman," a piece Louise practiced constantly for her school recital. While I cooked, she played the piano. It was a duet.

When it was Beth's turn to take music lessons, she too chose "The Irish Washerwoman" for her recital. I could hardly believe it. Perhaps through familiarity, Beth thought she would find courage when she sat down to play. Whatever, for what seemed like years and years, there were the staccato notes of an Irish jig while I was making dinner. When the lessons were over, the girls retired from the concert stage, and we moved the piano from the kitchen to Beth's upstairs bedroom. It wasn't easy, getting up the stairs, going across the second floor of the house, through one bedroom after the next, around a corner to Beth's room. It took three professionals and a chorus of moans to get the job done. And as Tommy said when it was finished, "Hannibal and his elephants crossing the Alps must have been a piece of cake!"

Although the music has faded from our kitchen, there are tunes of other vibrations. It's where we make decisions and raspberry jam, where I weave baskets and neighbors weave country intrigue over teacups. It's a studio, a workshop, the core of Christmas. It's probably my best friend if friendship depends on being there whenever needed. And of course we cook. But the kitchen staff is only on half-time these days as for most of the year there are only two for dinner.

I've made do with what we had, as they say in the country, when it comes to the kitchen. True we had that efficiency expert, but all he did was install new equipment, hang a few doors as well as four round overhead lights which look like biscuits before they rise. The one structural change was taking down the wall between the two rooms. We lifted the curtain for a bigger stage. And the only real growing pain was the efficiency expert, not the kitchen.

A professional decorator might think the black-and-white blocks are too formal for a country floor, but what is more country than a checkerboard? And I'm sure there are all kinds of Italian country kitchens in the same pattern, most likely in marble. Country furniture, which often looks like its mother forgot to tell it to stand up straight when it was a child, sits well, looks well on such a definite platform. It's a contrast, but very amiable. The floor does what it's meant to do, it ties the kitchen together. It was a bold step, putting down that floor, but I can't imagine any of those designs which look like amoeba floating around on our kitchen floor.

The stairway railing is another departure which has been at home in our kitchen for all these years. The original spindles were square, crude sticks supporting the banister. I took them all away, used them as kindling. And instead of wood, we wove a long length of thick rope up and down from step to banister, threading it through inch-wide eye hooks that we screwed almost at the outer end of each step, screwing hooks as well on the underside of the banister. While the hook on the step is centered, the hooks on the banister are spaced off to each side of that lower hook. This makes the rope travel up and down as if in a continuous line of big VVVVVVVVVs. I painted the banister Chinese red, and the rope has turned a lovely shade of tea.

Firmly attached at either end of the stairway by a newel post, and in the middle by an iron rod hidden by the rope, the banister has stood the test of time—children using it for take-offs, the elderly for support. This stairway could look nautical, but somehow it doesn't. And I think the inspiration probably came from the Reisterstown hardware store where we would browse on Saturday mornings as if it were a bookshop. I'm sure we saw that coil of rope and suddenly saw our kitchen railing.

All the walls are white, and always have been, but there are more traces of red, in addition to the banister. Around the wall framing each deeply recessed window, the three of them, I've painted a red, two-inch border. I did the same around the two doors. It cheers up the white, gives the windows and doors the look of a tidy package. The kitchen is like that old chestnut about newspapers. Black and white and red all over.

Each window has an inner ledge, a shelf about fourteen inches deep, the generous proportion the result of the thickness of the stone walls. Here I put plants, photographs, a piece of china that pleases me. These ledges have become my mini-galleries of changing exhibitions, personal prides.

In another deep window, hanging like a child's swing, is a double shelf. Tommy made the two shelves from logs, planing them even on one side, then hanging them together with baling twine. I usually put vases of single roses here, alongside a small collection of pitchers and bowls. Trimming the top of this window is a valence of needlepoint roses I once bought at an auction, a little tired but still elegant. I like the mixed bouquet—rough wood, my own pink garden roses, and old worn embroidered ones, all over the kitchen sink.

And facing each other, on either end wall of the kitchen, are two bulls' heads. You don't feel, I'm happy to say, as if you're in a hunting lodge in Austria, nor are the bulls such serious trophies. But they are prizes nevertheless. Woven of raffia, we captured them, by strenuous bargaining, from a street vendor in Seville. And the Spanish bulls have been with us ever since. One now wears, rakishly over one horn, a white safari hat, the kind Frank Buck wore, that I bought in a thrift shop on Nantucket. It is a perfect fit. I haven't yet made Kenya, but my hat is ready. That's why I need space in the kitchen. I'm never quite sure what I'm going to put on the walls, on the ledges, almost anywhere. It's the freedom of choice.

At the end of the center counter, I've surrounded the wall telephone with a montage of photographs. There's a grand sepia one of Mamoo as Queen of Atlanteans, New Orleans, 1910; another in black and white by Bill Brandt of two English "parlourmaids," 1933, stiff in white aprons, one of whom Tom says I strongly resemble. The other photographs are of a Main Street fete on Nantucket with little girls in lace dresses, straw hats, and innocent poses, taken by Jessie Tarbox Belas in 1918. When I'm on the telephone, impatiently waiting, these ageless friends keep me company.

The kitchen is where Tom and I sit before dinner to discuss our day. And it's where we seem to make decisions, much more than any other room of the house. It has a positive air, and ease as well. Where the piano once stood are two lady chairs, small armchairs which once graced a southern bedroom dressed in brocade. Now covered with a big red-and-white checkered pattern, they are usually the first stop before dinner. And dinner is on an old oval pine table that can stretch to embrace any number of family, while the chairs are still the six from Spain via Bloomingdale's, the chairs where our children first practiced their table manners. Behind it is a new addition, an old pine cupboard filled with my teacups and teapots, ready for afternoon tea.

Warming the entire room in the winter is the Norwegian woodburning stove our children gave us for our twenty-fifth anniversary in 1975. Todd, the organizer of the gift, said close your eyes, and we did. It sounded as if they were bringing in a chain gang or some heavy artillery. And over the last ten years this stove has kept us cozy with the wood we cut from Thornhill.

# *Chapter* Eight

I don't know why Tom started to cook. Maybe doing over the kitchen was an appetizer. I'm not sure. It just happened, and as it turned out, with a great deal of fuss. But before that first dish, he never announced his intentions, never staked any territorial rights. Like our older son Todd, he ate everything that the resident chef put before him. He never complained, never explained why he decided to stir his own pot. Maybe it's because he likes to eat. Whenever we go to a restaurant, Tom always orders the unexpected, the slightly exotic, definitely the over rich. I'm far more conservative. Oysters, for instance, I like neat and naked. If God had wanted them bedded with spinach He would have grown them in a vegetable patch rather than in a sea of seaweed. Lobsters I prefer simply boiled.

The next morning Tom often pays for his follies, his culinary adventures. And how he does repent, especially after he has weighed himself. I've even heard him weigh himself in the *middle* of the night. But I don't think he'll ever change. He is, above all, a curious man. He savors a challenge, whether it is in the kitchen or in a conversation. He enjoys a difference. Which is why, he says, he married me. And I certainly was not the girl next door in her Peter Pan collar. But he also has an eye to the future. Even before we were married he sent me a cookbook, perhaps with hope for years to come.

Tom is bolder than I am, much more of a kitchen extrovert. To him the stove is a magic carpet rather than an electrical appliance. It can take him to faraway places, and he approaches it with great expectations. Sometimes it works, and sometimes it doesn't. He's addicted to parsley flakes which his maiden Aunt Alice used as a delicate accent. For Tom it is more often heavy rain, no matter what the dish. He thinks parsley flakes can cure anything. And when he sprinkles on the parsley, I'm sure he is thinking of his own Aunt Alice, scenes of his childhood. Every man should have an Aunt Alice—gentle, loving, devoted to her only nephew, the maiden aunt always there, the one comforting back-up in family life.

Then there is Tabasco sauce, an import from Louisiana as he is, which he shakes on with the importance of the pope giving a blessing. I use it, two tablespoons to one gallon of water, as a mixture to pour over my flowerpots so the chipmunks won't nibble my pansies, but Tom uses it to enhance, he thinks, the flavor of every possible dish. Even today when he cooks scrambled eggs, I plead, with caution and with reason, "hold the sauce, *please*!" And although there is that New Orleans heritage, Paris was the birthplace of Tom's palate. But his first venture into the kitchen was at Thornhill Farm.

It was a calm winter Sunday afternoon about three. Tom and the children had taken possession of the kitchen. I was taking a glorious nap. The surprise for dinner was to be a Winter Green Chicken Casserole. And most of Saturday afternoon had been spent on a mystery mission, buying the food.

The recipe wasn't that involved, but the kitchen staff didn't quite read all the directions. Instead of putting the casserole *in* the oven, they sat it proudly on a front burner. The better to watch it. And Tom and company soon learned about culinary combustion. The casserole went off like a bomb. Everywhere.

My new white fluted Christmas casserole from France. But to Tom the appeal of cuisine was only increased, even after cleaning up the scattered debris from this major debacle. It was only the beginning. It whet his appetite. He has another quality. He never gives up.

## WINTER GREEN CHICKEN CASSEROLE

- 6 chicken breasts
- 2 boxes of any frozen green vegetable, such as spinach, broccoli, or green beans
- 1 cup yogurt or sour cream
- ½ cup mayonnaise
- 1 tablespoon lemon juice
- 1 teaspoon poultry seasoning
- ½ cup cheddar cheese, grated
- ¼ cup wheat germ
- ¼ cup nuts, such as walnuts, pecans, or sunflower seeds, chopped

Bake chicken for 40 minutes and remove meat from the bone. Cook vegetables slightly and drain. Mix chicken and vegetables and put into a greased casserole. Combine mayonnaise, yogurt, lemon juice, and seasoning. Pour into dish. Top with cheese, wheat germ, and nuts. Bake for 30 minutes at 350° F.
Serves 6 to 8

From then on Tom started practicing on his family once a week, doing the shopping himself for his special meal, *always* bringing home yet *another* box of shallots. His heroines, Julia Child and Simone Beck, used "two tablespoons of finely minced shallots" with the same fervor as he still uses parsley flakes.

Tom, now an international trade consultant who loves to discover obscure products, was partial to Simone Beck because he once had a business arrangement with her husband, Jean Fischbacher. Jean introduced Tom to an oyster cream, said to be used by Brigitte Bardot, supposedly made from the reproductive organs of French oysters, and Tom was to spread its wonder all over America. He loved talking about it. It never did quite cover the face of America, but it did get us an invitation to dinner cooked by Simone Beck in Paris. I was so nervous I can't remember anything we ate, except the dessert which was a chocolate extravaganza. Ever since Simone Beck's husband was freed from a German concentration camp after World War II, she has made him a chocolate dessert for dinner *every* single evening.

Tom often used the cookbook she wrote with Julia Child, and as Julia and Simone were cooking à la Française, so was he, a natural Francophile.

One of his first high wire attempts was Filets de Poisson Pochés au Vin Blanc. It was, he feels, a turning point in his career. It also turned our children into food critics at an early age.

"How did you like it?" asked their father, waiting to blush at every word.

"I think . . . a l-i-t-t-l-e too much lemon in the sauce," said Louise, probably all of twelve.

"No," said eight-year-old Beth, "needs more butter."

"Fish is *fish*," said Tommy, a wise ten. "It was good, Dad." Todd, a bottomless fourteen, as I said before, would eat anything. The French had their Sunday painters and we had our Sunday chef. Even today, if he's in the kitchen, it must be Sunday. It's the day *he* entertains at lunch.

It is his *spécialité*. We go to eight o'clock church at Saint John's, and have one o'clock lunch at Thornhill. We think it quietly civilized, nicely country, these Sunday lunches. More important, at least to me, is having Tom involved in the domesticity of life. I find it entertaining. When we were first married he hardly knew ice came from a tray.

Not all our friends find this formula as agreeable as we do.

"Why don't you ask us for dinner?" they say. And understandably so. Who would want to interrupt their Sunday with lunch when you can stay home to play with your children, read, relax? And too, Sunday is a catch-up day in the country. But Tom and I feel we have come of age, can be as frivolous as we like on a Sunday afternoon. It's one of those rewards you give to yourself as the years pass. Lunch definitely does punctuate a day, right in the center, but to us it is a graceful hyphen. And there is something a l-i-t-t-l-e, as Louise would say, naughty and Evelyn Waughish about sipping champagne in the middle of the day in the middle of the country. Especially on Sunday.

We try for surprise, but no explosions—no country Bo Peep with a city Bluebeard, no ex-beaux or old loves. Then Tom telephones the invitations, decides on the menu. I do the marketing, set the table.

We usually serve a mushroom dish, practiced and true through trial and error and at least a dozen burned patty shells. Tom is big on mushrooms as Foster's Mushroom Farm is nearby, and the mushrooms are as delicate and full as a white rose. His other secret, silent accomplices are Genie Elder's luxurious Guernsey cream and the deep yellow yolks of Cynthia and David Fehsenfeld's brown eggs. And although Tom prefers to be in the kitchen alone when he cooks, I often hear the roar of the lion, "Where did you hide the thyme?" "I told you to buy more celery seed!" "Where did all the whole-wheat flour go?"

To settle his nerves, he sips wine and quotes the Bible, after all it *is* Sunday, I Timothy 5:23: "Drink no longer water, but use a little wine for thy stomach's sake. . . ." I think that verse should also include "And your wife at your side." When things really get rough, I act as his scrub nurse, handing him his instruments as he operates on the mushrooms. And I insist that he make his mushroom mixture *before* the guests arrive, even before church if possible.

## TOM'S MARYLAND MUSHROOMS

- 1¼ pounds mushrooms, sliced thick
- 4 tablespoons butter
- 3 tablespoons parsley, chopped
- 2 tablespoons whole-wheat flour
- 1 cup chicken stock
- 1 teaspoon salt
- 1 teaspoon pepper
- 4 egg yolks
- 1 cup heavy cream
- 8 patty shells

Place mushrooms in a pan with butter and parsley and cook until lightly browned. Sprinkle with flour, then add stock, salt, and pepper. Lower heat and continue to cook for 15 minutes. Keep pan on stove but turn off the burner. Mix egg yolks with cream and pour over mushroom mixture, blending well. Keep pan on stove 5 minutes. Warm patty shells in oven, then fill with the mushroom mixture.
Serves 8

When the guests arrive, it is my turn to become nervous. Tom, on the other hand, is as peaceful as a lamb, as gracious as if he had a staff of ten. His charm is appealing, but his timing is terrible. Tom becomes a guest, enjoys the champagne, the ambiance. He is an easy meld, having such a good time at his own party that it often seems cruel to remind him of his kitchen duties.

We try to smooth the passage from oven to plate by preparing most of the lunch earlier, and then all he has is the "final approach," a term he loves to toss in from his World War II flying days. And for even more of a safety valve, I make the first course—usually oyster stew. Maryland oysters are plump and delicious and they start the lunch with a creamy panache. Although awfully rich, once a month, when in season, we feel oysters are the only way to begin a lunch in the country, far from the Chesapeake Bay, but near to the palate.

## THORNHILL OYSTER STEW

- 4 tablespoons butter
- 4 cups milk
- 4 cups light cream
- 1½ teaspoons salt
- 1 teaspoon celery seed
- 1 teaspoon pepper
- 2 shakes of Doxsee Clam Juice
- 4 dozen oysters, already shucked
- Butter
- Minced parsley

Put the butter, milk, cream, and seasonings into a heavy pot along with the oyster liquid and clam juice. Bring to a simmer and cook for 2 minutes. Add the oysters and cook for 3 minutes longer, stirring almost constantly. Serve in bowls, with a dab of butter and parsley.
Serves 8

The oyster stew, which I often make the day before, and it seems to be tastier that way, starts things rolling, but it is Tom's earnest attempts at cooking that both amuse and entertain our guests, compensating for the sometimes crazy service. It becomes a communal effort. The guests carry plates to the kitchen, open the wine, keep the party going. And if there is a lag in the conversation, Tom mentions the time he once had lunch with Craig Claiborne in Baltimore.

Craig Claiborne, Food Editor of the *New York Times*, was writing a column on Maryland food, and through a mutual friend, Tom was invited to join them for lunch at Marconi's, a Baltimore tradition where the waiters still wear formal black bow ties and short black jackets, even for lunch. Wanting to have some tasty repartee with the food expert, Tom asked me over breakfast if I knew any Maryland food stories. It *was* early in the morning, and I murmured something about the fact that in the early 1800s city officials seriously thought about putting a crab on top of Baltimore's Washington Monument, a very tall, classical column, instead of the father of our country, George Washington himself. This was, in 1815, the first column ever to honor Washington. And he won out, I told Tom, over the serious contender, the Maryland crab. Tom went on to tell Mr. Claiborne his local tidbit. Within a week we saw this crab lore as the lead on Claiborne's column on Maryland food and restaurants. It took me another week to tell Tom that I couldn't remember whether I had read this somewhere or if I had made it up. And *that* story gets us through dessert at Thornhill.

Sometimes you can fool some of the people some of the time, but you can't fool James Beard. And one Sunday, not so long ago, he came for lunch. Yes, James Beard, the guru of American cooking, the pontiff of our country's cuisine, had lunch at Thornhill Farm.

I didn't tell anyone. I didn't dare. He was giving a Saturday cooking lesson for the benefit of the Baltimore Museum of Art, and they didn't know what to do with him on Sunday. A country lunch, they decided, was the answer, Thornhill Farm a likely site.

I tried to keep it a secret. James Beard at that point could have been James Bond. It seemed that fictitious, and I was scared. I only told one or two friends, but when James Beard, a noted syndicated food columnist whose articles appeared across the country, including the *Baltimore Sun*, came to town, word got around. Even the State of Maryland heard. The head of seafood marketing called me on the phone, offered "one bushel of oysters, red crab fingers, and all the crab meat you can eat." I accepted immediately. Sunday lunch was Tom's province, but this time I thought we needed help. This was showtime for Maryland, no time for a second road company. We needed the best we could get. We were on parade.

Learning that JB, our code name for that certain Sunday, was going to be entertained on Friday and Saturday evenings by two local cooks of renown, I boldly called them. I requested that they not serve oysters or crab. They replied quite grandly that they didn't need Chesapeake Bay as a crutch, and told me their menus. Friday night: Scotch salmon rolled with cream cheese and fresh dill, poached chicken with duxelles. Saturday: frogs' legs mousse, turkey with green peppercorn sauce, and a different bread, braided, beaten, and beautiful, with each course. I quickly realized this Sunday lunch could be the grand *Titanic* of Thornhill Farm. Tom took it in his stride, and I took to the telephone.

I called in the troops. I called friends who were known for their cuisine. Tom, as laird and Sunday chef at Thornhill, could do the main dish with the help of the State of Maryland, but I needed a wreath of friends around our oval dining room table to help me survive even the thought of serving lunch to James A. Beard, Master Chef.

They all accepted readily, enjoying my agony and their ecstasy. It's not every day, after all, that one has lunch with James Beard. David brought his Eastern Shore vegetable purée soup, Minnie, her watercress and Chinese cabbage salad, Cynthia, her beaten biscuits. Ned gave the whole lunch a bit of tone with his English cold lemon pudding. (*He* once had dinner with Prince Charles.) I kept repeating *our* part of the menu to give me courage. It was like saying my beads: "Crab fingers, oysters, crab meat royale, crab fingers, oysters, crab meat royale."

Rita, who *never* works out on Sunday, only days with *R* in them, 7:30 A.M. to 12:30 P.M. prompt, agreed to work only because James Beard was her chosen hero. Just having her there added color. Rita looks like Dolly Parton drawn by Toulouse-Lautrec, her amazing red hair a Belle Époque crown. There's also a touch of Annie Oakley. Rita once shot her pistol into the air over the heads of dogs that were chasing our sheep. For James Beard she left her blue jeans at home, arriving in pure white.

We all fluttered around, letting down the front of the living room desk to make a buffet with platters of oysters and crab fingers. David had come over an hour earlier to shuck all the oysters. *That* is friendship. But when we opened the lid of the long box, we discovered the State had already performed this tedious job. We saw rows of shucked oysters, like big buttons, all tidily tied with red rubber bands, but *no* juice. Quick as a flash David, raised on the Eastern Shore, then a Baltimore investment banker, removed the rubber bands and lavishly squeezed lemon juice over the thirsty oysters.

Then James Beard, all six foot three of him, walked in the front door, looking for all the world, at least to me, like Peter the Great. He was a monument of a man, Buddha-size when seated. He immediately put us all at ease. We learned how he once hoped to be an opera singer, and that you "cut dill, chop parsley, but mortar rosemary." In between courses, Rita nearly choked him with hugs of joy which he received with reluctant grace, and kept smiling for her shaking Polaroid. We all had a wonderful time!

And although he was meant to be on a diet, he ate his plate clean. He even asked us for our crab recipe. We had, at least in the eyes of our friends, finally arrived at the table.

## CRAB MEAT ROYALE

- 1 pound Maryland crab meat
- ½ cup mushrooms, chopped
- ¼ cup margarine or butter
- 1 tablespoon onion, chopped
- 1 teaspoon Worcestershire sauce
- ¼ cup dry sherry
- 3 tablespoons flour
- 1 cup milk
- Salt and pepper to taste
- Grated cheese for topping

Remove cartilage from crab meat. In a large frying pan sauté mushrooms in margarine or butter for 5 minutes. Add onion and cook until tender. Add crab meat, Worces-

tershire sauce, and sherry. Make a paste of the flour and milk. Add to crab meat mixture and cook until sauce thickens. Add salt and pepper. Put mixture into individual shells or ramekins. Sprinkle cheese over top. Bake at 350° F., until cheese melts and mixture is bubbly, about 5 minutes.
Serves 6

What I really like to serve is our own lamb, but when in doubt, and with state aid, I serve crab. As well as Maryland wine, a "Boordy" grown in a vineyard only about a half hour from Thornhill. And Tom enjoys the role of wine steward almost as much as being the chef. He is especially enticed by the language, and I wish he would describe me, just once, the way he applauds his wine.

"Provocative," he says. "Full-bodied, splendidly robed, civilized." I wouldn't even mind being called "nonvintage," which I translate to mean "ageless."

This romance of Tom's started when we lived in Paris. But then it was only a mild flirtation with the grape. *I* would purchase the wine, along with my other marketing, and every time I would buy a bottle of Beaujolais because that was the only wine word I knew.

Now at Thornhill it's fun to serve the local wine. And it gives pride as well to have our own lamb and vegetables from the garden. But at another lunch, quite soon after James Beard's, only the wine was honorably native. Tom thought that once we had entertained James Beard, we could do anything. And he phoned me from his office to say that in twenty minutes he was bringing home two Italian businessmen from Milan. I had fifteen minutes to prepare an American lunch.

"*Supèrbo*," said the older one who looked like a movie director with his coat draped over his shoulders like a cape, as he ate cold chicken from the nearby Butler's Pantry. "*Delizioso*," chimed in the young one with eyes as black as olives, as he consumed his fifth croissant made from a can of quick dough. And, with thanks probably to the Maryland wine, they kissed my hand, called me "Madonna of the Cucina." It was intoxicating. It was the middle of the day. Life on the farm had never been like this. But it's still a lot easier just having lunch alone with Tom.

Sunday is his lunch day, but during the week, it's my treat. His office, in the small town of Cockeysville, only ten minutes away, is almost right at hand. And in the middle of the day in the middle of the week our house seems to be at its most peaceful. And nothing is nicer than a slightly clandestine lunch with your own husband. Years ago an older woman told me, "Just remember, a marriage may be for better or worse, but never for lunch." She has it *all* wrong. . . .

# *Chapter* Nine

LUNCH is a favored repast at Thornhill in any season, but when the children were younger a high point was high tea in the middle of winter in front of the living room fire. And it was quite an elegant array—little jam sandwiches, lacy oatmeal cookies, fat brownies, real china teacups, the big silver teapot, its spout the head and beak of a goose. It was also quite a mess. Sticky lumps of sugar, *always* spilled tea, cookie-crumbed tea trays. But there we were all together acting grown-up. Pint-sized patricians, or so they thought, pouring tea.

On a Sunday afternoon if it wasn't too cold and there was snow, we'd take our sleds and toboggan and the tallest thermos filled with tomato soup over to Sheep's Hotel. This is a hill below the barn, covered with a canopy of trees, where the sheep always sit in the summertime trying to cool off. Every morning they troop down, one after another, to sit on the rocks under the trees as if on the veranda of a resort hotel. Poised for the day, they seemed almost human, watching the world go by. And in the winter we borrowed their hill for an afternoon of coasting.

Now that our children have gone off to other hills, I seem to focus my winter energies on the house itself. And I *always* spring clean in the winter. That long stretch of winter months is the only uninterrupted time I have. And there is a certain inner contentment when I know the cupboards are neat. I'm especially pleased with myself after I've done the medicine cabinet. Once a peasant, always a peasant, and in good company. I once read that Sophia Loren, when she wants to relax, scrubs a floor. I understand perfectly. If my house is tidy, so is my mind.

In the spring there is too much else to do—there are the gardens, the front fences to be painted brighter white, the lawns to tidy. And who in their right mind would want to be in when springtime is out—waiting. No, it is in the winter when the house and I consult, sometimes console, even indulge ourselves with a splurge or two. A little indulgence in the dark of winter always gives cheer.

And so my January decisions often have interior motives. Once the Christmas trees have been disrobed—their boughs cut to cover the garden beds—our house looks empty, a little lost. And I feel a little lost too, the party's over. Not to worry though, in an old house there is *always* something to do. And once the house is cleared of its Christmas frivolity, it's easier to see what must be done in the new year, or should have been done in the last.

Often it's more practical than creative. Tom and I finally replastered the cracks that had wrinkled the library ceiling like the face of an old man—but not half as photogenic or as appealing. A house of many years does not grow old gracefully. It simply falls apart. And you have to catch it, watch it, care. You become constant custodians.

We feel we rescued Thornhill from a dubious past. We staked a claim, made a commitment, much more of one than we probably realized. But we'd have it no other way. As Thornhill has grown stronger, we have grown wiser—at least in the ways of an old house. And we lean on each other. More simply, we need each other. But wouldn't it be lovely if there was a Society for the Preservation of People Who Live in Old Houses?

Tom and I are just now insulating the attic, a job that should have been done years ago. It's our Mount Everest. It is so hard to climb through that hole in the upstairs hallway and it is still the only entrance to our attic. So far the squirrels, the prolific inhabitants of Upper Thornhill, haven't complained. This sort of chore, the art of insulation, a plumbing disorder, cajoling a suspicious furnace, I like to leave up to Tom. I'm all for show. I prefer the "fancy" work.

That's what I did to Beth's bedroom her first winter term at college. I prettied it up. On her bedroom walls I wallpapered a bouquet of flowers. And in the connecting bathroom I put a smaller floral print. I wanted pattern on pattern, shades of Matisse I kept telling myself. This was a treat for both of us. I was covering over our original paper, seemingly tired with age. And it was time. If wallpaper could speak, this one would have said, "I am seventeen years old."

When she came home she went right to her bedroom. She looked and she sighed and told me I had taken away her childhood. There was no intended rudeness, just apparent sadness. And she was right. *I* had intruded. I had disturbed *her* past, if only out of love.

I always felt that Thornhill, once I accepted its disabilities as well as its potential, was mine to have and to hold from that day forward. But I was wrong. I was only one of six. Thornhill, especially to Beth who was born of this house, means a great deal. And that's just what I was trying to achieve once we decided that this was our house forever. I wanted our children to have a house that was a core, a centerpiece. To care about Thornhill as much as we do. But somehow I never dreamed that this feeling for a house was going to reveal itself so dramatically because I simply papered a bedroom wall. You never know when emotion is going to strike.

Once she got over the shock of her lost youth, she hugged

me, she thanked me, and then proceeded to get on with her life by unloading a month's worth of laundry on the kitchen floor. But now, before I paint or paper, I think more carefully. I try not to trespass into worlds that our children obviously want to hold on to for a bit longer. And I haven't touched Beth's room since. In the summer I do plump it up with roses from the garden, those sturdy pink old-fashioned ones, very much like Beth herself. They open more and more every day.

There are even more roses in the living room, all year round. Dressed in a new cover of chintz, abundant with English roses, our living room, long and awkward and always a problem, has finally become a lady. This was a winter restoration without tears, unlike Beth's bedroom, but a long winter of indecision. It took two women, both born in the nineteenth century, to help me make up my mind—my mother-in-law Agnes and Edith Wharton. One gave a roomful of family furniture, the other the inspiration.

Mrs. Wharton, author of fashionable novels about early New York society and friend to Henry James, will never know the decorative impact she has had on one small farmhouse in Maryland. And it's all because I once saw, and never forgot, a photograph of her living room in New York City. *Everything* was coming up roses, even the lampshades. The same lush cabbage rose pattern climbed the walls, curved at the windows, covered the tufted Victorian chairs. I loved it. I wanted it. But I never dreamed we would have it. And it took me twenty-five years to turn our living room into a much milder replica of that Wharton brownstone.

It would never have happened without the family furniture. Since I am married to an only child, I knew the furniture would someday come our way. But I never thought about it, nor did I want it. I needed space more than heirlooms. With four children using it, the living room, the largest room in the house, was often a gymnasium, sometimes a bowling alley, and on rainy days, a campsite. Those rainy days produced young pioneers. In with the card table, down with the tent flaps, made from a heavy blanket tossed over the table. Such an early settlement in the center of the living room kept them happy for at least half a day.

The family furniture came to Thornhill when my mother-in-law Agnes, at ninety-one, went into a nursing home. Her mind was fuzzy, she didn't quite know who I was, and told Tom, in all seriousness, she was glad he had been at her wedding. I think she thought she was looking at her husband Harry when she looked at her son Tom. Harry had died eight years earlier of pneumonia, and at ninety-two Agnes died quietly, without any fuss, in her sleep.

How I miss her, more than I can say, but she's always around. I see her handwriting on the notes she taped under each piece of furniture. When I was younger, she'd point to a chair and say "That's Boston," to a sofa, "That's New Orleans," to a table, "That's Aunt Leila," and a fat footstool was "Uncle Will." I didn't take it all in, I was too busy counting children. But now I know where it all began because of her notes. And now I hear our son Todd telling me I should do the same thing as I am the last link, the last curator of family chairs.

I know he's right, but when we first inherited the furniture I secretly wondered about taking it all on. It was certainly welcome, a natural provenance, but I worried about inheriting the taste of others, *not* always my palate. It was grander than ours, that was obvious, had much more of a family connection, and I did always admire that elegant Boston sofa. And so it all moved into Thornhill.

It was a challenge and a tug. We had lived happily for years with our first-do, the original colony of furniture at Thornhill, covered in red, white, and blue. What should I do now with the sofa we bought as newlyweds when we returned from France, the wing chair, our first important treasure that we could afford to buy only because it was marked down, the furniture already in residence, our old friends? I soon learned. As the living room became more and more crowded I learned to edit, to make decisions. Forget emotion, I kept telling myself, *try* to be practical.

I also played house a lot, moving furniture around, taking it upstairs, downstairs, out into the barn to save for Beth. Some of it went into U-Hauls to start another life in our children's houses. It was like the children's game of musical chairs with pieces of furniture gradually being taken away. There was never any thought of putting the furniture up for sale, or even adoption to unknowns. That never entered our minds. This furniture was too important. Over the years it had become a chronicle of our lives.

Once Mamoo's furniture took its prime place in our living room, I realized this was *the* moment. Everything needed to be upholstered. My dream of roses blooming everywhere *might* be possible. The thought of a new look softened the missing of old friends. It's amazing how quickly I recovered. And recycling of some sort was definitely necessary. The Boston sofa, covered in a safe yellow silk, was showing its knees, as well as its elbows. And the New Orleans settee was still in faded rose velvet from a great-grandmother's parlor. I had a wonderful excuse to make whoopee, Edith Wharton whoopee, and suddenly the winter didn't seem so dark.

And it was love at first sight. I found a heavy English chintz filled with roses, Rosa Mundi by name. It was stiffly glazed in the tradition of English chintzes, a material to last forever with broad yellow and white stripes topped by rose and mauve blossoms growing everywhere with succulent abandon. Rosa also cost, per yard, about the same as a cord of country wood. This, alas, was an impossible dream. I needed yards and yards. In pursuit of another chintz, I went everywhere, found chintz of lesser price but only minor beauty. American chintzes, try as they may, are just not as generous, as striking or daring with colors as their English cousins. But as I was going to have a full-scale invasion of upholstery—two sofas, one settee, three chair seats, three window seats, and *no* lampshades—I could not think lightly, had to make the right decision.

It was slowly becoming a winter of discontent. Rosa, it seemed, was not to be ours, and nothing else made me as happy as my first choice. Discouraged, but not completely dismayed, I began to think how I could possibly wrap our furniture with this very expensive ladylike English chintz. When you really want something, as I wanted this chintz, one's mind often exhibits unusual initiative. I went to the source. I wondered how my English roses grew in London. After endless letters to my friend Bettina who lives there, I discovered that Rosa Mundi grew almost half price in its native land. This I could afford.

Bettina bought me twenty-seven meters, gave it to my visiting friend Mary Jane, who fortunately always travels light, to carry to Thornhill at last. The odyssey of my chintz was complete, from first love to London and back. I had accomplished my mission. By letters, logistics, and determination, Rosa Mundi was going to be at home at Thornhill Farm.

Having won a victory of sorts, I began to wonder how this hard-earned chintz would *really* look on our furniture, a mixture of ancestry, some from the North, upright and proper, but more from the South, tufted and curvaceous. And for one fleeting, very short moment I feared, shades of a New Orleans bordello, 1910, all those roses, all those curves. But once the furniture was upholstered we had, very much so, an Edith Wharton sitting room, a garden of roses all year round, a living room that is indeed a lady sitting in a Quaker farmhouse. And with the chintz of my choice covering all, the furniture, although inherited, became mine. Then I started thinking about the dining room.

Edith Wharton went so far as to carry her same cabbage rose

pattern right into dinner. I thought about using my chintz in the same manner, but somehow it didn't quite digest. Our dining room opens by a wide archway to the living room, and so the two rooms could definitely be related—by chintz or by color. But enough of Rosa Mundi is enough. I decided to go for color. Once I start winter decorating, it's hard to stop.

All of the walls on the first floor of Thornhill are painted white—except the library which is geranium red, a daring step a few winters ago. The red, with all the woodwork white, woke up the whole room. It was a surprise and a success. Red is a wondrous color as long as there is some paler color to tame it. And so I painted the woodwork, the bookcases, and ceiling with a glossy white. The red did so well, I wondered how yellow would do. And that is the color I painted the dining room.

Its proper name is gold finch, but to me it is as rich as butter, the same yellow that is in the chintz. While all around, our neighbors still seem to use the muted colonial colors of Williamsburg, tested and true, our color chart is more primary—red, now yellow. But still I wasn't convinced that I was doing the right thing. It is very hard to plan a room with a paint chip about the size of a domino.

After the first wall was finished I was in shock. It looked like a wall of egg yolk, the yellow you find in brown country eggs. "Wait 'til it dries," advised the patient professional, the painter who is a veteran of women changing their minds and wall paints as quickly as their nail polish. "I like it," he said. I was sure he was lying. Nothing could convince me that I hadn't plunged into the wrong pail.

When it dried, the yellow wall still looked as startling as a headlight in the dark. After all I had never painted a wall yellow before. Once you paint a room a bright color for the first time, I've discovered you've got to give your eye time to grow accustomed to the change. You have to be brave. Nevertheless I added more white to the already mixed yellow, and somehow we all seemed to settle down—especially the room, particularly me.

The professional went on to paint all four walls yellow twice, and then the woodwork white. It turned out to be the right decision, once we became accustomed to its sunny face, a bright room in a house of white walls. And soon the windows were swagged with Rosa Mundi chintz. I couldn't resist.

"This room looks great," said our daughter Louise when she saw the burst of yellow for the first time, "but the floor looks terrible." I knew that. I had purposely not waxed it for two years. I had been thinking about stenciling a floor for *that* long. And a likely candidate was the dining room. I had always wanted a stenciled floor, and this one needed help, so it seemed a good place to start. I would never decorate one of the original random-width pine floors, those floors are sacrosanct. The dining room floor was of oak, a later addition, probably about 1907, and undistinguished.

First I studied all the books I could find in the Cockeysville library, and learned that stenciling started with the Chinese, became more fanciful with the French, and was continued in America until the mid-1800s. Itinerant New England painters decorated walls and floors with stencil patterns—substitutes for imported rugs and wallpaper from Europe. These journeymen would place their stencil plates on a surface, then tap out bright colors. The more I read, the more excited I became about giving our 1843 Maryland farmhouse a design from its own time.

The floor was ready, I bought precut stencils from Historic Deerfield in Massachusetts while on a trip, and most important I recruited our daughter Louise, who has an eye for design combined with more patience than I. For my first steps in stenciling I needed a pal.

The experts might howl, but here is how one woman faced a floor—and it worked. I wanted to retain the look of seasoned wood. The floor was already smooth and I only intended to stencil a wide border rather than embroider an entire floor. So I didn't bother to sand the floor, as most of the stenciling books suggested. That would have probably been the best idea, but I didn't ask for perfection. Besides I wanted the stenciled floor to look as if it had been around for some time. So instead of sanding, I scrubbed away the patina of the past, especially the faint blush of wax, to prepare the floor for a look into the 1800s.

The actual stenciling, although not difficult, is time-consuming. It took us one entire day, nine to five, to stencil our eight by twelve foot border. First we practiced on newspaper, dipping the tip of the round, fat stencil brush into acrylic tube paint, a few drops of water added to the mixture. Then we proceeded to "pounce" on each stencil opening, one at a time. Pouncing spreads the paint evenly through the bristles. I held the brush like a pencil, so it remained perpendicular, and tapped and stamped, up and down, up and down.

Rehearsal over, we set the stage by removing all the dining room furniture except the center oval table and the chests at either end. These pieces knew their place, and the border had to oblige. Next we plotted our design on the floor—the border, a black leafy garland, yellow-and-green pineapples in each corner, and another pineapple in the center of the two longer sides. Then with a string attached at one end to the floor by masking tape, we measured straight lines for the six-inch-wide garland. The fourteen inch pineapples were stenciled first, guidelines made with chalk.

As we did each section, we secured the stencil to the floor with masking tape. And I used my free hand to press down the edges of the stencil opening closest to the area where I was stamping color. When we lifted the stencil, if there was any leak of color, Louise quickly removed it with a Q-tip. Every day for the next three, I brushed a clear satin urethane over the entire floor. And now with its warm chestnut hue and stencil border, the floor is handsome, in a nicely New England way.

Stenciling can be like eating peanuts, on and on, or strawberries dipped in honey. And I went on to stencil jam labels, book plates, stair treads, brown paper bags for carrying presents. But the first time was the most fun, the best of all. Louise and I had a wonderful day working together. She was introduced to a new craft, and I learned an old parlor trick.

Working on the interior of the house is one way to keep warm during the winter days, but it is our undercover agents, our hot water bottles, that keep us toasty at night over those long country months. Water bottles are standard equipment at Thornhill. They are a natural part of our way of life in the winter.

I carry mine around the way a little boy carries his teddy bear. I hug it, I put it at my feet when I type, in my lap when reading. What comfort this oblong object has, simply by being filled full of hot water. If I were running for president, or even vice-president, part of my platform would be ". . . and a hot water bottle in every bed!" Maybe an old-fashioned idea, but not a bad one considering the price of oil.

The British bottles are best. Maybe that's because central heating came much later to the English. I once read that when the Prince of Wales was introduced to Mrs. Simpson at a country house party, his first words were, "Don't you miss your American central heating?" *She* soon learned how to keep warm. And so did I. I became addicted to the hot water bottle, meeting my first adult one in St. John's Wood, a bus ride from central London where my stop was "Lord's Cricket Ground." It was winter 1947, I was a copywriter with British *Vogue*, and rationing was still on. I gave all my sugar and meat coupons to my landlady who in turn put a hot water bottle in my bed every night.

She also nourished me on around-the-clock tea, the Englishman's antifreeze in those days, and "gin was mother's milk," as

Eliza Doolittle was wont to say. I was introduced to both. And bacon was a bright moment in the morning.

I no longer eat bacon, the English tea I prefer is prone to caffeine so cups are counted, the gin I learned to drink neat is now mixed, but the hot water bottle is still, and forever, an island of winter pleasure. In our family we each have one, the girls carried theirs to college. I give them as Christmas presents. I *believe* in hot water bottles. Once married, and more traveled abroad, I remember hot water bottles and beds the way Proust remembered things past.

So do the English. They hang them in their hotel rooms with polite notes that say, "This is provided for the comfort of guests *whilst* here." Then they mysteriously appear, warm and cozy and filled, at the bottom of your bed at night. And some English affectionately still call a hot water bottle a "foot muff."

Their bottles *are* like muffs, wrapped in a plush cocoon, with the stoppers of metal rather than plastic. At Thornhill Farm we turned one naked American hot water bottle into an English model by making a wrapper of flowered flannel. But the real test of a hot water bottle you put in your bed at night is the *next* morning. Given the toe test, is the heat still there?

There are also some game rules. Don't use boiling water. Only fill about three-fourths full. Gently press the bottle to remove air and steam, cap, and put to bed an hour before you turn in. This gives the hot water bottle time to become acquainted with your bed, time to spread its warmth.

You don't have to live in the country to appreciate hot water bottles. And even those who sleep under electric blankets might want to savor their old-fashioned charm. A hot water bottle, quite simply, gives your bed a warm heart. And when our furnace balks, we at Thornhill are ready. Last year our furnace, like a star baseball player, didn't quite make it to early spring training. It went on strike. We just went to bed earlier with our bottles. Oh the joys, the warming joys of winterhood!

# *Chapter* Ten

OUR winter guests have come to expect hot water bottles at Thornhill Farm. I guess it's become one of our signatures. Nowadays, especially in America, you don't usually find a hot water bottle as a bed companion. And if by chance, with the excitement of guests and a good dinner, I forget to slip one in the bed before our guests retire, I'm often told the next morning how they missed their cozy friend. I hope it isn't really their way of telling me to turn up the oil heat. I like guests with old country values.

Our guest room has its own special hot water bottle. It is in the shape of a white woolly lamb and I bought it when I realized that after many, many years we were again going to have a guest room, a *proper* guest room, a space once occupied by children, but now a room on its own.

A guest room, it seems to me, is a lot like a boomerang. In early years of marriage you often have one, suddenly with children it disappears around a corner, then, eventually, it comes back. Like almost everything, a guest room is another circle of life.

When we first moved to Thornhill there was a grand guest room, the middle room with the four windows looking out over the land. And it was like a Victorian valentine—lacy curtains, a high four-poster bed covered by a white webbed canopy crocheted by my southern mother-in-law Agnes. It was straight out of *Gone With the Wind*, or at least that's what I thought in my youth. Ante-bellum perhaps, but this guest room also had the usual appointments—the writing desk with pens, a clock, books by the bed, even an empty closet, the epitome of luxury.

Then quite soon Tom and I too had another modern appointment—Beth Hardie, born of Thornhill Farm. The guest room became a nursery, and with it all its fancy ways faded from memory as well as from this old house.

But we *still* had guests.

And it always seemed to be a momentous occasion. "Guest room" became the name we gave to a room after evacuating the children in order to offer hospitality to family and friends from out of town. It was a lot like getting ready for an old-time birth—clean sheets, lots of hot water, which meant the children couldn't bathe all weekend, flowers in the bedroom. Women guests were channeled to Louise's room, men directed to Todd's, and when we had a couple, double accommodations were found by taking Tommy's bunk bed down a peg or two for a twin-bedded room.

If it was warm outside we pitched a tent for the children. They had a much better time than the guests—eating wild berries, wearing torn T-shirts, rejoicing that they didn't have to take a bath, were free, at last, from their mother's yoke. We hardly saw them. There was, however, every morning in the kitchen a trail of peanut butter and jelly, evidence of the vanished race.

Bryan, a bachelor guest from San Francisco, put it ever so politely. "Your children," he would say, "certainly don't get in your way!" I would have preferred a touch more of congeniality, a mannered handshake or two, even a quick conversation. But for the most part, they were invisible.

# *Chapter Ten*

For a while Beth's room was off limits. Although smaller than the rest, she wasn't as transferable, her equipment not so mobile. As she grew older and graduated to a larger bed, her bedroom became the chosen one. It was bigger than Louise's, had a better view than Todd's, and wasn't in the middle of the house as was Tommy's. If there was a trace of privacy in this house, Beth had a corner of it.

But she was not what one might call a graceful hostess. There were tremors. "Awww," she would cry, age about eight, "you're making my room look grown-up!" Which was exactly what I was trying to do—age a room overnight. It wasn't easy. First we had to relocate the zoo—two stuffed lions, one elephant, a mastiff, and Raggedy Ann. All were about as high as Beth's middle, and as difficult to tame into a closet as it was to tame Beth into dresses. The closet was a challenge, already engaged with everyday essentials such as a fishing rod, a set of assorted doll's china, wooden shoes, and ugh, said Beth, girl shoes.

Then we would catalog her very own Smithsonian Institution. I wonder, I would ask her, where Mary Jane, our guest for the weekend, would like to see that skeleton head of a sheep? No Beth, not on the bedpost. And what about the spider web? No Beth, it does not look like a mobile. It was the most negative maneuvering, but I had to persevere. Eight year olds can be cunning adversaries.

What about the turtles? Under the bed? What else, I asked her, was under the bed? Only, she would reply, her creepy crawlers, Barbie and Ken, and her punching bag, a birthday present from her godfather Jerome who thought it a perfect present for Beth. From then on, when in doubt, we put *everything* under the bed. And somehow by the time Mary Jane arrived on Friday evening the room was presentable with flowers everywhere and paper parasols, in lieu of shades, poised on the deep sills of the windows.

I sometimes wondered how Mary Jane, a magazine editor, survived those weekends, coming from a handsome New York apartment where she slept in a wide antique Spanish bed, lavishly dressed with flowered French sheets. It must have been the peace of the country, just sitting around in the sun. At times though it wasn't so peaceful.

One weekend Mary Jane was determined to teach me how to do needlepoint. And by Sunday our ancient friendship was almost dissolved. She kept telling me to work on the diagonal, putting the needle from the side hole to a lower hole of the canvas, next row, side hole to a higher hole. I couldn't even find the right hole, and all the while she would exclaim, "Watch it grow, watch it grow!" The fact that our children had hidden themselves under the dining room table where we were working, listening to their mother's ignorance, didn't help at all.

On another Mary Jane weekend, forty-seven bachelors invaded the farm at 8:00 A.M. on a Saturday morning while Mary Jane was trying to sleep. Bachelors, as to all of us, are always acceptable, but these young men were only eleven years old, and it was the day of Tommy's class picnic. I wish Mary Jane would come back, now that our guest room has really grown up!

From the west coast, Bryan would fly in and simply walk off the plane into our waiting car. He *never* checks his luggage. Instead he would be carrying two hand bags, and his faithful traveling companion, a very small pillow. And from those two small bags Bryan managed to meet every occasion—walk the fields, ride a friend's horse, dress for dinner. He later admitted that he always included pajamas on his weekends because he never knew whether or not he would be "unpacked." Shades of P. G. Wodehouse!

But then Bryan is a professional weekender, a true Englishman, although he has lived in San Francisco, his adopted city, for years. And if any one in the world knows how to weekend,

An early-morning walk around Thornhill in spring 1971. *From left to right:* Rosie (one of our Saint Bernards), Beth, Todd, Dee, Tom, Louise, and Tommy. In the background our flock of Hampshire sheep are wondering just *what* is going on.

Twelve-year-old Todd feeding six-month-old Patrick. Although his mother has abandoned him, Patrick still bends his front knees as if nursing from his mother's milk supply.

Thornhill sitting in a nest of snow, the boxwood somehow surviving the weight of winter.

The side kitchen door with boxwood wreaths and Christmas snow. The goose decoy propped up on my child-size cupboard, where I keep my gardening tools, was used years ago by hunters to lure geese into cornfields. Dirty pool if you ask me.

A portrait of John T. Hardie, Tom's great-grandfather, who had twelve children, looks over our production. In the back and left, our daughter-in-law, Diana, with Todd; and right, Scott with Louise. Tom is centered on the Rosa Mundi chintz sofa by Beth and me. It took me hours and many groans to get everyone to pose à la John Singer Sargent: the girls in white, the boys in bow ties.

When this photo was taken, seventeen-year-old Tommy and his friend Brad had just spent two days chopping wood. He looks pleased with himself, and well he should. We were always rich with firewood.

An eighty-five-year-old Mamoo looking at a portrait of her grandson Tommy, painted when he was five.

it is the English. To them a country weekend is a tradition, a ritual, a formula, a *must*! And Bryan does it very well indeed. By the end of his first visit our children were calling him Uncle Bryan with sincere affection. I think it was because he never asked them how old they were, or if they liked school.

These were the questions they usually received from our business guests and often in different languages. Tom always insisted on putting up these foreign visitors. He had a theory, I think, that if they slept overnight at Thornhill, the next morning he could sell them *anything*. I was never of that persuasion. I didn't like mixing business and pleasure. But I must admit those foreign guests, once I adjusted to them, opened our eyes to other avenues of the world. And Tom really brought them home for other reasons. It was simply that he was proud of Thornhill. And Tom, a natural ambassador, loved showing foreign visitors, if only for an evening, a slice of country Americana.

There was a flow—an Irish poet whose family owned an important factory in Northern Ireland, an Italian princess on her honeymoon (*that* made me very nervous), and a gentleman from Finland whose name was so difficult to pronounce that we all called him "Mr. Finland." He loved it as well as his schnapps which he claimed was just as warming as our hot water bottle.

From a completely different climate came a man from Tanzania, from Dar es Salaam to be exact, on the east coast of Africa. *He*, rather than Tom, was trying to make a deal. To flower his path he brought me a slender pocketbook made of zebra skin, a wide ivory bracelet, a huge photograph frame made entirely of small shells that spelled LOVE, and a carved wooden woman, completely naked, with the most amazing anatomy. It was like the Dutch bringing trinkets to the Indians of Manhattan.

This African trader had a purpose. He wanted Tom to sign a paper saying that he supplied him with a million dollars of business a year. This would have helped him enter the country legally to settle down in the good old U.S.A. It sounds bizarre, and it was. It was absurd. There was no way Tom could oblige, and our guest left most abruptly for Texas where a marriage agency had guaranteed to find him an American wife for the bargain price of $200.

After that startling episode, I felt Thornhill needed cleansing. It was time, anyhow, for our children to take over the stage. Almost too soon, it was their turn to play host, bringing classmates home from school, from college. It wasn't so hard to realize that our children were that age, but it *was* difficult to realize we were old enough to be their parents. As Bryan often says, "You're always as old as you feel, and never as old as you look." And I just didn't feel *that* old.

Yet our halcyon days were our children's house parties, wonderful country weekends, wall-to-wall backpacks. Sometimes our guests' hours were so different from ours that I only met them at the refrigerator door. I loved it. One time I nailed blue enameled numbers, some I once bought at a French hardware store, on their bedroom doors so when they awoke they would think they had gone away to some snappy place, say Stowe or Saint Bart's. But they seemed to prefer Thornhill. The price was right. I sometimes called Thornhill the "Last Resort," but a frequent guest simply called it "Hardie House." And the sign she made for the front door still hangs in a hall. I don't think there were any better times.

Now our children have entered their adult worlds, and their bedrooms are like small museums of their childhood. Fully booked over the holidays, these bedrooms can be awfully lonely in between. It is inevitable. But sometimes it's harder for a mother to grow up than a child. She has to do it twice. First on her own, then when her children come of age. But the time had come, I realized, to be practical. The time had come to shift gears and change sheets. Without looking back—well, hardly—I turned one of the bedrooms into a guest room, a *real* guest room. The boomerang has returned, making a full circle.

Once I stripped the bedroom of its boyish past, I felt almost like a bride, putting together a new room for our guests. Again there's an empty closet, one that hasn't seen space in years, a cubbyholed desk with Thornhill writing paper, matching envelopes, and some eyelet-trimmed sheets I never allowed myself to buy for our own double bed. If we were going to have a guest room, it might as well have sheets as big as the Ritz. And this room has a certain position, holds a definite rank, five-star territorial rights. It is for guests only. It is not a warehouse for accumulated clothes never worn, nor is it a refuge for extraneous collections. I don't even hide Christmas presents in the closet. This way the room knows who it is and why. This is a guest room.

I once read that the poet W. H. Auden liked to have a bowl of cold potatoes by his bed when he was a guest. Sounds like a strange snack to me, but I do think nibbling, in the bedroom, all alone is fun. On the dresser I put Aunt Alice's last two surviving crystal glasses with a small decanter of Maryland wine, some beaten biscuits, and if there is any Thornhill fruit in season, there's a bowl of it by the bed. Better, I think, than potatoes.

At the end of the double bed, plump with an eiderdown, is the small curved settee where my father-in-law proposed to Mamoo when the settee lived in New Orleans. Now it is always on hand for afternoon tea or the first chat of the visit. It has a very cozy, intimate feeling, this settee. Perhaps that's because I know of its past romance. But more than that, it is a wonderful place for gossip, even a little scandal carried to Thornhill from the outside world.

Far more sedate is Tom's grandfather's plantation desk, a

desk that once helped count up bales of cotton. Now it merely helps to write letters, holds sharp pencils, a dozen black felt-tipped pens, postcards already stamped, a portable radio.

For reading, and that's *my* idea of a perfect country weekend, there is a tufted Victorian chair that wraps around you, literally embraces. And for all that is said about those staid Victorians, they certainly did make some affectionate furniture. This chair is a fine example, and next to it is a small table holding new magazines and a pile of my favorite old English mysteries. If our guests prefer a good read in bed, there are sturdy backrests waiting in the closet, along with extra light bulbs that I bought over the telephone from the handicapped, meant to outlast all others. I've had them in the wall lamps on either side of the bed for two years. A pine chest holds more blankets and it is the right height—low enough for unpacking a suitcase, high enough to sit on.

Over the dresser is a large square English mirror and a small hand mirror helps with other views. Near the clock and sewing kit on the dresser is a pair of small binoculars. On a clear day you can see forever in this Maryland countryside. Even closer is the bird life, an extravagant array from bluebirds to cardinals to gold finches. Early in the morning, early in the evening, their songs are constant.

I try to fill this guest room with independence. Treat it as an island, if that is what is necessary. Our guests, after all, have come at our invitation for some country quiet. It is *our* guest room, but *their* harbor. A place to get away from it all, to rest, to recharge.

You can make a room beautiful, but how does it sleep? That's what we had to find out. Guests, unlike the story of the princess and the pea, can often be too polite to tell you that the mattress button has pierced, nightly, their lower dorsal nerve. And so Tom and I planned a weekend, a weekend as our own guests.

It was like going to another country, or perhaps just a better hotel. Everything was so neat and tidy. There were even enough hangers. Padded ones at that, in lovely shades of lavender and peach. We liked it. One night though, we decided, was not enough. It takes two to feel at home. The double feather pillows were especially nice, we agreed, and the new shades did keep out the morning sun. But the top drawer of the old dresser definitely needed waxing. It didn't open as easily as it should. Room service could be improved, but other than that it was a pleasant room with a view, and we just might go back again. Half the fun, we discovered, was staying right at home.

Tom became so enthusiastic he thought we should have more guests. He even suggested nailing a small, card-size frame on the guest room door where we could slide in the name of the weekend guest. He came up with this idea after reading an English novel by Nancy Mitford where all ten guest rooms had such a way of identification. I figured it must have been a remnant left over from the days when Edward, Prince of Wales, was looking for Lillie Langtry, or one of his other girls in the middle of the night, but I didn't want to discourage any ideas coming from Tom. There is now a small frame on the guest room door waiting for the next visitor. And beside it, in enameled blue is the number "1."

Room #1 has been used much more than we thought it would be. And it is being used by another generation. Our children, much to our pleasure, have given us a wonderful legacy. We seem to be inheriting their friends. Thornhill, we realize, is the real draw—a walk in the woods, a day in the country, an overnight of sleeping *very* late the next morning. And sometimes there is even breakfast served in bed.

When these young people come to call, the house wakes up, and so do we. We thrive on it. Oscar Wilde, who was often witty, but often wrong, wrote that it is a shame to waste youth on the young. Born a hundred years too soon, poor Oscar may have had good reason for this thought, other than just being clever, but Tom and I relish this age, the mid-twenties and on. While we are on hold, they're just beginning. And it is exciting to be around for their first acts. Our own children, making their way in life far from the farm, are pleased that their friends like to visit. I like to think they might even be a little proud. One friend, looking for an apartment in Baltimore, stayed at Thornhill for a month.

More likely it's an overnight and Sunday lunch—away from the push of graduate school, or the pull of being a young intern in a crowded city hospital. They need Thornhill to relax, as much as we need them. Sometimes they may even need roots. It's a reciprocal joy.

They keep in touch, call us up, come out to play. We eat and chat and catch up. Tom loves dissecting words with Hugh who was an English major at college before going into medicine. And I love having a doctor make house calls, his only diagnosis trying to decide what herbs I put into the salad that day. There are other times though when he comes out on his motorcycle to thump my back, look at my throat when I just can't seem to get over a bug. He is our resident physician, often staying in the guest room. And when he leaves town, his motorcycle lives in our barn.

Chris and Jimmy, who came to Thornhill long ago as childhood friends of Tommy's, make periodic checks on how we're doing, and in the summer if we're away, Chris watches over Thornhill. A writer of books on Chesapeake Bay, he finds Thornhill a peaceful place to write or polish whatever he has written before. It's extraordinary how these young people come back into our lives, never expected, always appreciated. And we try to keep the flame bright.

Another gentleman caller is David, our godson, now with an auction house in Washington, D.C. He usually comes around four and drinks tea with a professional eye, noticing my pride of teacups. Something, I'm sure, he never thought about when he was young. When he became engaged to Polly, their first official lunch was on our porch at Thornhill. We're all growing up together.

They come and they contribute. Louisa, our daughter Louise's chum from the first grade on, takes photographs of Thornhill in every season, on every visit. And sometimes we cook together. With Francesca, Beth's best college friend, now studying for her Ph.D. in Art History, Tom always makes a flamboyant feast of pasta, stirring in his Italian along the way. And Todd's friend John has introduced us to a most delicious lettuce soup he first met while working in England.

Soon after lunch, they all seem to have the same idea. They all want to stretch, take a long walk over the farm. It does clear the mind from the full glass of wine that Francesca says is Thornhill—gives them a chance to think the week over—or perhaps think about what they're doing with their young lives. And we never walk with them, unless asked. As they want to clear their minds, *I* want to clear the kitchen.

They walk to the top field, higher than the rest of the countryside, the land that looks over the house, over layers of green meadows in the spring, beige fields of corn in the late summer. Every season a different view, but always a view seemingly undisturbed by man. Still the same as when we first moved to Thornhill.

Then our young guests wander through the woods. There are ten acres of them, filled with white oak and beech and mountain laurel. This is where the Quakers hid their two horses from the Yankees marching through Maryland on their way to Gettysburg, and where we took our children, not so long ago, on pony picnics.

They invariably bring back souvenirs—leaves for pressing, walking sticks with the right curve and height, new memories.

If it's September, they gather the pears, apples, and chestnuts that have fallen near the house, a bounty to carry home. Then it is time for tea, maybe a nap before supper.

Lately they've been bringing friends with them to go on those walks, to sit by the fire—Hugh with a new girl, Francesca with a new beau. We, I think, have been accepted, perhaps for ourselves. Suddenly the steps between the ages are growing shorter. And as these young guests are *not* our children, we treat them as adults. And through them, we learn about our own. It's a wonderful exchange. Tom calls our new role *in loco parentis*, but I like to think we're just pals.

# *Chapter* Eleven

ENTERTAINING is one thing, *celebrating* is another. And we never celebrate without reason. A celebration should have a centerpiece, an importance, a joy. It makes setting the stage so much more fun, the planning so much more creative. And at Thornhill it is often a family connection—a birthday, wedding, christening, and of course, Christmas. Or a well-charted sit-down dinner for friends.

We have never, for instance, given a party at the drop of a cocktail napkin. Not that I feel any kindred spirit with Carry Nation, that fierce woman who threatened saloons with hatchets in the early 1900s, and I have certainly enjoyed the lavish libations of others at their own parties. But for the most part I find cocktail parties confusing—endless stand-up conversations, embarrassing moments when you can't remember someone's name, sometimes food, sometimes not. I find it an exhausting ritual. Rather, I think guests should be fed, cared for, and seated, no matter what age.

My friend Janet, who gave great parties filled with imagination, once told me that a party was like a medieval fair, with jugglers and magicians. The jugglers, she said, always seemed to get everything done, even at the last moment. But it was the magicians who brought the wonder, that touch of make-believe that turns a party *into* a celebration, makes the real world more pleasing, if only for brief moments. And if there was anyone who could wave a wand, it was Janet.

I'm certainly no magician, but I do struggle with those sleight of hands, my own hands as I always make our invitations. Tom says it's just because I like to cut and paste, like a child, but it is more than that. Granted, it takes more time, but to me it's having fun before you get there. It gets me in the spirit, and if I'm inspired, maybe our guests will be too.

For a tennis party I once made small racquets from the rattan cane I had left over after recaning a kitchen chair, and for a young girl's tea party I made garden hats. On white poster paper I pasted a yard of lavender-and-white gingham. Then I cut shapes of wide-brimmed hats, and trimmed them with a thin red ribbon, writing the particulars of the party on the other side. For a friend going on a holiday to Japan, I sent party invites on paper fans from the five-and-ten. And when we had a lunch at Thornhill before one of our country steeplechase races, I made colored luggage tags look like paddock tickets, the white envelopes striped with colors of racing silks. But the invitations I wish *I* had sent were made by our neighbor Minnie.

On stiff paper she painted circles of color, abstract designs, wrote the details of her soirée, then cut the stiff paper into a jigsaw puzzle. The minute I opened the envelope, the party had begun. And after I fitted the pieces together, I knew it. We had been invited for "fun and games." That's one invitation I've kept. So original, so Minnie. I collect designs that will make invitations more interesting, and I file them under "I" in my office. That's often about as far as they get. Just like all those recipes I'm always cutting out of magazines and newspapers.

If there are more than twenty-five invitations to be made, I resort to block stamps. Again I guess I'm like a child, stamping away. I have a beautiful one of a sheep looking as if she just walked in from a meadow in England. I stamp it with a blue pad, or a green one, depending on my mood, onto white postcards. I also have a stamp of a coronet which I bought from a London stall, one of those moveable shops that appear on Sundays along the fences of Hyde Park. But I've never dared use it. We've never had a party that royal.

Another easy, and reasonable, invitation is to copy old prints. My source is my collection of *Punch*, an English magazine started in 1840. As these prints from the pages of the magazine were the cartoons of their day, especially in the mid-1800s, they are often amusing, making fun of bloomers and bustles, mustaches and manners. I just put the page of the book on Tom's copying machine and out come the invitations, one after another. I use a long enough sheet of copying paper so I can write the specific details of the party at the bottom of the page, as well as simple directions to Thornhill Farm.

When our children were younger, I enlisted them to make their own invitations. After all it was their birthday party, and to me the drawings of children can be as provocative as those of Picasso. At least that's what *most* mothers think. I rationed these parties as there were four children born, different years of course, but all within a span of five months—late November, early December, late January, early March. It could have been quite a circuit. To survive motherhood, as well as the social scene, I gave each child a birthday party every other year.

Tommy had his boating party, the kitchen camouflaged as an ocean liner, and for Todd's "Thornhill Express," I turned the furniture of the living room into a long line of trains led by a locomotive—the wing chair—and ending up with the caboose—the settee. Each guest was given a red handkerchief to tie around his neck and a striped engineer's cap to make him feel more important. There were a lot of whistles blown that day, and I had a wonderful time punching tickets.

"Miss Beth's Sunday Salon," with all the guests arriving in their parents' faded finery, celebrated Beth's fifth birthday.

And when Louise was twelve there was a "My Fair Lady" fete. I canopied the dining room like a huge umbrella with streamers of blue-and-white crepe paper, gave each fair lady a paper parasol, and immediately after lunch whisked them all off to the movies to see Eliza Doolittle dance at the ball.

These parties entertained the children, and they also gave mothers a chance to get together and chat, and probably, compare. It's only human. Even at that age there is a party dress code—little dresses heavy with smocking, little boy legs in the shortest of pants. When Todd was invited to his first birthday party, he was probably all of four. I dressed him in a bright new pair of red corduroy overalls. I thought he looked irresistible, but the moment we entered Geordie's house I saw all those little boy legs in short navy blue pants. I felt miserable, I felt I had failed my son. It seems so silly now, but at the time I felt as if I had sent my son to a black tie dinner in a pin-striped suit. And maybe it's one of the reasons most of *our* children's parties came in costume.

As our children grew up, so did our parties. For Todd's sixteenth birthday I organized a surprise coon hunt, led by the local plumber's hound dogs. Tom and I had been to an adult version of this party, and it seemed unusual, a new twist, although it had been a Maryland country sport for years. What I hadn't taken into account were the sensitivities of teenagers. In the dark, flashlights in hand, we all scurried through the woods of Thornhill chasing some terrified raccoon who was smart enough to climb a tree and disappear. I later learned that Todd hated every moment of it, thought it all barbaric—which it certainly was, and I blush when I think about it. In my quest for something original, I had completely misread the cast. Gone overboard. Lost my reason. Sometimes, no matter how well you plan, a party just doesn't work. And that's one party I like to forget.

Next we tried a dance. But we didn't take any chances by

giving it for one of our own. We gave it for Laurie, the eighteen-year-old daughter of Alice and Frank, and we held it in the nearby Butler firehouse. The thought of giving a dance in a firehouse, long accustomed to covered dish suppers and bingo, but never a waltz, gave me pleasure from the very beginning. We asked everyone to wear something red, and we called it "The Fireman's Ball." It was fun, and the exhilaration of knowing a party worked kept us going into the early hours while the Hardie family did the sweeping up. But then nothing is ever perfect, and it took us a day or so to find the missing firemen's helmets which some of our male guests thought were party hats.

That dance must have put some sort of bee in Beth's bonnet, as in a few years she and two pals, Wendy and Jenny, asked to have a dance on the front lawn of Thornhill. We were delighted. The other two mothers and I decided to hire a tent. Since it was our first tent, we shopped around, discovered all that canvas can be a costly item. And as it was May and the grass was green we quickly crossed out "dance floor" from our list. The tent we finally found *was* reasonable, so cheap that it leaked all evening long as rain fell over Thornhill Farm. Our front lawn was a complete mud bath. Bare feet danced up a storm, and the spring seersucker suits of the young boys became so splashed with mud that they began to look like gingerbread men. And they loved it. Because of the mud, they had an excuse to act like children in a grown-up environment. Sometimes it is the unknown, the unexpected that makes a party go. Even if it's mud.

But *most* important is the music. That's where the party money should be spent. If it is contagious and catchy, it can, like a bridle, hold a party together, and like reins, lead the dancers on. Without good music, you can lead a guest to the dance floor, but you can't make him dance the next dance. It took us a while to learn this.

We did have enough sense to dance into the barn—where we should have been in the first place. It was perfect with its sturdy floors, wide arena, no tent necessary. We never thought of using the barn before because we never knew what to do with all those stored bales of hay. But if we waited, we discovered, long enough into the spring, the sheep devoured most of the hay, and the rest of the bales we piled up into corner pyramids, making grandstand seats for the guests. And we gave a country gala for Kate, Cynthia and David's young daughter.

Since it was our first venture into the barn we thought it would be appropriate to have a square dance, a good old-fashioned hoedown. I wonder what the sheep in the stalls below thought was going on? There were our two professional callers, done up in ten-gallon hats, ruffles, and twirls, and the music was their country records. It was a resounding flop! Our young guests didn't particularly want to doe-see-doe, or promenade with their partners. No indeed, they wanted to shimmy and shake, dance through the night to the beat of the wild. Another bonus to good music is that the young guests dancing on through the night often have little time to tap the beer kegs and they'll eat anything. But I always make it a point to have a long table, actually an old paneled door, supported on both ends by hay bales, filled with do-it-yourself sandwiches, bowls of popcorn and pretzels, platters of different cheeses, lots of fruit, a keg of beer, sodas. And later, continuous coffee.

Thornhill sounds like an all-night dance hall, when in truth we've probably given five dances at the most. But now that we have the pattern, I see more on the horizon. Yet dinner parties are much more frequent at Thornhill. Maybe it's because I love to dress a table. Tom enjoys the warmth and action of a good party, the people, the conversations, a buoyant evening. I enjoy all that too, but I'm not as relaxed as he is. (Southern blood *does* show when it comes to entertaining.) Then too when he sits down to a dinner party at Thornhill, it's like seeing the show for the first time, while I've been on the road for days, getting the props and the program ready for opening night. But that's what I like to do. And it's comforting to know that he can handle the dialogue. Sometimes he handles it so well that he forgets he's the host. Then I feel obliged to run around asking guests what they want to drink, then giving Tom a shove toward the bottles. Still, when the final curtain comes down, I'd rather do dishes with him than anyone else.

Center stage is our dining room table, oval and old, once used by Tom's grandparents. A late Victorian, it is steady, heavy, and ugly. Maybe that's why I keep it under cover most of the time. It seats six comfortably, eight closely, and ten intimately. For twelve we need to put in a leaf, and it's like a tug of war pulling the heavy table apart. Then I decorate. Nothing much matches, chairs or china, but that's my usual pattern.

And our tableclothes, at least the ones I like best, seem to have tumbled right out of bed. There's the dark blue-and-white striped one made of ticking, the way mattress ticking used to be, and I use country quilts all the time. Sometimes in the summer I turn the tables by using cotton tablecloths, born as such, as flowered canopies on the four-poster bed.

I've been known to set the dinner table three days in advance. Tom thinks this is hilarious, but I know it's security. It's also having fun, like making the invitations, even before the party starts. I think this must be my mother's influence. She didn't entertain at dinner parties, but she always decorated our family table, no matter how modest the holiday. And although she was Swedish, there were shamrock surprises every Saint Patrick's Day, lovely valentines, and on the first day of May, always a May basket and bows tied on our bicycles.

When I set the table, I choose the cloth first, or borrow it from a bed. And I like my napkins big, really big. There's quite a wardrobe as over the years, I've cut many of them from materials I couldn't resist at Blank's, a fabric store where Mr. Lurie unearths bolt after bolt of cotton fireworks. Talk about magicians, he can find any material you want. For a more elaborate evening, we use the inherited white damask napkins, dignified and pure as the driven snow, the raised monogram embroidered as flowers more than seventy years ago by the Ursuline nuns in a New Orleans convent.

I wreath the napkins in real flowers, sometimes wild ones from the fields or baby's breath from the garden. And I stretch ribbons across the table so it looks like the chest of an Italian ambassador presenting his credentials to the Queen. But not all at the same time, mind you. I have a very good time with this table.

There are usually place cards, easy identification. Sometimes they are like medals—made from a stationer's gold seal with ribbons below. As we grow older I write the names larger so our friends don't fumble around in the candlelight. And there are always candles as we have a family source. Todd's beeswax makes marvelous, mellow tapers. And if Louise or Beth are around, their calligraphy on the place cards is a lovely, flowing touch. I place the cards against egg cups I find in Emma's antiques shop, fill them with small zinnias. In the autumn I use leaves instead of cards. The yellows and reds of maple are sturdy enough to take the writing of a black felt-tip pen.

I like party favors, too. Perhaps I've never grown up from those children's birthday parties. Favors do make a table more festive. Sometimes I use cool silver Christmas balls in the middle of a hot summer. Even a wooden spoon tied with a pansy, a favor I used for an engagement party, has a certain air. Or in the fall, a paper arrow as a name card stuck in a round red apple always starts a conversation—which is what every dinner party needs from the very beginning.

Once I've set the table, and it pleases me as I walk by, my private party is over. It's time to make my entrance in the kitchen. That takes time, as I'm usually in a stew. Cooking to me is much more of a challenge. But having my supporting cast, the dinner table already in costume, gives me courage. Then all I have to do is try to make a star out of spinach, or whatever is in season in our garden.

The one time I wasn't too stirred up by the menu, or what-in-the-world-will-we-serve-our guests, was, surprisingly enough, at the largest dinner party we've ever given. Without consulting me, Tom invited the *entire* Australian Ballet, then on tour in Baltimore, for Sunday supper at Thornhill Farm.

I was aghast, at first, by the thought. Tom claims he told me earlier in the month, but then Tom has a way of announcing major happenings when I'm totally involved in something else. It's his protection, his trick. I have a one-track mind, and he knows it. And when he told me about these young stars of the ballet, I was decorating the Christmas tree, my mind miles away from Australia.

But this island continent was very close to Tom as he had just been there on a business trip. It was his first visit there, and he was enthralled with the people, their wines, the spirit. Everything from Down Under was high priority to Tom and he wanted to return their hospitality. I didn't feel quite the same, and as I sat there writing eighty-some notes saying "In Honor of the Australian Ballet, an Open House at Thornhill Farm," I kept telling myself what a good sport I was, wondering how were we ever going to fit eighty people in our farmhouse on a cold winter's night.

Somehow I learned that these young dancers, while on the road, were only given an allowance for two meals a day. My heart was beginning to soften. My maternal instinct began to stir, even blossom. Their dinner, I decided, would be Very American. We made Maryland beaten biscuits to go with the ham and turkey, brown bread to serve with the baked beans. There were bowls full of Boston lettuce that I managed to find at the Lexington Market in Baltimore, and platters of Thornhill lamb, casseroles of southern yams. When I told Tom I was going to have popsicles for dessert, he was horrified. "You can't serve popsicles to the ballet," he said. But somehow all those brownies, apple pies, *and* popsicles disappeared immediately.

It was a memorable evening, our Thornhill filled with fifty elegant willows, lithe spirits, the enthusiasm of youth. They were everywhere. From the bedrooms to the kitchen where they were playing chopsticks on the old upright with Todd, then sixteen, and Tommy, thirteen. They taught Louise, a graceful fifteen, how to point her toes, showed twelve-year-old Beth how to wear a tutu. And they were so appreciative, so happy to be in a home again after months on tour. There was a wonderful warmth wrapped around Thornhill on that cold winter's evening. Sometimes the party you don't *really* want to give turns out to be the best of all.

Although there was never a repeat performance of the ballet scene, it has become one of our children's memories. Memories, traditions sometimes happen all on their own, but often you have to *make* them. I guess that's what I've been trying to do all these years. I wanted our children to have the continuity in a house that I never had. I wanted Thornhill to be the heart of the matter. It takes nourishing, but it's something that no one can ever take away. And there's no other place in the world, other than Thornhill Farm, that our daughter Louise, when she was twenty-one, could have had her wedding reception. It was a natural.

When Louise's engagement was first announced, I was told by a country father of four daughters that the first wedding in the family is like the first waffle. You're never sure how it will turn out. He was so right. And there's a vast difference, I was to discover for myself, between a marriage and a wedding. A marriage, if you're lucky, especially in these times of easy change, goes on and on and on, while a wedding is a one-day festival that takes months to plan. And I learned a lot, planning Louise's wedding, about dazzle and decisions. It's their wedding, so don't compete with the Carnival of Roses. Not that I didn't try. After all, this was our first family wedding.

Although Louise and Scott chose to be married in early October, I was determined it was going to be a summer country wedding. That was the kind of wedding Thornhill *should* have, and besides I can't stand chrysanthemums, a flower I feel suited only to football games. And when I found a lovely white chintz patterned with pink ribbons and lavender pansies, I felt we had taken the first giant step. From this material we made tablecloths for every round table that was going to be at the reception on the lawn. Even Beth, the maid of honor, was to wear a long pinafore of the same material. And in the middle of each table was one of our house baskets filled with garden flowers.

Then Louise wanted to sit down and draw floral bouquets as the invitations. It sounded charming, but not very realistic. There were going to be 120 invited to the wedding—that's all Saint John's will hold—and a hundred more invited to the reception. She would have been at her drawing board until she walked down the aisle. Tom vetoed the idea immediately. He wanted the traditional. There were tears, there was compromise. Louise wrote the invitation in her elegant calligraphy and they were properly engraved, with the Hardie family seal embossed at the top. Tom also insisted that, as the father of the bride, he was going to wear a morning suit, striped trousers and all, even though he would be the only member of the wedding dressed so formally. There was no dispute here. He has certain inalienable rights.

The next decision was food. Louise thought apple pies, made from our own apples, would be perfect for the reception. *Only* apple pies. It began to sound more and more like a country fair rather than a country wedding. We finally agreed on clam chowder, in case it was a cold day, and because of New England grandparents, and the best of Maryland—lots of crab, a raw bar with oysters. Once the food was settled, I wondered what else there was to worry about?

The twenty-one-year-old bride refused to have her china in one pattern. No, she wanted each plate to be different. Guests questioned, but generously gave Limoges "Vieux Chine" mingled with Wedgwood's "Morning Glory" and other flowered fancies. And she was absolutely right. When she sets her dinner table for a party, it looks like a Matisse. She returned all the steak knives, as she figured they wouldn't be able to afford steak, and the casseroles kept marching in.

We thought we had it all figured out. Then the morning of the wedding a sixty-five-mile-an-hour wind swept through our farm. The tent, much finer than the sieve we had for Beth's dance, although planted a week in advance for security, was flapping its wings like an old goose about to fly away. Nearby five very tall locust trees careened over like fallen Redcoats. And there was no " 'lectric." We had planned this wedding months ahead, with a strategy that a general might envy. And then a sudden country storm sabotaged us. We put boxes of champagne on the bottom of the tent flaps to hold them down, ignored the fallen trees, left the caterers to worry about heating the food with sterno, and somehow got to the church on time. And when we returned from the afternoon wedding, everything was working again at Thornhill Farm.

Then we all quietly hibernated over the winter, recharged our batteries. But when June came, it was Tom's turn to be feted. I thought he deserved it. It was his birthday. And I gave him a balloon, a big rented one striped in red and yellow and blue. Birthdays, I decided, especially as we grow older, shouldn't be wrapped in the anonymous pretense that they are just like any other day. No indeed, they are days to celebrate, your very own fete day, champagne rather than cider, days to exaggerate. Besides, I had never been in a balloon, and Tom and I have a way of giving each other presents we would really like for ourselves.

The balloon puffed up to giant size right in our front field. It grew and it grew. Then we climbed into the wicker gondola with the pilot, someone I tried to imagine wasn't there. I wanted this to be a romantic interlude. A celebration just for two. And it was. We gently rose into the sky, the world below became miniature. Thornhill, the barn, the cornfields grew smaller, soon so small they looked like they belonged under a Christmas tree. We sailed over treetops, we ran with the wind. We were, I like to think, only a little lower than angels. After forty-five minutes we floated down and a flock of farm children rushed out in wonder. I'll never forget it, nor can I remember just how old Tom was on that beautiful day.

# *Chapter* Twelve

FOR some, traditions are like pigtails. When you grow up, you cut them off. But *not* at Thornhill Farm. And holidays are easy traditions. They've already been created, they're built-in celebrations. The Fourth of July is a wonderful excuse for decking Thornhill with a regalia of red, white, and blue. And I *love* the American flag.

That may sound awfully corny, but once you've lived abroad, those stars and stripes mean even more. Or maybe it's because as a twelve-year-old Girl Scout *I* carried the flag in a small-town Memorial Day parade. And I'll never forget a window box I once saw in front of a rowhouse in Baltimore. The façade of the rowhouse was as anonymous as all the others on the block, but the window box was filled with small American flags stuck in between the flowers. It was like the front line of a miniature parade.

At Thornhill we have our own supply of flags. There's a silk one, dating from the Spanish-American War, which I found in the Nantucket Hospital thrift shop, and ten others, made of cotton, came from a garage-antiques shop in Concord, New Hampshire. These flags are about a yard long, with forty-eight stars in the top left corner and WONOLANCET CLUB written in block letters in the lower border. Since we had forty-eight stars as far back as 1912, I like to think these flags have celebrated many a glorious Fourth, complete with fireworks and dancing under the stars. And as they only cost fifty cents each, I felt the least I could do was to have them cleaned for a Fourth of July at Thornhill.

It's not often one says, "I'm taking my flags to the cleaners." And I didn't. Instead, when Monday came, I asked Homer, who has been collecting here for years, if his laundry did flags.

"Of course," he said with his usual country brevity. Since I had ten of them, I asked how much they would cost.

"Flags are free," he answered.

I couldn't believe it. Could this really be, I wondered, or was it just small-town patriotism, a vestige of old-time America? I gave them to Homer, with gratitude, then called several dry cleaners in Baltimore. I discovered that yes indeed, the cleaning of an American flag is always on the house. In fact they'll clean any other country's flag as well. Suddenly, somehow, the whole world looked a lot better. Flags are still free, it seems, at least at the cleaners.

For Easter, another reason to puff up Thornhill, I bring out the baskets rather than the flags. These are baskets I've made for our children while vacationing on Nantucket where I can rent the molds, big Lightship baskets that I hope will be part of the Easter tradition forever. I fill the baskets with surprises—writing paper, lettuce and carrot seeds from England, flowered dress buttons, books, whatever catches my eye throughout the year or on our travels. One year I put a pair of scissors and a pot of paste in each basket as my own desk supplies kept disappearing.

I sprinkle the baskets with jelly beans, stealing most of the licorice ones for myself, and I bow the handles with plum and peach moiré ribbons from my favorite store, the Cockeysville five-and-ten. It's a lot like decorating an Easter hat. Beth's basket is always addressed to "Elizabunny."

I enjoy filling these baskets even more than Christmas stockings. Christmas is *so* gifted that the family stockings, some made from retired quilts, are often my last thoughts, while an Easter basket is the *one* treasure of the day. And I hide them, childish as it may seem, in the woodpile, the boxwood bushes, behind the spring tulips. Then it's time for lunch.

The lunch table is set with Beatrix Potter Wedgwood china which I have been collecting, with anticipation and great expectations, for years. I only use these Peter Rabbit plates on Easter, but I hope in time they will be usual fare for visiting grandchildren. I can hardly wait to set a children's tea table with Peter Rabbit running away from Mr. McGregor's garden. I'm going to thoroughly enjoy my second childhood.

Maybe even as much as Christmas which is *the* celebration as far as I'm concerned. Tom says I celebrate Christmas all year round which is as exaggerated as Christmas sometimes is, but I must admit I do hoard throughout the year, often thinking, in the middle of June, that I've found the right present for the right person. It's my own little game, mix and match. I push these presents into a pine cupboard in our bedroom. Then in early December I have a marvelous time rediscovering my loot. Christmas is the one time of the year when I don't have to take down the props the very next day. There is a time for tinsel, and this is it.

Christmas, if you look at a calendar, happens all by itself, as do all the holidays, but Christmas, most of all, needs no invitation. Yet to celebrate, truly celebrate, takes time and care. I have one friend John who combs our woods at Thornhill for pine cones, then ties them with bright tassels to decorate gifts. A neighbor Jane makes a succulent pea soup, braids homemade bread, to serve on Christmas Eve when the carolers come by on horse. After those hearty bowls of soup, the carolers mount to go home, riding away with extra-tall flickering sparklers, saved from the Fourth of July, and given to them at the front door. It is quite a sight.

### JANE'S SPLIT PEA SOUP WITH CURRY

2 1-pound packages green split peas
6 quarts of water
2 pounds ham, preferrably a leftover butt-end piece or one provided by a butcher, but a small picnic roll may be used
4 onions, sliced
6 bay leaves
1 teaspoon ground cloves
Salt and pepper
Curry powder

Soak peas overnight in 6 quarts of water in a large stew pot, or cook a few minutes and let stand one hour. Combine all ingredients except curry. Simmer 3 or 4 hours or until most of the peas turn into a paste. A blender can be used as a shortcut to soften peas after putting the meat and bone aside. Add water as needed to keep mixture liquid but not thin and watery. Serve with chunks of ham in it and curry powder sprinkled on top, the more the merrier as this makes all the difference.
Serves 20

Robert, another friend, always has an orange and onion salad because as a boy in France during the war there *were* no oranges. Except on Christmas morning. He thought then it was Père Noël's gift, but now he realizes they were harvested by clandestine methods, known only to mothers. Especially French ones.

## ROBERT VIRET'S ORANGE AND ONION SALAD

- 2 oranges
- 1 large onion
- generous pinch sugar
- salt and pepper to taste
- 3 tablespoons olive oil
- 1 tablespoon vinegar

Peel the oranges and onion and slice evenly. Put a layer of oranges in the bottom of a serving bowl, sprinkle with very little sugar. Put a layer of onions on top, salt and pepper. Repeat. Whisk together oil and vinegar. Pour over orange and onion mixture and let stand a few hours in the refrigerator before serving. Especially refreshing after so much rich Christmas food.
Serves 4 to 6

It was in France that Tom and I celebrated our first Christmas together. He met me a week before Christmas at Orly Airport in a new fourteen-year-old Citroën convertible, a low chariot of azure blue. In the rakish *speed-aire*, the rumble seat, was standing a Christmas tree, and up front was a bunch of violets.

That tree later proved to be the only decoration in our apartment on the Villa Guilbert for the lunch before our wedding on December twenty-third. Bob, an art student, had magically touched the forlorn little evergreen, decked it with whatever was on hand, whatever was in reach. Baroque paste pearls, strings of them, sausagelike links of second-class metro tickets, red-and-white checkered napkins tied in broad bows, and at the top, a gleaming tin cookie cutter in the shape of a heart.

On Christmas morning, two days later, Tom and I were in Marseilles on our honeymoon, our *lune de miel*, eating oysters at the port. After the gray of Paris, the first sun we had seen bounced off the white bellies of the wet fish, and Moroccan vendors wandered around with their shoulders of rugs, looking for all the world as if they were seeking a manger.

## *Chapter Twelve*

We still have oysters at Christmas, and we always have trees. I can't possibly imagine Christmas without a tree. They are our constant Christmas glow, our exclamation points throughout the house. And we usually have three.

Every year I forget how tired I was the year before. Every year I become a born-again Christmas addict. And by the second week in December our trees are dressed in glory. The tallest tree is in the living room, and at the top is a fine Woolworthian parrot. Now an ancient age twenty-five, the parrot was bought, jointly, by our children. It's one parrot that never talks back. And under the lowest bough of the tree is a collection of toys—the wooden horse our children once rode, a miniature Welsh dresser, *my* china doll from England, Fiona Barley. The tree itself is looped with golden beads, hung only with bright balls. We save the ornaments, ones we've made, been given, or gathered on trips, for the dining room tree. Each ornament has its own story, makes us remember.

The dining room tree must be plump as a goose, must reach at least to my nose. Sometimes I think if we could only have one tree I'd choose to put it in the dining room. It makes every meal an occasion, and eating dinner by the sparkle of a tree is magic. I first saw a dining tree in Finland, and the Finns, who have the darkest of winters, keep their trees up forever. Our dining room tree doesn't take itself quite as seriously as does the one in the living room. Perhaps because it's short and fat and fun.

Standing in the kitchen is the living tree, planted later in a border hedge around a field. This tree is decorated with sheep cookies Beth has made, tied on with thin red ribbons. She always makes extra cookies to give away to friends who come by during the holiday. Sometimes I box them as a present, other times we just give one or two as tree ornaments. It depends on how well the baking goes, how many bake into a tasty flock, how many we burn in the attempt.

## BETH'S SHEEPY SUGAR COOKIES

1 cup butter
1½ cups sugar
2 eggs, well beaten
3 teaspoons vanilla extract
½ teaspoon lemon extract
3 cups flour
2 teaspoons baking powder
½ teaspoon salt

Cream butter and sugar together, add eggs, vanilla, and lemon extract. Beat well. In another bowl sift together flour, salt and baking powder. Add to the first mixture. Mix well. Chill for about 1 hour. Roll dough out very thinly on a floured surface, then cut with any type of cookie cutter. At Thornhill we use a tin cutter shaped like a sheep. The sheep is about the size of my hand and makes about 24 cookies. Bake 6 to 8 minutes in a 350° F. oven. While cookies are cooling on the sheet, sprinkle some cookies with white sugar, others with brown sugar. The two sugars make an interesting flock of sheep.

The kitchen tree is decorated as well with a bouquet of spiced pears, oranges, lemons, and limes, embroidered with designs of cloves. The scent is delicious. To make the job easier, I first make the holes in the fruit with an ice pick. I also make colonial kissing balls the same way. Using grapefruit, I ice-pick the holes, then completely cover the grapefruit with tiny sprigs of boxwood. Soon the grapefruit looks like a round green porcupine. After making a few, I hang them with broad red ribbons around the archways of the house.

In earlier years the children even put a tree in the barn for the sheep. Decorated with biscuits dipped in honey, it seemed appropriate, again going back to the manger. One year Tommy and I went to a tree farm to cut one down. Right next to us, doing the very same thing, was his idol, the great Orioles third baseman Brooks Robinson. We were so excited we left the saw behind. And perhaps showing off near his hero, Tommy carried the cut tree by himself—absolutely upright. The way he carried the cross when he was an acolyte in church. A family went by and said, "I see a tree with legs," and we all laughed and it was fun, the way spirits should be around Christmas. Seeing Brooks Robinson, I'm sure, was Tommy's best Christmas present of all.

Another early gift for children is the felt Christmas calendar my friend Margaret makes. She used to pretend that her own children had made them, as she didn't think much of her own stitches, but these calendars are charming. The calendar is a square of bright yellow felt, twenty by thirty inches, with a large green Christmas tree sewn in the center. Along three sides, the left, lower, and right, she sews a row of small yellow pockets each numbered in green felt, from one through twenty-three, up until a red pocket heralds the twenty-fourth of December. In each pocket is a tiny token attached to a tiny safety pin—a star, a butterfly, a golden acorn, a bumblebee. Each day a pocket is opened, the present pinned onto the center Christmas tree. And each year she replenishes the pockets with new surprises.

I use ribbons more than felt, and in the yellow dining room I tie big red bows on the brass sconces. In the red library I hang floor-length streamers of green ribbons from the very top molding. But first I staple a three-inch ribbon with the Christmas cards we have received, each about five inches apart. Rather than sitting the cards in the bookcases or piling them in a bowl, I find these streamers and cards add a gaiety to the room. They greet friends almost immediately, and flutter when the front door opens. It's like a roomful of miniature pictures. I also sew silver Christmas balls to graduated lengths of red ribbon, then hang them in a Palladian curve over entrances of bedroom doors. Once I get started, I can't seem to stop.

Now that the children are grown, I seem to have more time. But it wasn't always like this. When our children were young, Christmas was another challenge of parenthood, like teaching them how to tie shoes. Would I, could I, ever get it all tied up and packaged by the big night? We overspent and underestimated our children's intelligence. And it was all so sadly calculated. If Todd gets eight presents and a train from Grandpa, what are Tommy's matching gifts? If Louise gets that doll, would Beth like a clown? And engineers we certainly were not. Little red wagons always limped along on Christmas Day because we always lost that last little screw. And there was that jungle gym that never did get put together, just put away before the morning eyes of children ever saw it. We learned *never* to buy anything that had to be assembled.

What I assemble now are wreaths. And I wreathe everywhere—from making a Christmas collar for the larger-than-life-size goose decoy on our front lawn, to putting circles of green on the stable doors of friends. These wreaths can be made of any evergreen—fir, balsam, moss cypress—but I always use boxwood because it is mine. I like its dark green shiny glow and that some of the wreaths last for months. One Easter Tom asked me if I didn't think it was time to take the Christmas wreath from the inside of the kitchen door. It was still green although it was late April. Sometimes for a spring party I make another boxwood wreath, pinning yellow daffodils and white narcissus against the green. Any flower will brighten the garland, and a more delicate, lacy look, I discovered, was when I put white lilacs and apple blossoms on the boxwood wreath.

Our boxwood are always waiting for us, no matter what season. When we first planted these bushes some thirty years ago, they were knee-high greenery. Now they are five feet tall, wider than Santa Claus, and just as generous. When Agnes first insisted we plant them, I thought of them merely as fringe benefits, but now they are an important part of Thornhill traditions. And if a bush can be part of a family tree, I consider these boxwood bushes close relations, always ready to give when asked.

I prune them in early December for Christmas. I break the limbs from deep in the center of the bush with my hands, never with clippers. And I gather enough for wreaths and garlands. Then I pat the bushes and thank them for their winter kindness. The boughs always spring back, as if to say, "Okay, we've done our part, now it's up to you."

The first wreath is the most exciting. Christmas is almost here. That first wreath goes right on the inside of the kitchen door. The others I make live outdoors. And as I often give wreaths as presents, I make them whenever I find time—often under the dryer at the hairdresser's. They are *that* easy. I arrive at Mr. Ryan's hair salon, which is in a converted barn, with a basket full of boxwood, a straw wreath form, and lots of fern pins. Both the wreath forms and pins, which are like miniature croquet wickets, can be found at the five-and-ten, my source for all my decorating, or at any florist.

The wreath forms measure fifteen to eighteen inches in diameter, edge to edge. I place the wreath on the kitchen table, or my lap, and start pinning the branches of boxwood around the circle counterclockwise or clockwise. It all ends up the same. I overlap, slightly, every bough. This way each fern pin is covered by the next fan of greenery. Then I pin the inner circle, and the last is the outer rim. To make a fuller, more complete wreath, I pin the backside as well.

Self-taught, I realize there must be a more proper procedure for making a wreath, careful steps to insure a perfect circle. And if any wreath of mine was ever entered in a garden club competition, I'm sure I'd be disqualified immediately for errant fern pins sticking out from under the green. But there is no way that is any quicker. And that's the fun of it. I can whip up a wreath in twenty minutes. If a curve of the wreath seems to be a bit wild, a bough out of line, that simply adds to its natural charm.

Our own front door wreath and the wreaths I give away I decorate with small ornaments that can be used the next year on the Christmas tree. Or sometimes I decorate with fresh fruit. Over the years I've used green grapes and small Madonna apples, wooden toys, and old lace. Whatever takes my fancy. I fasten these ornaments with fern pins, or tie them with *very* narrow ribbon. The big bow is often of Scottish plaid or a deep red grosgrain ribbon. I hang these door wreaths with ribbon by looping it through the circle, then taking both ends and thumbtacking them high to the unseen top edge of the door frame. If I have time to make inside window wreaths for the red library, I leave those wreaths, solidly green, adding no additional color.

Our dining room table is the last scene to set. And again I often do it days ahead, much preferring to dress the table than the turkey. A great-grandmother's cloth, like Mrs. Cratchit's gown in *A Christmas Carol*, "twice-turned but brave with ribbons," covers the oval table. It is turkey red, and in the center I use a boxwood wreath as a green nest to cover a large patch of age. I fill the nest with golden balls sewn to tartan or red ribbons. The ribbons stream from the nest like a Christmas maypole and on each ribbon, written with glitter, is the name of a member of the family or a friend. These ribbons and balls become place cards as well as souvenirs of a Thornhill Christmas, our guests taking them home to put on their own tree. At each place at the table I also put a Christmas cracker, the kind you pull at a child's party, complete with paper hats—a tradition I borrowed from England. I like to think they fit the occasion. Christmas, after all, is our biggest birthday party of the year.

With the house decorated, food cooked ahead as much as possible, presents for my family that please me, I take off. I *never* go to the marketplace the week before Christmas. I find it helps my spirit, makes it easier to follow the star. Instead I go to the Baltimore Museum of Art to feast, to look once again at the French Impressionist paintings and the fine collection of American furniture. This solitary venture is a gift of time, a gift to myself. Then I go home and open a bottle of champagne with Tom. I like Christmas to bubble from the very beginning.

# *Chapter* Thirteen

LIVING in the country, I found collecting was second nature to our children. They filled their shelves with unlimited enthusiasm—cracked robins' eggs, Mason jars of lightning bugs, birds' nests, butterfly wings, and old nails (but *only* those over seven inches long). Todd eventually graduated to coins and stamps, while Tommy stuck with teddy bears, without any shame, until he was about twelve. Then he packed them all up, labeled them carefully by name, and put them in his closet where they're still waiting for someone to play.

Their mother, however, continues to collect. It's so easy. One old teacup is a treasure, two starts a collection. It's that simple. But then collecting is often unintentional. Like love, it just happens. It's that sudden sparkle between you and a lusterware bowl in a small antiques shop. It can also be an unlikely marriage that no one understands but you. But that's the sport—for some an innocent game, for others an expensive leisure, for many, a quiet passion. And once you let it embrace you, the hunt is on. Part of the pleasure is the pursuit.

When I look around Thornhill now, I realize there is a collection in almost every room. They warm us, give us a certain sustenance, an ambiance that makes our house our own. No first editions of books, just first photographs of our family and how they grew. On a corner living room table a bevy of photographs instantly starts a conversation when strangers bend over to scrutinize the faces. On the wall of the upstairs hall is another gallery of photographs, the steps of our lives. And in the library on two of the shelves is a collection of wooden toys and a zoo of wooden animals, some carved by a man who worked for a circus, all enclosed in a pen of popsicle sticks.

In the kitchen the pine cupboard holds a covey of teacups from England, France, assorted aunts, and early America. I collected them because I like tea in *china*. To me it tastes better. Mugs are not my métier. And when I serve a tray or table of tea, these fine bone-china cups, splashed with painted bouquets, give a pleasant air just by being there. It doesn't take much to add a little grandeur to small moments in the day.

On top of the cupboard sit six teapots of various sizes—inherited, inveigled, beloved. I only bought one of them, a small black pot dotted with bright pink rosebuds. On the lid, printed in gold, a noble FOR ENGLAND AND FOR DEMOCRACY. And on the bottom, "World War II, Made in England, Escorted to U.S.A. by Royal Navy." My mother didn't understand why her thirteen-year-old daughter was spending three of her dollars to buy a black teapot. But I knew. I knew my teapot had outwitted those turtlenecked sailors on those German U-boats, I knew *then* there'd always be an England. What I didn't know was that first teapot was the beginning of a love affair that would last all my life, an unshakable admiration for anything English.

That year I collected other romantic ideas. In my closet in a shoe box under the hat box were my prizes—a Red Sox baseball from the summer Ted Williams hit .409, a summer I spent in the left-field bleachers of Fenway Park in Boston watching my hero's every move; an autographed photograph of my then and forever idol, Katharine Hepburn, wearing white crepe pajamas and carrying calla lilies; a blotchy stone, like the face of an adolescent, from Lizzie Borden's garden.

Lizzie Borden, around the turn of the century in Fall River, Massachusetts, took an ax "and gave her mother forty whacks. When she saw what she had done, she gave her father forty-one." One way or the other, she did them both in. Or so I think, although she was never proved guilty.

She did, however, prove irresistible to two young amateur detectives. And when my older cousin, Neal, and I visited our relatives in that former textile city, we made pilgrimages to Lizzie's house, her garden, and, I shudder to remember, even her gravesite. Then we'd go to a second-floor restaurant owned by Anna May Wong's brother (she of silent film fame) for soggy chow mein sandwiches, ten cents each. It was there Neal produced this unusual stone. "See those blood-red spots," he whispered, and I paid him a nickel for it. He went on to become an FBI agent; I went on collecting.

My habits are still the same. At one point I even collected country names, names with a Dickensian ring and purpose. Mr. Sprinkle was once our laundry man, Mr. Bear, the taxidermist, and Mrs. Nest is still in real estate. But I've been told half the world is different, half the world knows when to stop. You either accumulate, or you pare down. There are some so self-disciplined that they haven't collected since they pasted a purple King Farouk in their stamp book. I admire their restraint, but where do their memories go? I've tried to tidy up, but how do you prune away the past?

My friend Ned understands. When he was ten years old his grandmother gave him a Federal eagle, and he has been collecting ever since. When you visit his house you would never suspect that this American bird is an endangered species. He has a majestic collection of quilts, all with eagles as a motif, his walls are mounted with eagle quarterboards, even eagle buttons from old uniforms. He collects with gusto and style, obvious delight. Show and tell is one of the joys of collecting, no matter what age.

Tom is of a different flavor. He claims he doesn't like "things," or "dust collectors" as he calls them when he accuses me of succumbing to a new fancy. I think he's a closet collector and just won't admit it. How else can he explain all those shelves of books on sailing, his collection of James Bond mysteries, but *only* in French, his boast that he's read and owned most of Georges Simenon? There is, whether he knows it or not, a little bit of a collector in every man.

Tom also collects men of the same name. There's Thomas Hardy, the writer, and our library holds all his books, and Thomas M. Hardy, captain of Lord Nelson's flagship, H.M.S. *Victory*. I've even heard my husband insinuate he's related to the latter. *That's* when *I* take cover. But it did lead us, when we were on a holiday, to one of the most fascinating collections I have ever seen.

On Nevis, a small Leeward Island in the Caribbean, is the largest private collection of Horatio Nelson memorabilia. Gathered over the last twenty-five years by Robert Abrahams, a Philadelphia lawyer, it is housed in the dining room of his island home, Morning Star Plantation.

This collection started simply because Mr. and Mrs. Abrahams wanted to decorate with something of the island. And as Nelson, England's greatest naval hero, sailed these waters as a young captain on the H.M.S. *Boreas*, and as he married in 1787 the widow Nisbet of Nevis, Nelson became the heart of the Abrahams' search. Their "evening" dining room, filled with furniture, china, paintings, endless memories of Nelson, is now a museum open free to the public. And when we were there Mr. Abrahams even showed us a drawing of Captain Thomas M. Hardy. *My* Thomas Hardie looked as pleased as if he too had won the Battle of Trafalgar. That's the magic of some collections. They help you relate to another era, put you at ease with a different age.

And Tom certainly enjoys the silver spoons I've collected in a fluted Victorian glass jar, once used for cigars before the lid was lost. There are sixteen of them always ready on the kitchen counter. Some are heavily engraved, others stylishly sparse. (The busy ones are from the South where there was once help to polish the silver, while the plain but elegant spoons are from the North.) Tom likes to eat his grapefruit with one pointed spoon and his morning cereal with another, one that his great-great-someone or other used in 1813. I use them all for tea.

I collect to use, and to remember, and to give. After a museum visit I buy a large supply of postcards for quick notes, invitations, and often with a special occasion in mind. I go wild, thinking this is one extravagance I can easily afford. I hoard them. And by my desk now are probably about 150 postcards waiting for the right moment. The challenge, the fun is finding the right postcard for the right person at the right time. And rarely do I send them when I'm traveling. More often I send them when I'm sitting at Thornhill, thinking of someone far, or perhaps not so far, away.

The Baltimore Museum of Art is a fine source of postcard art, its treasure the Cone Collection, Matisse after Matisse, plus Picasso. (The Cone sisters, Dr. Claribel and Miss Etta, first started collecting modern art early in the 1900s while others only laughed.) There is also a wonderful gathering of Baltimore painted furniture, decorated in the early 1800s by two Irish brothers, John and Hugh Finley, who became famous for their "fancy furniture." My favorite postcard from that collection is a slender black settee painted with portraits of Baltimore houses that no longer exist.

The Metropolitan Museum in New York to me is Postcard Heaven. Once a year I buy enough to send a collection to friends in Europe, a neat packet to use as they wish. So far they haven't complained, but I often wonder if they are tiring of my taste. Their postcard gift is usually heavy with American furniture and American art. A little chauvinism doesn't hurt, showing the old country what has happened in the new.

You can also get caught up in friends' collections. Beware! Once you associate a friend with his or her collection you have to be careful. It becomes too easy to give. For example, my friend Alice's nickname is "Owl," so for a time she was up to her attic in owls. Then she married Frank, a dairy farmer, and went into cows—herds of Staffordshire and Guernsey milk pitchers. Some of them she now confesses she hates. You must *know* your friends' collections, know what they like so you won't embarrass them into exhibiting something they can't stand. Alice's best china cows graze beautifully over the living room of her Hope Hollow farmhouse, and she has collected long enough to gain the courage to weed out the heifers of lesser stature. This comes with age, I think, and more financial independence.

My most important collection is far more rustic. For years I have been in baskets. Living in harmony, high in our kitchen is a border of baskets, fourteen of them, an assorted chorus line of curves and squares, waiting to show their stuff. I use at least one of them every day, taking them down with a long pole topped with pinchers, the kind grocers used when butchers still wore straw boaters, and clapped their wrists in paper cuffs.

Hanging in all sizes from huge to tiny, they are woven of willow, reed, oak, sweet grass, seaweed, honeysuckle, grapevine, and one basket of olive branches was found in a Jerusalem market. They are my pals, my constant companions. I carefully choose them on travels, and they help me at home. Their given names, often reflecting their shape or use, are lovely—melon, tea, trinket, egg, market, lady, flower, berry, bread, lunch, and, of course, picnic. Each one has its own past, its own character.

Mentioned in Genesis, baskets come from the very beginning, so I don't find anything unusual about using them anytime, anywhere. But others do. I have been accused of carrying everything from counterfeit money to chickens, often ridiculed, thought a bit strange. But country women have been carrying them for centuries, and country women don't fool around with extra baggage.

And that's how I got into baskets in the first place. When I was a young woman working in Paris, I bought a set of graduated wicker suitcases, very cheap, and I thought, very stylish. When I came home my mother lined them all with bright calico. And although these suitcases have been retired after years of service and delight, I still carry baskets in the city. No canvas bags for me, thank you very much, no plastic sacks printed with status symbols. My baskets recycle themselves with natural grace.

I have hardly ever turned my back on a new basket, but I gather them for a reason—their past or their presence. And I have a few rules. I always buy baskets with handles or side arms, for once in my possession they become part of a moveable staff. Baskets can be light, such as berry baskets, but they *must* be secure. And I *try* never to buy a basket that needs repair, no matter how beautiful. I also look at baskets the way other women examine china plates, upside down, for the quality of a basket starts from the bottom up.

A friend once told me that there is an African word for basket meaning "a house for little things." A charming thought, but with a taskmaster such as I, my baskets have to think big. These baskets, after all, help keep my life in place. The ones in the kitchen have obvious roles. The Vermont backpack, given to me by our son Todd, is for hiking, but I also use it when I walk the mile down the road to the Butler Pantry for groceries. My largest basket, made by an eighty-year-old man in Appalachia, carries books, and can handle ten cartons of country eggs at one time. The low willow oval from England takes mail to be answered, magazines to be read, to the weekly hair appointment with Joan. And all of my baskets, no matter what size, hold summer's flowers.

Sometimes I'm asked to loan my baskets for other people's flowers, especially big parties. I always do, but with security measures. On each I put a label as a name tag: "I BELONG TO DEE HARDIE. PLEASE RETURN." I take my baskets seriously, and the loss of a treasured basket is a disaster. Yet to some people a basket is a basket is a basket. And one basket, to them, looks the same as another. These are the ones you educate.

I give baskets as presents, but always filled, the handle tied with bright ribbons. Just choosing the blend of ribbons is fun. It takes much longer to fill a basket, for different occasions, than simply going out and buying a present, but the basket work brings out a creative spurt which I enjoy. I use baskets made in China. Strong, reasonably priced, they come in every size, are available most everywhere. And like the clowns who file out of one small automobile at the circus, a basket holds a great deal, and at *almost* any angle.

It doesn't take too much imagination to fill a basket. It's the combinations that add to the unexpected. For a young girl going away to school, much to her mother's sadness, I gave a basket filled with writing paper, pens of every color, a stamp on every envelope, and five dollars worth of dimes for the first telephone calls home. For our godson David, when he was a bachelor, I once filled a Christmas basket with a bottle of champagne, two antique champagne glasses, two theater tickets, and one very small tin of aspirin. Then there are bridal baskets, baby baskets, tied, of course, with pink and blue ribbons.

For my own pattern of life, I have gone to any length to find one that would fit. And fitting is part of the problem when I come home with treasures from a foreign country. I once traveled from London, via Morocco, to Baltimore with a wicker market basket on wheels, the kind Englishwomen push in the villages. I find that when I see a basket I want, I buy first, think later. The airline was considerate, took my market cart in their stride. Now there is even a wicker wheelbarrow from France, one big square basket, at Thornhill. But that was easy. I bought it on sale from the display department of a local store.

This isn't just the whim and the desire to possess. Instead, I manage to use all of my baskets. In the car there is always a tea basket, with a thermos and china teacups, ready for a trip, even a short one. They make it more of an occasion. There is also a resident basket, a deep, rectangular one from Nova Scotia which holds maps, a flashlight, paper towels. For carrying summer food from the kitchen to a porch lunch, and for cleaning up afterward, I use long, low baskets. If I have a high basket that has lost a handle, which does happen, it becomes a container for tall stalks of wrapping paper, ribbons, tape, scissors. And square wine baskets with sections are handy for storing tennis ball cans all year round. I gave a basket to Barbara, a young woman who works with Tom, to carry the morning mail from the post office to their office. She tells me she is now known as Little Red Riding Hood, and she seems to enjoy it.

Nor is it all work and no play for the baskets of Thornhill. The oldest basket in my collection is trunk-size, a hamper of wicker, probably used years ago for a family's linen when they moved to a cooler summer house. *This* is our picnic basket. We load it with food for twelve guests, cloths, plates, and we walk approximately three minutes, taking turns holding each side of the trunk, to the top of our hill behind the house, to a sweeping view below of the whole valley. Baskets make picnics a party, and this is our summer jubilee.

My most prized, and probably my most valuable baskets, are my Nantucket Lightship baskets. Perhaps I feel this way because I made them myself. This doesn't sound very modest, but it took me years to weave a friendship with Mr. Reed, a fine name for a basketmaker, who rented me molds, helped me make baskets. A Lightship basket, compact and precise as a Quaker's bonnet, can *only* be made on a wooden mold, and these molds are guarded as if they were crown jewels.

To add these baskets to my collection I first had to learn how to weave them, as one large open Nantucket Lightship basket can cost as much as $500. That's the price for a new one. The older ones are in museums. Their beginnings were much more humble. First woven in the mid-1800s by the crews of lightships anchored near the dangerous Nantucket shoals, the men eased their lonely vigils, often three months at a time, by weaving baskets for their women at home—big open ones for marketing and sewing, smaller ones for blueberry expeditions. These baskets are now heirlooms, and the trade for new ones is brisk. While visiting the island of Nantucket, over the years, I managed to learn how to weave them, filled out my own collection, and made them for all our children. This was my aim. Now finished, I am about to retire.

I realize collecting is often influenced by the stages of one's life. While some of my collections have simmered down—I'm finished with Ted Williams and it will take an *extraordinary* basket now to seduce me—I find I'm becoming possessed by new collections, collections I could never have afforded before, more in time than money. For instance, I have spent afternoon after afternoon with Angela Thirkell.

Mrs. Thirkell wrote thirty-two novels, between 1933 and 1961, about English country living. And I am besotted. Frank, the lawyer, now judge, who introduced us to Thornhill, gave me her first book about a year ago, and that was it. I have been on her trail ever since. I not only want to read *all* of her books, I want them piled by my bedside.

Witty and wonderful, they make me relax, make me laugh out loud. I now own twenty-nine of her books. Determined to own all of them, I have set up a network of scouts. Shamelessly I send lists of her books to friends everywhere, or if I know a friend is going to London, such as my college roommate Katey, she goes with my list in hand. It *is* a passionate pursuit, and I have a remarkable bonus coming my way. Bettina, one of my best scouts, found a Thirkell book in St. Petersburg, Florida. It is a first edition, and slipped into the dust jacket is a personal letter from Mrs. Thirkell herself. I am in ecstasy.

James, a scholar at Oxford, has just received the same typewritten list because I know that university town is filled with secondhand bookstores. Although popular in her time, even coming to America to lecture at Columbia, Princeton, and Yale, Mrs. Thirkell is now, alas, out of print. I *must* know what happens to Captain Belton and Clarissa, especially Lady Emily Leslie. The same characters are woven throughout, but each is emphasized in a different novel. Mrs. Thirkell, and that's how she preferred to be called, takes me away to another land in another time. After all, collections are meant to make you dream a little.

Sometimes they also make you scheme. Along with Mrs. Thirkell's books, I have developed an unquenchable thirst for painted furniture. If it were possible, and of course it is not as we have a full house of family furniture, I would collect only pieces that are painted or decorated, plain or fancy. Maybe this has something to do with my Scandinavian heritage, however latent it may be. Maybe it's because I saw the most beautiful dark green closed-cupboard in a Nantucket shop, painted completely with a New England village over its façade—the white steepled church, the square, the tall houses. Suddenly there was that sparkle. I visited this cupboard every day for a week. I patted it, I walked around it. I brought my friends. Everyone just smiled.

And then I bought it.

I had examined my conscience, and there was no doubt in

my mind. It *had* to be mine. I felt no guilt. I made the money, I spent the money. And it was only the beginning. I now own a small table covered with painted American flags and a field of stars, and a hope chest, circa 1880, painted in faded blue with red trim. The front is decorated with curly monograms wrapped around each other, his and hers. From Sweden, it now sits at the end of our bed, filled with blankets and linen. Known also as an immigrants' chest, whenever I look at it I think of my own Swedish grandparents coming to the new world.

Tom's grandparents gave us another collection. As the wife of an only son of an only son, I have recently become the curator of family silver, some of it quite out of step with our country life. For instance, there is a covered butter dish that looks like Kirsten Flagstad's helmet in *Die Walküre*. Our life on the farm is far more simple than their turn-of-the-century entertaining in the Garden District of New Orleans. As dazzling and as comfortable as that era must have been, I prefer a country dawn over Thornhill. And whatever inherited silver our children don't want, I'm going to sell with relish. Collections should be *enjoyed*, not deposited deep in bank vaults.

There are other collections I'm much more interested in—a whiteness of swans, an exaltation of larks, a paddling of ducks on nearby ponds. Even more I want a gaggle of grandchildren, lots of little children to play with. I have just found a dollhouse, a miniature salt-box from Massachusetts. Now I'm hot in pursuit of a three-inch ladder-back chair.

# *Chapter* Fourteen

THOMAS Jefferson once wrote, "No occupation is so delightful to me as the culture of the earth, and no culture comparable to that of the garden. Though an old man, I am but a young gardener." And that's just how *I* feel. In early spring any minor tip of green makes me jubilant. It's new birth, new hope, another beginning. Together we have survived winter. And my perennial bed is my first hurrah, my first garden party. When I am in the garden, I am never alone.

I talk to my tulips, coax my jonquils into spring, hope they'll enjoy my company enough to come back the next year without asking. And now I only add new perennials in the spring. One early year at Thornhill I planted them in the fall, as many gardeners do, but for me it was a disaster. The winter was a fierce one, killing many of the bulbs, and by the time spring arrived my writing on the identifying stakes had been washed away. It was a secret garden, and I was frustrated. Some did survive, but I didn't know one young green leaf from another. I've tried keeping a diary, writing notes to myself from time to time as I inspect the garden, tried drawing charts, but I find my scribblings in my gardening book are more notes of remembrance and reproach. "The lupine is lost *again*!"—"admit delphinium doesn't like Thornhill, give up"—"poppies are impossible"—"divide EVERYTHING"—"lilies last and last." Now rather than record, I plot a little, plant in the spring, and pray a lot.

Our perennial bed, the first garden planted at Thornhill, grows along a low white fence beyond the front lawn. This is the fence Tom and my father put up years ago, and it still borders the garden filled with my new experiments and older flowers given to me by friends when they have divided their own gardens. A mixed bouquet of many years, my garden is, in a way, a neighborhood party, a friendship quilt. There's Cynthia's New England hollyhocks standing tall. Frances's perky blue forget-me-nots, Bunny's delicate columbine next to Betsy's bright yellow evening primroses. Flowers do tell, they say, and these gifts are so like their owners. Betsy, for instance, is a lovely blond. And leaning over this front fence are the full June blooms of Janet's white peonies, each looking like the woolly face of our English sheepdog when she was watching for the children to come home from school. In the center of the garden are the two pink rosebushes that were here when we arrived, as well as the faithful pink peonies we carried with us from Pumpkin Hill.

This garden is also a family affair. Anchoring one end is the white oak our son Tommy planted as a seedling when he was twelve. It cost a dollar of mine, and one of his, to buy this descendant of the famed 400-year-old Wye Oak, Maryland's state tree and the most majestic, enormous oak tree I have ever seen. Our little seedling, about three inches high, even came with credentials, a large diploma of proven lineage. Tommy was so proud, and I was so proud of Tommy's young interest in trees, one he never outgrew. Our oak is now only sixteen years old, but I can't reach the top anymore.

At the other end of the garden are Aunt Alice's ferns from North Carolina. Like graceful ostrich plumes, they are a fanfare every spring and with them we remember Alice. Near them I've planted jack-in-the-pulpits which I've transplanted from our woods. They seem to agree with civilization, protected by the shade of the old chestnut tree.

This perennial garden, stretching over the years, grew with ease, and with us. Then I disturbed its peace. I joined a garden club—my first venture into the sociability of group gardening followed by afternoon tea. And I became ambitious. I like to think it was for my garden, but I'm not so sure it wasn't for myself. I wanted to have a garden just as glorious as the other girls'. And as I was a late bloomer in this small garden club, the Garden Club of Twenty, I *had* to try harder. But it was time, time to learn more about gardens, and the other members are all entertaining and interesting women.

Studying garden catalogs, trying to become more knowledgeable, stumbling over botanical names of flowers, I soon realized my thumbs weren't so green, but how green was my envy. *Everyone* knew so much more than I did. I crammed, read, wrote off to nurseries for new plants. I tried to recast my perennial garden, give my old friend a new face. I was told, at a lecture at a club meeting, that a perennial garden should be planned on graph paper. But that seemed too much like painting by numbers. I just tucked in new plants next to old standbys. Near Bunny's columbine, for instance, I planted the Duke of Windsor, a small but stylish narcissus. I thought she would like that. Strange bedfellows perhaps, but good company.

A big hurdle was learning a new language, Garden Latin. In casual conversations, members of the club would sprinkle around the botanical names of plants like fertilizer. If this was meant to make me grow, it didn't help at all. I felt as if I were back in high school, failing Latin all over again.

I do call coreopsis, a daisylike flower, by its botanical name because that is how we were first introduced. Besides it is one of the *few* I can pronounce. It's also more appealing than its more common name of tickseed. But I would truly rather address myself to columbine instead of aquilegia, and hollyhock, *not Althaea rosea.* To me, certainly not a member of the gardening elite, it sounds pretentious. Perhaps I'll never be a serious gardener. Perhaps I'm just jealous of more accomplished gardeners. But scholarship takes away some of the charm, the wonderful names I remember from childhood. It will always be bleeding heart to me rather than dicentra, and sweet william is so much sweeter than dianthus. And there is simply no contest between the name gypsophila and what is known to me as baby's breath.

I must admit though to a slight feeling of superiority, after studying the genus, family, and common names of plants for a year, when I visited a flower mart with our daughter Louise. Every plant for sale was staked with its botanical name. Without even a second glance, I knew what they were talking about as I walked down the aisles. Dee, I said to myself, maybe you aren't too old to learn, after all.

The only time I use Latin is when I'm arguing with nurserymen. I feel it strengthens my position, makes them think I know more than I really do. I don't argue often, but sometimes what you order by mail is not what you receive. You must make a stand.

One spring I planted what I thought was digitalis, which in my more innocent days of gardening I called foxglove. This foxglove turned out to be an uninvited, and unwanted, *Fritillaria persica*, or checkered lily. After a lengthy and heated correspondence with the nursery, complete with crumbing leaves as evidence in every envelope, I finally received the plant I originally ordered. Another time the new poppies never popped, and the Raspberry Queen peony was all white. Those were the times I thought about throwing in the trowel. But then every winter garden catalog brings a new spring challenge.

Sometimes the mistakes are my own. I ordered a batch of tulips that I thought were going to be the color of deep red wine. When they burst forth in bloom, the red was *so* bright they were as noisy as a trumpet in a garden that was meant to be serene. I gave them a chance, I tried. But I finally had to dig them up, even before the green leaves had turned brown. I didn't want to forget where they were, have to face that same music the next spring.

It helped me learn that one or two tulips in the right place are worth twenty in the wrong. It's the site that counts. Now I have white fluted tulips against the green boxwood, yellow ones near the pink roses. Peace and harmony have been restored.

As we grow old together, this perennial garden, the first garden one sees when approaching Thornhill, is in a way like a long-time mellow marriage—some surprises, some disappointments, love and affection with spurts of passion, sometimes even a revolt, like those bright red tulips. But always there. And I'd miss it terribly if it went away. I must admit I do offer it a chance to flirt with younger gardeners as I give plants away when they need to be divided. And these plants help to start other young gardens just as ours began so long ago.

Harvey Ladew, an old gardener in my life when I was in my thirties, didn't give me many plants, only some hydrangeas which never survived, but his advice I remember. "Don't forget, Dee," he'd say, "tulips love gin." So did he. "When they start drooping in the house, give them a little nip, and in no time at all they'll be standing at attention." He's right. It works with tulips, and he, as a matter of fact, lived to be ninety!

Looking like a mischievous Somerset Maugham with a dash of Douglas Fairbanks, *his* era Fairbanks, Harvey was endlessly entertaining, and he was the first to teach me that gardening could not only create a pretty picture, but an amusing one as well, filled with imagination. Who else would have thought of putting a statue of Adam and Eve in the apple orchard? A bachelor, his gardens became his family. Like rooms, each garden leads to another. And his topiary, his sculpture of shrubs which he designed and clipped himself, won an award from the Garden Club of America as "the most outstanding topiary garden in America without professional help." He was then all of eighty-five.

Some of his gardens are all of one color—the white garden, the yellow, the pink. And he loved telling about his pink flowers. "A friend was showing me his garden in Vermont," he would say, "and I saw these lovely flowers that looked like pink lilies. I wanted to get some so I asked their names. My friend couldn't remember, but he said in Vermont they call them 'naked ladies.' I forgot about it, but a month later I received a telegram—'Can send you 50 naked ladies at 50¢ apiece if you think you can handle them.' " Then Harvey would laugh and hope I enjoyed the story as much as he did. I always did. And how I miss him.

In Harvey's garden a Chinese proverb is engraved on a stepping stone—

> *If you would be happy for a week, take a wife.*
> *If you would be happy for a month, kill your pig.*
> *But if you would be happy all your life, plant a garden.*

Harvey's house and gardens, now a foundation, are open to the public from the middle of April to the end of October, nineteen miles north of Baltimore. The address: Ladew Topiary Gardens, 3535 Jarrettsville Pike, Monkton, Maryland 21111. This house and gardens, with topiary swans gliding on waves of high hedges, are as unique and original as Harvey who once crossed the desert with Lawrence of Arabia and slept every night in his dinner jacket because he was cold, ate snails, he would tell me, in bed with Colette. To me his flower beds are even *more* fascinating than his bedtime stories.

My perennial bed, in comparison, and there is *no* comparison, is such a simple one. And even simpler is my herb garden, a garden I never thought would be mine. It all began when my friend Sidney asked me to drive with her to Stillridge Herb Farm in Woodstock, Maryland. I enjoyed the ride, but early on the road I told myself there was no way I was going to get involved with a new garden, no herb garden for me. I already had my hands full, my beds filled.

And then the curtain went up—there I was at the herb farm, completely taken by a field of yarrow, as only yarrow can be yellow, tiptoeing around tansy, pinching lemon balm, sniffing the leaves of pineapple sage, listening to Mary Lou Riddle, the owner, pour out her lore and love of herbs. How Roman warriors bathed in tubs of thyme for strength, how the Pilgrims used sprigs of bible leaf to mark pages of their prayer books or chewed its minty leaves to keep awake during a long sermon. Who, I ask you, could resist names like my-lady's-mantle, lamb's ears, which feels as velvety as its namesake, lion's tail, Indian ginger, or simply sage? I didn't succumb—I was seduced. And with summer half spent, I invested in an herb garden.

Herbs should ideally be planted when you begin your vegetables in the spring. Yet in the middle of July I was rearranging the small flagstone terrace we made when we first bought Thornhill. Sheltered by three sides of the house, it has sun at least half a day and sandy soil which drains well. As Mrs. Riddle warned, "Herbs do not like wet feet."

I took away at random some of the irregularly shaped flagstones which Neal and I had set in soil mixed with sand years before. I didn't have a design. I just wanted to sprinkle the terrace with growing herbs, leaving enough stones to walk and work on. My limits were already determined by the dimensions of the terrace, about twelve feet by twelve feet.

My first garden four years ago held lemon verbena, pineapple sage, lavender, thyme, rosemary, basil, chives, and rose geranium. Learning that there are three kinds of herbs—fragrant, culinary, and medicinal—I didn't know whether I was going for scent, the kitchen, or playing doctor. As it turned out, I chose all three. And my pineapple sage tea, or "infusion," is wonderfully soothing for a sore throat. Steep 1 teaspoon of dried pineapple sage in 1 cup of boiling water for 10 minutes and serve.

That first garden grew and grew, the bargain of the summer. I watered a little at first, stopped a few weeds from invading this new kingdom. In between the flagstones I poured buttermilk which helped grow moss, a soft trim for the herbs. It was a most satisfying garden and I was enchanted with it. Every visitor, even Homer picking up the laundry, had to smell and taste and feel. I sent fresh leaves of pineapple sage and lemon verbena in letters to our children, tied small stalks of lavender together to tuck in our linen closet. It was as if *I* had discovered herbs. And I had.

The second year, along with our own garden, I felt herbwise enough to give a kitchen window box as a house present to a friend in Nantucket whose backyard is handkerchief-size, already filled with vegetables. I planted two of each herb—thyme for her clam chowder, parsley for bluefish, basil for pea soup, sage for chicken, chives for salads, and dill, of course, for the pickles she makes from her cucumbers.

And what to do with herbs once the season changes? First, I give pots of them to our daughter Louise for winter green in her small house, then I save the rest for drying. Mrs. Riddle hangs hers to dry from an old wooden towel rack spread wide like a fan on the wall and as a curtainlike border around windows.

I put mine on a cookie sheet and bake in a 200° F. oven with the door left slightly open until they dry but don't crumble. Then I strip the leaves from the stems, keeping them in airtight

Mason jars—the rosemary for Thornhill lamb, the basil especially good in olive oil. And in the winter, I go into the small garden to check on the perennial herbs. I put more hay around the lavender and pinch a spike of rosemary, sniff it, and remember what joy I'll have come herbal spring. I've also added some friends from other families. In the center is a lilac bush, now about two feet high, a miniature rosebush that will never grow up, and on the low wall, a small stone rabbit who sits very peacefully watching over all.

This rabbit, carried home one time from a trip to England, is a much safer bet than the native rabbits who watch over the vegetable garden, longing for entrance. So far I'm winning—against the rabbits, against the weeds. The philosopher Ralph Waldo Emerson once wrote "What is a weed? A plant whose virtues have not yet been discovered." I think he had it all wrong, and I'm sure someone *else* cared for his vegetable patch. The evangelist Billy Graham knows better. He once told Aunt Alice, a neighbor of his in North Carolina, that he thought it was perfectly all right for her to tend her flowers on Sunday, but certainly not her vegetables. He knows a vegetable garden is work, and to him, one doesn't travail on the Sabbath.

One year I wanted to divorce my vegetable garden which I'm sure Mr. Graham wouldn't approve of either. I wanted to give complete custody to Tom. I didn't even want the right to visit it every other weekend. It was simply that I had gone away one week to visit my parents in Boston, and when I returned there was a full scale invasion of the unwanted, promiscuous weeds everywhere. It took me days to clean the garden and reconcile. But I've learned. Mulching is the answer. And our vegetable garden is completely blanketed by summer hay or leaves raked and saved from last autumn's lawn. It keeps the weeds down, the soil moist.

Our well-mulched vegetable garden is now a calculated garden, planned parenthood, certainly not the glory that was ours when John was the helping hand at Thornhill. The menu is more limited, but there are always peas, tomatoes, lettuce, sometimes okra, sometimes not, spinach, squash, broccoli, beets, and especially in the spring, asparagus. We've learned that a small vegetable garden, like a small dinner party, is sometimes the most fun of all.

And that's the way Tom says I plant my vegetable garden—the way other people choose their dinner guests. Maybe that's true. I do expect a lot after all my work. I want my vegetables to be delicious as well as decorative, start conversations at the table, be tidy and on time. Asparagus is our most elegant guest, and there is nothing quite like fresh asparagus quickly steamed, with broiled shad and shad roe, all lightly laced with lemon or melted butter.

The older the asparagus beds, the thicker the roots grow, the more the family increases. I like that idea. It also pleases me that the lily and asparagus are of the *same* family. I'm not a bit surprised. Breeding does show. And four years ago I decided to increase the asparagus population of our vegetable garden. I needed more space, so it was good-bye to cabbage, so long kale.

It was a big step. Other vegetables come and go, brief encounters, but asparagus is almost forever, lasting, if properly tended, up to twenty years or more. I weighed my age against that of the two-year-old asparagus roots, and made the plunge. I'm glad I did. Even in the autumn the asparagus gives us a lift. The stems have grown into feathery ferns and when the morning sun sweeps the garden, the dew on these ferns sparkles like decorations on little country Christmas trees.

Next to our vegetable garden is our raspberry patch. Here is where my heart lies. I inherited these raspberries from our son Tommy, who inherited them from his grandfather Harry. Other family possessions have been passed down, fine silver, old tuxedos, but the raspberries come alive each year, every year. Tommy planted his grandfather's raspberry roots at Thornhill, and I'm continuing the family line. So are other friends in the neighborhood. These raspberry bushes have become so abundant that every spring, before they berry, I give dozens away.

Once they berry, it becomes an intense affair. And the pleasures and passions received from these raspberries, I must admit, are far more emotional than any pea picked, any tomato from the vegetable garden. That first tomato, round and red, gives a certain sense of pride. It's the first merit badge. But soon I begin giving them away easily, without regret, their wealth often overwhelming. But the raspberries are my aristocrats. As elegant as the asparagus, but more evasive, more difficult, more treasured.

They hide like children who don't want their hands washed. But knowing what's good for them, I invade their privacy. With unusual self-confidence, obvious greed, I must be quicker than the birds, and more clever, hoping they feast instead on the deep purple fruit of the nearby mulberry tree.

Four weeks of my life, the last of June and the beginning of July, are ruled by this precious crop. Other summer fun fades. I try never to leave the farm for more than a day because the berries seem to multiply overnight, and quite frankly, my berry fingers are much more accomplished than my tennis backhand. I think only raspberry. In the morning, before it gets too hot, I start picking.

I've fashioned a comfortable working basket by tying a long rolled cotton scarf to each side, the loop going around my neck. A belt does as well. The basket hangs at my waist, leaving both hands free. This is important because you need one hand to pick, one hand to push aside the branches to find the berries. And while I pick, I hoard, reluctantly offering to anyone passing by perhaps one or two berries, no more. Tom isn't much help because he always seems to eat more than he picks. I'm not much fun in the raspberry patch. Only after the berries are made into jam do I become more generous. Somehow then the deed is done. I have captured as many as possible and can begin to share.

It takes a good hour each day to pick the raspberries. Strawberries, which I no longer have, look up at you, but for the raspberries I get down on my knees. And the taller branches I bend back into wide curves, like Fred Astaire leading Ginger, to find the hidden red domes of the berries below. To entice me, to lead me on, there are a few raspberries that dangle like ruby earrings from the branches, but for the most part it is a diligent search. I part the branches, the way I used to part our children's hair so I could see their faces, I hunt and I collect. And there must be a raspberry Mafia out to get me because my arms become scratched, my feet tangle with lower branches. I've learned to wear my Wellington boots, even on the hottest of days. But a full-berried basket is worth the risk. My eye measures five cups of berries, four jars of jam.

The jars are waiting for me on the kitchen counter, waiting to be filled. These have been saved over the year, small containers that once held everything from artichoke hearts to bouillon cubes. Their lids have become camouflaged with flowered fabrics, labels written with careful calligraphy. If I have an especially large crop, I have to buy jelly jars from the grocery store. They make my production look much more uniform, but not quite as much fun.

I first rinse the berries, then crush them in a two-quart pot, adding a box of fruit pectin. Then I bring it all to a full boil, stirring constantly with a wooden spoon. Next I stir in three cups of sugar for five cups of berries. I have tried less sugar, but it just doesn't work. I also add a dot of butter which reduces foam while boiling. While I stir, the berries bubble and come to a wild, rolling boil. I let this continue for one minute. I love the excitement. I'm stirring the pot, as country women have been doing for centuries, repeating a pattern of love, making sweets for family and friends. It's old-time therapy in a busy world.

After boiling for only one minute, and *that* I find hard to clock, I remove the pot from the stove and skim off whatever foam there is with a metal spoon. Now I'm ready to fill sterilized jars—usually four, sometimes more. Then I top each jar with paraffin. Each day the cupboard shelf grows closer with jars of jam. My record last year was a full complement of a hundred jars.

At last the day comes when my summer collection is complete. And there they stand and wait. The joy and pride is the giving, one by one, slowly over the year. Many, of course, leave at Christmas, but I enjoy, maybe even more, giving a decorated jar for a honeymoon breakfast. That lid is covered with old lace. My raspberry jam is my own cottage industry. The day I pick the last berry, the first peach always seems to be ready. But it isn't quite the same. Maybe peaches are just too easy. They practically beg to be taken, while the raspberries tease you into pursuit.

# *Chapter* Fifteen

TOM moved us to the country because he thought it was the best place to raise our children. Then he led us to church every Sunday because I think he thought he needed help with his flock. And like Thornhill Farm, our church, Saint John's, has been a thread throughout our lives. Sometimes that thread has grown a little thin, but Saint John's has seen the happiest of our days, and the saddest. And it is always there, waiting without question.

We weren't even Episcopalians when we started attending services. Tom comes from a long line of Scottish Presbyterians, devout without fuss, and I was raised in the Methodist Church, the nearest my mother could find to the Swedish Lutheran of *her* childhood. And my father was Roman Catholic. It's much better, if possible, to attend the same church, and Saint John's just happened to be the nearest, five minutes from Thornhill, straight down Butler Road.

Our children didn't always agree that this was the best route on Sundays. Especially since it meant getting dressed up. Tommy rebelled against his short pants when his older brother Todd was allowed to wear long gray flannels, and Beth would jump up and down on her bed screaming that never again would she wear a "baby" dress, a beautifully smocked one that

Mamoo had brought her from London. Beth was also ingenious at hiding her little red English shoes, which she detested. Louise was far more lamblike, her long blond braids the last to be plaited before we all leapt into the car as if going to a fire instead of Sunday church.

Once corralled into a pew, fourth from the front on the left, I must confess I was proud of our production. And Saint John's does somehow wrap one in a feeling of security and peace. It is a small church. As well we know. When we were planning for Louise's wedding, years later, we had to count heads (or bottoms) very closely. No matter how you squeeze, Saint John's holds only 120 people.

A small, Gothic church of stone, Saint John's was rebuilt in 1927. Beautifully so. And when you approach it on a late fall day it arises from bordering fields of corn with much the same moving simplicity that Chartres cathedral in France arises from fields of wheat. With snow on the ground nothing seems quite so peaceful. Around to one side is the graveyard, paths fringed with boxwood bushes, where children play leapfrog over the ancient stones. In the springtime the dogwood blooms soften the stones, and the black-and-white dairy cows from the next farm try to poke their heads through the rail fence to nibble on sacred sod.

The very first Saint John's was built of limestone in 1816, supported by gifts of the faithful rather than the sale of pews, the usual custom in those days. And there have been others in between, one church burning down a little more than a hundred years ago on Christmas Eve. The ministers have been as varied as the styles of architecture. One, a Virginian, who left the parish before the Civil War, eventually enlisted and became a brigadier general of artillery. Legend has it that, before barking out orders, he would cry, "Lord have mercy on their souls! Fire!"

## *Chapter Fifteen*

The minister who reigned when we first came to Saint John's wasn't quite as militant. In fact he would not allow the singing of "Onward Christian Soldiers," the hymn I marched to with vigor every week at my Methodist Sunday School. He simply didn't like it. It took me a few years to discover why they never played my song. But when I did, it lit a fuse. Or maybe it gave me an excuse to find a Sunday School with a larger enrollment. In those early days Saint John's was almost the mission church it had been in the very beginning.

I certainly wasn't one of the faithful. I talked Tom into moving on to Saint Thomas's Church in the Green Spring Valley, a handsome colonial brick church with a healthy-size Sunday School. Here I could sing "Onward Christian Soldiers," splendidly arranged with trumpet fanfares. Now *that* was music to my ears. Of course it took us a half hour longer to get to Saint Thomas's, a half hour more struggle. But I was trying to prove a point. *No one* censors the hymns of my youth.

Our friend Janet, who could walk to Saint John's from her Octagonal House, couldn't understand how we could leave our neighborhood church. She too had certain disagreements with the minister. "But Dee," she would argue, "that's not why you leave a church." In time we did return to the fold of Saint John's. And when Tommy was fifteen, he was the only acolyte at Janet's funeral. I think she would have been pleased that the little boy she once thought smelled like a goat was her very last honor guard.

While at Saint Thomas's we became bona fide Episcopalians. That Sunday morning when the bishop placed his hands on my head, a heavy one, I must admit, as we had been out late the night before, I thought I was going to topple. But God works in wondrous ways, and Tom and I even began to teach Sunday School.

It had to be the sixth grade. None of our own children, all

of whom were younger, wanted us. They begged us to stay away from *their* classes. Maybe they were right. Tom opened the first class with a joke I had never heard before.

"How many animals did Moses take on the Ark?" he asked our twelve-year-old students.

I corrected him immediately. I didn't want our class to think we were *that* stupid. "Oh, but Tom, that was Noah, not Moses!" And right then and there I ruined his story.

As an embarrassed hush came over the class, one of our young male students, who later turned out to be a star, piped up, "That's exactly why I'm *never* going to get married."

And as a matter of fact, he hasn't. We may have changed his life, and he and his classmates certainly changed ours. We became, in a way, early Christians. Early to bed on Saturday and early up on Sunday mornings so we could practice what we were going to preach. These twelve-year-olds were on their Sunday toes, and we had to keep up with them.

We soon tossed aside the proposed text. It wasn't good old Bible stories, blood and thunder, or even the Golden Rule in modern dress. Instead the official class text told of contemporary episodes of daily life. The children thought them boring, and we agreed. So Tom and I decided to try our hand at something we were more familiar with—publishing a newspaper.

And that's how *The Jerusalem Free Press* was born. The students dove into the project with gusto, and for the rest of the year we had perfect attendance. Brian was our news editor, Laura, art director, Billy pushed want-ads, especially "slightly used chariots." Jimmy's sports column was titled "Seen in the Arena," and Barbara's page on fashion was all you'd ever want to know about togas. When Jervie asked to be "Execution Editor," we began to wonder what havoc we may have wrought. What, we wondered, did these children tell their parents when they came home from Sunday School? The copy became even more gory when we asked Lisa, our food editor, to use some other ingredients in her recipes than lions and snakes. She immediately suggested, with a sly grin, "People!" We quickly put the paper to bed.

We weren't *really* asked to leave Saint Thomas's, give up our jobs as Sunday School teachers. We left because we wanted to go home. There was a new minister at Saint John's, Erv Brown, a whole new spirit. And as Todd was now twelve we wanted him to be an acolyte at our first church. As more and more people moved to the country, the congregation grew, Erv giving more hope every Sunday. And now our only clothes problem on early Sundays before church was Tom looking in his sons' closets for his favorite tie.

Over the years our lives have become intertwined with the activities of Saint John's. When President Carter asked churches to toll their bells for the American hostages in Iran, I pulled that long thick rope, hanging down in the narthex, fifty times at noon, fifty times for the American hostages. Our small country church suddenly became part of a nation's sadness. Usually our scope isn't quite so broad, usually far more provincial. Tom and I have moved jumps at the annual fall horse show, served bowls of strawberries at the June festival, held summer picnics at Thornhill for the Sunday School. And many a Christmas Eve we've watched our daughters in the Sunday School pageant dressed as cheesecloth angels with wire hanger wings. One year we were even the parents of Joseph—Tommy layered in grain sacks borrowed from the barn.

As Tommy grew older, he became, as his brother had before him, an acolyte at Saint John's. Miss Evans says he was the only acolyte who ever lit the altar candles in the proper order. A force to be recognized, Miss Evans, a retired social worker, knows what she is talking about, and lets it be known. And whenever she's a lay reader on Sunday, she is the only one who quotes her verses from the Bible by heart, looking straight at the congregation, her strong voice reaching easily the last pew, her eyes scrutinizing any nonbeliever.

I liked it when our sons served as acolytes. I felt Someone else was helping to shape them up. It gave them, if only for a few years, a ritual, a discipline, a Sunday morning routine. I felt they were contributing to a world that was beyond their young years, but a world that might leave an impression when older. One Christmas Eve at the late service, Tommy carried, for the very first time in church, a golden processional cross. He held it high and steady and I felt proud. It was pomp and circumstance with a touch of the medieval, certainly a bit of showmanship, and I loved it. Whenever I see that golden cross on a Sunday morning, I think of Tommy.

When he was sixteen, he wrote our minister, Erv, a letter. Tom and I saw it a few years later, after Erv had gone on to another parish.

12–Nov–72

The Reverend Ervin A. Brown
St. John's Church
Western Run Parish
Glyndon, Maryland 21071

Dear Rev,

I write to you on a most sorrowful subject, but I have decided to retire from my post at the altar. No it is not because of insufficient pay or non-fitting gowns, but rather I feel I no longer can compete with the young rookies and my knees are getting creaky from old age and excessive kneeling. Although I know this retirement from the team makes me ineligible for my pension, I am convinced it is the best choice of action.

I have greatly enjoyed our past years of success. Good

luck in the new season. I know you have a great team in the making, but a word of advice: be careful of that youthful lad under you who may have aspiring eyes for the top position.

Regretfully and Sincerely,
Thomas G. Hardie, III

When Tommy retired, I thought perhaps it was my turn. There is a section of our prayer book I particularly like that reads "We have left undone those things which we ought to have done; And we have done those things which we ought not to have done . . ." Serving on the vestry was probably one of those things I should have left undone. Tom was on the vestry years before, and I'm sure he contributed, but my performance was pitiful. I was terrified to open my mouth at the monthly meetings, I became puzzled, discouraged, by the cross tides of politics, and the finance was over my head. But as it had taken 150 years for an earlier woman, Miss Zouck, to be elected to the Vestry of Saint John's, I was honored to be there. But I was a silent token, nothing more, nothing less. I felt much more comfortable with missionary work, and that's how I thought of our blood program.

When I mentioned it to Philip Roulette, our minister who had followed Erv into the pulpit, he was all for it, giving just the right enthusiasm to make me feel perhaps at last I was doing something I "ought to have done." I talked Sally Bradford into helping, although as a diabetic she could never give blood, and together we started the new program. The first collection day was in December as I wanted this giving of blood to be a Christmas present to people we would never know, who would never have to say thank you. It was a present with no strings attached. And for the last eight years, we've delivered our presents early.

Rather, the congregation has. But it wasn't easy. The Baltimore Red Cross didn't believe we could do it. How could a church as small as ours, they asked, warrant the bloodmobile going twenty miles out into the country? They wanted us all to climb on a communal bus and come into the city! But that's not how I wanted this present wrapped. I wanted that big, white, red-crossed van right *there* at the church door on the first Sunday in December.

All right then, they said, we need a pledge of 100 volunteers. Not an unrealistic number, but our congregation was only 250 families, many old, many young. And what we needed were able-bodied bloodworthy volunteers between the ages of seventeen and sixty-five.

We turned to the telephone. And it's amazing what happens to some strong men at the mere mention of "blood," or the thought of a "needle." They suddenly remember that they had jaundice in World War II. There was also a rash of anemic women who are summer-fierce on the tennis court. Other conflicts were a final Colts football game on the same day, and flu was everywhere.

But it is also amazing what a crew of contemporary Clara Bartons can do over the telephone. Especially Sally, who could, I swear, squeeze blood out of the proverbial turnip. We still had to turn to bribery. In the *Epistle*, our monthly church letter, I promised a "Bloody Mary Party" at Thornhill Farm for all donors and families a week after the big event. That alone certainly didn't turn the blood pressure our way, but we finally realized our quota of 100 volunteers.

Our church may be small, but our new parish house is spacious, and on "B Day," as we called it, the huge central room, filled with nurses and cots and donors, looked like a segment from "M*A*S*H," or even a heavy dose of early Ernest Hemingway. It was glorious. It was also confusing. Everyone wanted to give as early as possible after church. We figured those who had the longest drive home should be the ones to be called first. But there were also those who could only stand and wait—and sometimes nearly fainted. Still they all came back the following year.

There was Betty who only had soybeans for breakfast and so couldn't give. (You must eat a proper meal before donating.) There was Andy who couldn't quite weigh in at 110 pounds on the Red Cross scale. Next year she wore heavier clothes and passed. And there was seventeen-year-old Lucy giving for the first time. The nurses couldn't find her left arm vein and were about to turn her away until Lucy offered up her *right* arm. That is young bravery. And when Neale arrived in his Naval uniform, bright with brass, we all felt a patriotism that sometimes fades in today's world.

This isn't all complete altruism on those Sunday mornings in December, once a year at Saint John's. By giving blood, our congregation is assured of as much blood as it might need over the year. We are protecting our young and old who cannot give, as well as those people I mentioned before, the unknowns who also need. And it is such a quick gift to give—no Christmas shopping, no last minute wrapping. The actual donation takes less than ten minutes, the whole procedure not quite an hour.

That "Bloody Mary Party" we gave at Thornhill the following Sunday was joyful. We were all so pleased with ourselves. I wore a long white apron I had made, complete with a big red cross on the bib. Again I thought I was a Hemingway heroine. I *do* like show. Cynthia brought an enormous tray of raw vegetables, Sally rolled in the wheels of Brie. We had proved to the Red Cross that one small church, once we put our minds to it, could be as proud as a cathedral. Our minister Philip Roulette beamed. Here gathered together was some of his flock, joined together by the bloodline of Saint John's.

He looked far more serious when he married our daughter Louise to Scott. And so did we. As if we weren't nervous enough, the tornado that nearly flew away with the reception tent on the lawn of Thornhill darkened the church as well. I wasn't meant to be at church so early, but the confusion of the caterers was too much to bear. I had to escape. While Nancy and Minnie arranged beautiful baskets of flowers on the altar, I tied posies and bows to the end of each pew. I had to keep busy, keep moving. I even scowled ferociously at Philip who had come over from the rectory to minister aid.

By the time of the afternoon wedding, everything was in place, but still there was no electricity. On a sudden impulse we placed seventy-five candlesticks, silver and gold, all over Saint John's. These were candlesticks of varying heights, borrowed from neighbors and meant to center the tables in the reception tent. But because of the emergency, they first had to go to church. And they gave a lovely glow. Then Scott and Louise were married by candlelight in the middle of a dark afternoon by Jim, Scott's father, and Philip, accompanied by a flute played by our friend Clinton. The organ, which is powered by electricity, was silent.

We don't hear the organ much anymore, even *with* electricity, as Tom and I often attend the early morning service at 8:00 A.M. When we do go to the later service, the choir is glorious, voices of angels. But somehow I seem more at ease at early church. So quiet you can hear the turning of a page. Tom likes to sit up front which often gets us in trouble. If there's no one in front of us, there's no one to follow. And sometimes we're up when we should be down. Even after all these years. And many times I've mumbled through the Nicene Creed because I can't find the right page. Often I just listen. That way I hear the words more clearly. Try to understand. Sometimes I don't think I have the right to say, "I believe in one God, the

Father Almighty, maker of heaven and earth, and of all things visible and invisible," because sometimes I don't know *what* I believe. It's hard to go to church when your heart hurts. But I always, always say the last two lines of the Nicene Creed because it gives me hope. "We look for the resurrection of the dead, and the life of the world to come. Amen."

# *Chapter* Sixteen

EVERY June when I pick our raspberries at Thornhill, I like to think I'm with Tommy. It's the only garden we have together. He planted the raspberries, I continue them. Yet he never had one jar of jam. He died too soon. The berries hadn't yet come to fruit and neither had he. He died when he was nineteen years old in his sleeping bag near a railroad track in a lonely summer field. Boots in a row, the clock set for six, and by his bedroll the book he had been reading, James Joyce's *Portrait of the Artist as a Young Man.*

We had big plans, an August project. Together we were going to make a brick terrace—a checkerboard. There was going to be a square of herbs, then a square of bricks, another one of vegetables, another of zinnias, and so on, the bricks alternating in between the patches of plants. I had seen the garden in a magazine and admired it. Tommy said, "Let's do it." I was thrilled. So happy to have him home from his freshman year at college, so happy just to be with him. And before he left on his early July cross-country hike to visit friends, he measured the space, drew a plan, figured we needed 3,500 bricks. I never questioned him, just put in the order for August first.

He didn't quite make it, but I wasn't bothered, there were

so many other things to do on the farm. Then when Rosemary, a friend in Cleveland, called to see why Tommy hadn't stopped, as planned, on his way back to Maryland, I began to worry. Tommy was never late for friends, hardly ever for family. As the days went by I tried to trace his route, called voices in Michigan and Ohio, strangers to me but friends of Tommy's from Williams College. I called my cousin Neal in San Francisco, a retired FBI agent and by long distance he tried to help. I started going every day to the local barracks of the state police, hoping for news of a son, now on the books as missing. They weren't too concerned. "Boys will be boys," they said casually. "Boys take their own time." And in the middle of the night I'd hear the telephone ring, but it never really did.

It seems idiotic that I didn't call Tom immediately. I look back on it now as ignorant bravery. But he was on a business trip to Spain and I didn't want to worry him unnecessarily, hoping that Tommy, for the first time in his adult life, was off on a toot, some summer fun. It turns out that we would always have been too late. Tommy died peacefully, unruffled in his sleeping bag after a long day's hike.

Tom and I were in O'Hare Airport in Chicago when we heard the news. It was our first stop on our search for Tommy. And when Tom came back from the phone booth I knew what he was going to tell me. I sat on the marble floor in that airport and kept saying, "I'll never see Tommy again. I'll never see Tommy again." That evening in an anonymous motel in Michigan Tom made all the arrangements while I cried in the halls and drank gin.

Our daughter Louise had received the news first, but didn't know how to reach us. It hurts when I think of a young girl, a blithe spirit of twenty at a summer dance, being approached by a policeman to tell her that her brother was dead. Beth was seventeen, doing a solo for Outward Bound on Hurricane Island, off the coast of Maine. She too was told by a stranger.

Only to Todd, our twenty-two-year-old son then working on a dairy farm in upper New York State, could we ourselves tell our great sorrow. And then it had to be by phone.

Tommy would have been appalled by all this misery to his family. He helped whenever he could. Even as a young boy, on the morning of a trip, he'd scramble like a monkey to the roof of the car to tie up the luggage, make it all fit, make it shipshape. Louise could never, she claims, have passed biology without him. And when he was around ten he raised his little sister Beth more, if not better, than we. Whenever I try to fold an awkward contour sheet after doing the laundry I think of Tommy. Tommy holding the other end, making it work.

He had big brown eyes, a face of freckles, a wide grin, and the only dimple in the family. He was that brown head in a field of blonds. And although he had the color of his father's hair and his name, we never knew where he came from. He had his own look. When it came time for him to choose a language at school, I suggested Spanish. French had always been a trial for Todd. But Tommy wasn't sure. He wanted to be like everyone else in the family, he said, but he never really was. Still he took my suggestion. He would be, as he put it, "the odd ball." And he had a wonderful time that first year rolling his eyes and his Spanish *r*'s, showing off, especially repeating "*Luisa tiene catarro*." What if it only meant "Louise has a cold"? He loved it, and so did I.

In those days he was open to almost anything. When he was twelve and I asked him to go to a Sunday matinee of *The Merchant of Venice*, he said, "Will there be music?" I said I didn't think so. "Will there be a lot of 'doth thou' stuff?" I said perhaps. We went and he was enthralled. After the show we saw the Duke of Venice and Portia getting into the car next to ours in the parking lot. And when the Duke of Venice waved to Tommy, I don't know who was more stage-struck, the mother or the son.

While I tried to educate him in the world of drama, he and Todd tried to help me musically. We'd drive in the car with the radio on and if I identified a song successfully by Booker T. and the MG's, or Gladys Knight and the Pips, popular groups of the day, I would have to give *them* a quarter each. It was "honest work" as they called it. And when they painted the front white fence, it was two dollars an hour. "For anyone else it would be a dollar," said Tommy, "but after all you're our mother."

Tommy somehow could do his homework while watching Archie Bunker on the television and listening to an Orioles baseball game on the radio. During the summer he'd have a game on while sitting on his bed doing a needlepoint canvas of his Saint Bernard. It may seem a strange scene, but there was a purpose. Since he hoped to be a doctor when he grew up, I wanted him to know a stitch or two, how to handle a needle. I got the idea from Dr. DeBakey's mother who taught him to sew as a boy. I also knew there was going to be a period of recuperation for Tommy and I thought this would help him pass the time.

When Tommy was twelve we took him to Houston, Texas, to have his pinched aorta corrected, a coarctation of the aorta that we had known about since he was five. It didn't bother him too much except for extreme leg cramps which we eased with hot water baths, and he couldn't run on those thin legs as much as the other boys. It was always with us, but we didn't dwell on it. Yet every summer was punctuated by, "Is this the summer for Tommy's operation?" We worked everything around it—summer camps, family trips.

I wasn't frightened about his future, I was confident, believing that everything would be all right, knowing that without the operation, he wouldn't reach twenty-one. I have this childlike faith in doctors. It would be painful, I realized, but as Tommy put it, "just a piece of cake."

Two weeks after we arrived back from Texas I looked into another room and saw two well-formed legs that I had never known before. They were Tommy's, and because of his operation, his blood stream had found new routes. I remember thinking that at last we had a complete boy for the first time in his life, and I had everything I had ever wanted in mine. Dr. Denton Cooley, the heart surgeon, told us the operation was 100 percent successful, that in six weeks Tommy could be playing football. Life was *so* sweet.

In a few years he became a determined teenager. But the roles were reversed. *He* questioned everything we did. Ralph Nader was alive and living on the second floor of Thornhill. Our dark-eyed crusader read stamped dates on milk cartons and studied consumer reports the way other boys looked at *Playboy* magazine. When we had meat for dinner, our table talk turned into a game of twenty questions. "Where did you buy it? When did you buy it? Why?" Tommy, I'm sure, formed his ideas on his own, but he was certainly influenced by his older brother Todd who became a devoted vegetarian in his freshman year at college. Whenever he came home on holidays I served crab, which was allowed, and carrot cake which was approved.

When Tommy was about sixteen he discovered the Inner City. It was a hard blend. Here he had parents in the green countryside who had dinner parties on Friday evening, and on Saturday morning early he'd drive to tutor children in the asphalt jungle who had beans for breakfast, beans for lunch, and if they were lucky, the same for dinner. His emotions couldn't weave it together with any understanding. He thought we were spoiled, frivolous. He didn't come right out and say it, but you could tell. We had everything, we had Thornhill, but what were we giving to the world? At times his silences were intolerable.

He still cleaned the rain spouts without being asked, tended the raspberry bushes, taught his sisters how to work an old sewing machine, changed the fuses, "paid his dues" as he might have said. He became utterly independent which is probably what bothered me. And I was jealous. I was even jealous of my mother-in-law, dear, wonderful Mamoo. As her house was nearer school, he often stayed there. It was easier for him, but harder for us. We missed him. But Tommy was usually where he thought he was needed most.

In his senior year I worked as a volunteer in the school library, thinking I would see him on his own ground. But as a senior, I later discovered, he wasn't obliged to have supervised study halls in the library. It's a wonder he even had time to study. He started the Ecology Recycling Center, a Work Day to clean up around school, and a project called Operation Green Grass which brought children out from the inner city. We offered to have their spring picnic at Thornhill. Tommy was off on a senior Encounter project for the month of April, living like Thoreau on the island of Nantucket, and Tom and I tried to stand in for him.

Tom drove the children around on the farm wagon, I gave them our daughters' school bloomers, since they didn't have bathing suits, to wear in the water. Then we wrapped them in towels, warmed them by starting a fire in the living room fireplace. One little six-year-old boy looked up at me with round brown eyes and said, "Don't this just feel grand!" It was easy to see why Tommy so wanted to help them. Tommy wanted to help everyone in need. We later discovered in his wallet membership cards for organizations to save the whale, the wild, the world, along with a torn stub from a Bob Dylan concert and a photograph of Ralph Waldo Emerson.

At graduation from Gilman he let me kiss him after he won the Fisher Medallion, the school's highest award. "He *must* be in a daze," laughed one of his classmates who knew him well.

And we were thrilled. I felt what we had lost those last few years had been recognized and rewarded by others. It was a good summer.

During the day he worked in a natural food store, and in the evenings we all laughed together as he sewed, from a kit, a coat for skiing. He was getting ready for a New England winter at Williams College. We still have the coat, but I can't wear it, and it's not because of the size. Tom does, however, wear the rowing jerseys Tommy won as a member of the freshman crew. The custom, it seems, was that the victors always claimed the jerseys of the losing crew. And now Tom, a Princetonian, wears, with great pride, jerseys from Yale, Holy Cross, Amherst, MIT, all a bit tattered, but he won't give them up.

Crew gave Tommy his greatest pleasure that freshman year. It was the first sport he had ever been able to participate in, become one of the boys. During the spring break when the crew traveled to Washington, D.C., to practice on the Potomac River—the waters still icy up north—they all stayed at Thornhill for a night. Tommy was in his glory, again giving refuge, taking care. His own dormitory life wasn't as satisfactory. Again he expected too much, again he was disappointed. He thought his roommates frivolous, and the one who enjoyed cocktails he called the "mixologist."

When he transferred to a third-year dormitory he found students he could talk to and he discovered as well the Ecology and Environmental Studies Department. Although he was premed, I'm sure Tommy's doctoring would have been in a remote spot near nature rather than a suite in the city. When he came home he seemed happier. He was laughing at us again, and with love. We were just beginning to be a family again. I was so happy. There was that garden to make together after his trip across the states to visit college friends. There was even a young girl named Rosemary. Then he went to the woods.

* * *

## *Chapter Sixteen*

Tommy is buried by a tall pine tree in a corner of Saint John's churchyard. He's quite alone, but there is always the sound of birds, and by the rail fence those black-and-white dairy cows often seem to be keeping watch. He was carried there by his classmates through the paths of boxwood. I was adamant about that. I didn't want to see any professionals in black suits hovering about, and especially not a trace of their long slick hearse. And his pall, the cover for his plain pine coffin, was all of wild flowers, made by our friends.

Early that Wednesday August morning the Jenkins family took off in their pickup truck, filling it with buckets of water. Chilly, the father, sat in a chair in the back of the truck directing his family. From his vantage point he could see the patches of the wild—the black-eyed Susans, goldenrod, asters, Queen Anne's lace, even joe-pye weed. Kitty, his wife, and their children, Charlie, Ellen, and Louisa, picked and picked, plunging the flowers in the buckets of water. Then they drove them over to Catherine's house, where she and Mary and Louisa spread Tommy's camping blanket on a Ping-Pong table and for hours tacked the flowers on the blanket. It became a bed of wild flowers.

With our own family we planned the service sitting under our pear tree. Todd, Louise, and Beth read some quotations that Tommy had written in his notebook, a notebook he always carried, even on his last trip. There was Shaw, Byron, Longfellow, Louis Armstrong, and of course, Thoreau. Beth said she wasn't sure she would be able to read, but she did, and our pride in our children, all of them, made it all bearable. And Clinton played the flute high in the choir loft.

We sang the sailor's hymn, my choice, "America the Beautiful" which Tom thought appropriate, and a Shaker hymn that Tommy loved. " 'Tis a joy to be simple, 'tis a joy to be free. 'Tis a joy to come down where we ought to be. And when we are in the place just right, 'twill be in the valley of joy and delight."

With a great flourish, as if in celebration, Clinton played Beethoven's "Ode to Joy" as we all walked out of the small church.

We all returned to the front lawn of Thornhill to share our sorrow, cry together. One classmate, Brad, told me through tears that now I would have to be his best man when he married. Skip gave us Tommy's letters. And Liz, a mother of much younger children, brought roses and a chocolate cake. When I thanked her, I said, "You didn't even know Tommy." And she said, "Oh yes I did. Every morning while I was waiting for my car pool, he'd wave to me when he drove by. It started my day right." It was a sad farewell that became sadder as the evening grew later.

The next morning we put a small stone lamb that had sat in a garden at Thornhill at Tommy's head. In time there was a proper headstone, but I had to wait until I found the right quotation for the boy who loved quotations. It was in Tommy's own copy of *Walden*, and he had underlined it. Now engraved on marble, it reads: "I went to the woods because I wished to live deliberately, to front only the essentials of life, and see if I could not learn what it had to teach, and not when I came to die, discovered I had not lived."

Around the stone is a small garden of ferns and wild violets from Thornhill. I've tried other flowers but only the wild from the woods survive. Nearby is a peach tree given by Edie, a woman who taught Tommy in nursery school, a woman who also lost a nineteen-year-old son. She gave a peach tree because she remembered that, even as a little boy, he loved peaches. Now in July when I see Sunday School children enjoying Tommy's fruit, I smile. It helps to know that somehow he's still giving.

Mornings were intolerable, I'd wake to clouds of despair. And in the middle of the night if I heard the moanful whistle of a train passing through the small Glyndon station, at least seven miles away, I'd think of Tommy by the railroad tracks. I couldn't read, I couldn't watch television. I couldn't understand. After Tommy's operation we never looked back. We thought everything was all right. And even after his death, we were never sure what had happened. Tom didn't understand why I wanted to know, but I wanted to know *why* Tommy died. I wanted an explanation, a reason. Tom thought it must have been his heart, but I wasn't so convinced. I had such faith in his operation. And we'll never know as we didn't find Tommy in time.

This darkness, this doubt was always with me. Only working in the garden eased the pain for a while. And I contributed to everything Tommy cared about—the Audubon Society, UNICEF—anything that came in the mail addressed to Thomas G. Hardie III.

I kept wanting to write him a letter, wanted to tell him everything that was going on, an art exhibit to see, all about Robert Redford getting an honorary degree from the Environmental Department of Williams. And Tom and I traveled a lot. They were business trips for Tom, but I was trying to run away. I thought I was safe in airports because I had never spent much time in them with Tommy. But I kept looking for him. I'd see a hand that reminded me of his, a boy with a calico handkerchief around his neck. One time I saw a red backpack and I dissolved. Even to this day if Tom and I see the back of a head of a dark-haired boy—in church, in the streets—we look at each other and we know what each is thinking.

Whenever I met people I found myself asking them how many children they had. I kept counting the families of others. And if anyone asked me how many children we had, I would say four, then try to find a way to escape from the next sentence. I couldn't exclude Tommy, even in death. Suddenly all my mathematical proportions, even at breakfast, were wrong. I had always cut three grapefruit six ways, and now that didn't work. Everything seemed uneven, unfair.

I was trying to replenish, replace, substitute, relate. I'd look up at the sky at the clouds and tell myself that Tommy was up there patching up the clouds just like he repaired the sails on his sailboat. I was irrational. I even wanted to adopt a child. At forty-eight I wanted to adopt a child. Tom wisely rode every wave of my emotion. Tom not only lost a son, he was losing a wife. My grief was so selfish. It's a wonder he didn't pack up and leave. You think death is going to bring you closer, which it does at first, but often despair drives in a wedge. I never felt that way, but I think Tom found the going awfully tough at times. I later learned that parents often separate, even divorce after the death of a child. I finally got to such a stage that I had to find professional help.

The first psychiatrist asked me if I felt guilty. The second asked me if I was happy with my husband. The third, suggested by Bill Fritz, my doctor and friend, whose son Billy had been in Tommy's class at Gilman School, just listened to me talk about Tommy, hardly said a word, smoked cigarette after cigarette, drank endless cups of coffee. It seemed to work. I felt stronger after six months of weekly meetings. I had to start rebuilding.

I had to learn not to depend on my family. I had expected too much—just like Tommy. I had asked for too much, my grief so self-centered. I wanted to touch our children, I wanted to walk as a unit. I wanted to talk about Tommy, and sometimes our children just couldn't. They had to comfort me when I should have been comforting them. I wanted to commiserate and they wanted to grieve alone. I hope I'm forgiven. I just didn't want anyone to ever forget.

It's important to keep busy, but important not to get tired. Once exhausted, life seems even sadder. Since Tommy had planned to be a doctor, I felt I had to do something medical. I was filled with good intentions, noble endeavors, but the first time out in the field I failed. I took a nurses' aid course for weeks, suited up in a light green pinafore, only to discover there was hardly anything for me to do at the hospital. I couldn't be Florence Nightingale. The nurses, the paid attendants did everything. I wasn't even allowed to practice my hospital corners. I didn't want to chat, I didn't want to push books, I wanted to dig deep. Again I expected too much.

My next idea was more successful, the blood program at Saint John's. Tom organized an Outward Bound Program at Gilman School that over the years has given boys a chance to test themselves, boys like Tommy who never made a touchdown. And on the stone wall at Saint John's Church there is a handsome sundial given by Mary Jane that keeps time in Tommy's memory year after year.

The good times are still the hardest to bear—a family wedding, Christmas, a christening. I *know* that's one reason I try to puff up celebrations, make them even more special. I want everything to count. I want to give to my family, and I want everyone to remember, even though one is missing. Our lives have certainly changed since Tommy died, and I think he would be pleased the way we've turned out. *That* remark would have him doubled over with laughter. But it's true. Our priorities, I like to think, are in order. We try to take each day as a prize, rather than a possession. And we'll never leave Thornhill. It's the house where we all were one.

Although Tommy's bedroom is now a guest room, there are still tangible touches of him everywhere. There are his raspberries that we tend, the white oak he planted as a seedling, now almost as tall as the second floor of Thornhill, and I know he would approve of my herb garden with the lilac in the center. And my friend Lucy who came to see me every day of that first desolate week, each day bringing a flower, still writes me about Tommy in the summertime.

Tommy's death hasn't made me any braver. Maybe harder, but not braver. I never read sad books or see sad movies. I can't. It's too easy to relate. And sometimes I wonder about being brave. Being human is more important. And being human means laughing and loving and crying.

It's been nine years since Tommy went cross country, and just when I think I've got it all together, I find myself crying alone, simply driving along in the car. And every time a young person dies, Tommy dies again. It hasn't happened that often, but any time is one too many. I'm plunged into the sadness of sadness because I know. I know. I have a hard time writing condolence letters because I know. Yet letters should be written. Those written to us gave me the chance to write about Tommy, be with him if only for awhile. I've kept a letter written by Hugh who was a senior at Williams when Tommy was a freshman. He wrote, "Whenever I have been forced to accept death, I am always taken back to a letter President Lincoln wrote to Mrs. Bixby of Boston who lost all five sons for the Union Cause. The letter is so powerfully humble and sincere that Lincoln is able to overcome the near impossibility of feeling out the depth of her anguish and that alone is unique sympathy. Both are overcome—that is condolence." That letter helped a great deal, and Hugh, now a doctor, has become our friend.

The most powerful solace comes from the visits of parents who have lost children. When you first look at their faces, there is immediate understanding. Forever a bond of sadness, but a bond, as well, of strength. They have survived. Somehow. And that's how Tom and I have tried to handle our loss, going out to others, especially when the shock is the strongest, the wound the most cruel. *Now* it's Clare and Van, Susan, Jackie and Moe, Augusta and George, Anita and Tad who have looked at us and said, "You know, you know," just as we looked at Rose and Arthur when they came to Thornhill when we needed them most.

# *Chapter* Seventeen

IT was time, indeed, for roses. It was time to bring a new beauty into our lives. A time to create, to grow again. I had always wanted a rose garden, but I never thought I could fit it in. There was certainly room at Thornhill, but not in my own schedule. Someday, I kept telling myself. Someday when the children were full grown, hardy, and could feed themselves. And so I kept putting it off, sublimating. I named one of our Saint Bernards "Rosie," I always seem to buy teacups festooned with rosebuds, and the chintz that climbs all over our living room furniture is Rosa Mundi, an ancient rose named after fair Rosamund, the true love of Henry II, although Eleanor of Aquitaine was his queen. Formidable women. And if roses talk to you as my friend Liz claims, I *already* had the most fluent of old pink roses. I knew that once I became involved with roses, it would be like walking into the nursery again, a lot of tender loving care. And that's just what I needed.

There were, from the beginning, those two old-fashioned rosebushes that came with the house and every June since have carried masses of pink and fragrance throughout the summer. Their fidelity is unquestionable, their blooms so generous that for weeks on end I cut them every morning, knowing full well that their family will increase by the next day. They never ask for any extra attention, except pruning. They simply perform.

And they *are* old, probably about my age. I was once given a wrinkled black-and-white photograph by a neighbor of her Uncle Bill who had lived in our house. Uncle Bill, grinning at the 1930s camera, was standing in front of one of my pink rosebushes. Perhaps he's the one who deserves the credit for these roses. Perhaps he gave them a healthy start, fertilizing with small favors from his barnyard. Whatever, they are a lovely gift. And it seemed the right time for me to add to the bouquet.

The decision, the plunge into the rose world was taken with deep thought. Although I certainly needed a new interest, an old trick of therapy, I didn't want to make any mistakes. Roses are much more serious than daisies, roses are an expense, both in time and money. And so I went on the road, toured the circuit. I visited public gardens, had private interviews with friends known for their roses. I made daily house calls on Liz's garden in the country, seeing how her garden grew, taking note of the roses I thought would make me happy. I auditioned gardens the way Flo Ziegfeld chose his own long-stemmed beauties. Looking back on it now, I was probably an awful pest, but people who grow roses are a special clan. They *love* their roses, love showing them off, but sometimes don't understand, even have hurt feelings, if you don't find the deep coral of Tropicana, or the slight green tint of a white John F. Kennedy as enticing as they do. Yet I now understand their pride, their affection. And when I first learned I was about to become a rosarian, or one who grows roses, I knew I was in the right bed. You *never* hear about a petunian, or even a foxglovian.

I even found a new friend along the garden path. Tom and I were at an afternoon wedding reception in town, and I was so blinded by the bouquets of roses everywhere in the house, I could hardly take in the bridal party. I asked where they came from. The answer—right next door. And so after a few glasses of champagne I climbed the fence and met Clover and her garden. The blooms were more beautiful than I had ever seen, but then Liz, my country expert, has always said roses love pollution, the exhaust of the city. Maybe she's right, but whatever Clover is a special rosarian, even tests roses for a national nursery. And she, a complete stranger, in one afternoon became my close friend, my rose expert in the city.

Clover, and what a lovely name for a gardener, encouraged me. She gave me books to read, called me on the telephone with ideas. I was completely hooked, insatiable, studying and always carrying a small rose handbook as faithfully as I remember the nuns reading their prayer books in the Paris Metro. It seems whenever Tom would be reading a newspaper, I'd be reading my rose book. And I certainly investigated rose pedigrees far more intently than Tom's before our marriage. But then when you're young, it's love rather than lineage. Anyhow that day in December when we were married, I wasn't planting a rose garden, I was walking down the primrose path, carrying the only white flowers we could find in Paris—tulips and lilacs.

I knew what I wanted—in marriage, and in a rose garden—and finally the day came to dig the garden. Most of the rose gardens I had seen were in squares or rectangles, symmetrical and secure. And my friend Beau plants his roses alphabetically. It's probably more convenient, easier to remember the names, but to me it seemed as if all his roses were in the Army. I always feel like saluting as if on review. Instead I wanted something more fanciful. I wanted a bowknot, a big bowknot of roses on the lawn.

I didn't want a rose garden like everyone else's, but still I needed help. I called up Liz, pleading with her to come over to give me courage. And with a garden hose, we laid out a rose bed in the shape of a bowknot. Once we were satisfied with the pattern, we carved a deep bow with a Rototiller on a gentle slope of the green lawn. It is on the west side of the house where the sun spends most of the day. You can see it from the herb garden, the kitchen window, and from the second floor guest room you see the full force of this bowknot filled with polka dots of color every June. But that first day I wondered if I had completely ruined the lawn merely because of a feminine whim. Told myself that there are times you should be "square." But this garden has appealed to the most unexpected. Rod who was repairing our roof, pleating together long sections of tin, told me that he sure did like standing on the roof, looking at my garden, the one shaped like scissors. Scissors to him, bowknot to me, the garden gives pleasure.

My original idea of having a lady garden, with only roses named after women soon faded when Liz told me I *had* to have the dark red of Mister Lincoln. I did everything she told me to do. But after living with him for five summers, I'm still not so sure. I admire the rose's namesake, but to me a red rose often looks florist-born. I much prefer the fragile pink blush of Michele Meilland. But that first May I was guided by the taste of others. And it shows.

Liz, a dark brunette, a vivid woman, painted her living room peach before others dared. Her suggestions were Fashion, Cherish, Tropicana, their colors from salmon to shrimp. Even to this day, when I look at those roses I think of Liz. Clover's roses were more subtle, more creamy rose like a summer shortcake. She introduced me to Sweet Afton, Garden Party, and Charlotte Armstrong, still among my favorites.

The names of roses make a garden more personal, you find yourself talking to them as if they were friends, more likely family. And Gertrude Stein was wrong. I can't believe she *ever* knew roses. A rose is not a repetitious sentence. They all have their own personality, their well defined lines, or their scattered beauty. That first spring I didn't have my choice of later years.

I *had* to plant whatever roses were available at the local nurseries. I hadn't planned ahead. I had studied, but I hadn't the confidence to order from January catalogs. It can be bewildering. And so I had to go with whatever pots were on sale nearby. In all, fifteen bushes, mostly hybrid tea roses, started the garden, with spaces left in between for bare-rooted ones I would order later. the next time around, from winter catalogs.

Bettina, a friend in London, the bride who was married at Thornhill soon after we moved in, knew I wanted a rose garden. She remembered, I'm sure, that at her wedding in June we threw grass seed along with rose petals. And just as I was about to dig the rose garden, I received a newspaper clipping from her. "The Queen opened the grounds of Sandringham to the public yesterday and offered long-stemmed roses at only half a crown for a bunch, grown on manure from the royal racehorse studs." My manure, although not as prestigious, was waiting for me in the barnyard.

But if it hadn't been for Mood Gibson, a most handy fellow I borrowed from my mother-in-law's garden, there might not have been a rose garden at all at Thornhill. I don't think I could have done it alone. Together we dug fifteen holes, two spades deep and wider than the rose roots—eighteen to twenty-four inches in diameter. We mixed the soil with peat moss and that well-aged manure for a fertilized bed. Then we anchored one end of the bowknot with Mister Lincoln, and at the other end we put Gypsy, named after a striptease artist who was famous when taking off your clothes was meant to be risqué. Perhaps she wasn't a fitting companion for a president, but as she was my only other red rose, I made a match. And Queen Elizabeth, a pink grandiflora, sat right in the middle of the bow.

It took us all day to make the garden. Mood, who looks like an older, darker Clark Gable, although he doesn't know it, never complained, just worked and watered. Born in North

Carolina, his only treat was seeing a rabbit or two which immediately made him think of dinner. My reward was a summer full of roses.

Although Liz warned me not to pick too many blooms, I couldn't resist. I did cut the stems short as you're meant to do in June (longer in August as growing time is slowing down). Whenever Tom and I went out to dinner, I buttonholed him, pinning a home-grown rose on his lapel. And at Tessa and Philip's June wedding we carried a basket of our own rose petals which we threw with joy and pride.

While working in my rose garden that first summer I felt as if I *were* back in our children's nursery again. Needed. Roses do take a lot of attention— formula feedings, formula spraying. And a wheelbarrow full of wood chips for mulching, to keep weeds undercover and edges in line, is a great deal harder to push than a baby carriage. But while working in that garden I was at peace. The satisfaction of going out to the garden and picking one perfect Pristine made it all worthwhile. If I went away for a day or so I could hardly wait to get back to see if Sonia, a pale peach, had bloomed from a bud to a beauty. And as Queen Elizabeth, the first grandiflora of all, grew tall and strong, I wanted to measure her against our closet door as we had once kept track of our children's heights.

This new family of mine kept me content until the middle of October. Then I mulched the bed thick with hay, protection against winter, and started thinking of what roses I would plant next March. There was one in particular that I *had* to have. Although a late bloomer myself, I had always been told of a white rose named Madame Hardy. I knew she was an old rose, a damask, introduced in France in 1832, and named after the wife of the head gardener at the Tuilleries in Paris. Any rose book you read is lyrical about Madame Hardy.

She was rare then and she's rare now. Only a few are grown

each year at a nursery famous for old roses. It's called Roses of Yesterday and Today, in Watsonville, California, and it's their decision, obviously, to grow what sells. I found myself writing weekly love letters to the nursery. I was determined. I explained my rose garden, I drew the design. I wanted to be one of the chosen few. "Who," I asked them, "should have 'Madame Hardy' if not I? Yours sincerely, Mrs. Hardie." I even told them I was married in Paris. I pulled out all the plugs.

I ordered other roses as well, seventeen of them—five yellow, five pink, five white, and two apricot, some from California, others from Oregon and Georgia. But it was Madame Hardy who kept me guessing, all through January and February, wondering if I was going to be able to plant her, come late March, right at the feet of Queen Elizabeth.

In Maryland roses are pruned after George Washington's birthday, his proper birthday. Under the tutelage of Liz, I had pruned my rosebushes by early March, cutting away, at an angle, the winter kill, removing inner cross branches. "You are," Liz kept repeating, quite dictatorially, "trying to shape a teacup, *not* a hat rack." It wasn't easy and when I was finished I could measure only about eighteen inches left of each of my original fifteen bushes. I wondered if I would ever see roses again.

That last week in March I never left home. UPS, good old United Parcel Service, was going to be my Prince Charming, riding in on a big brown truck, delivering my treasures of spring. And all the roses I ordered, except Camelot, came to my rose garden. As for Madame Hardy, or "mah-DAHM are-DEE," as she is spelled phonetically in the catalog, she was right on time.

I called on Mood again. I enjoy working with him, he makes me feel young. Although he is only five years older than I am, he still calls me "Miss Dee." On this visit he saw a deer in the upper pasture which made him salivate even more than when he saw the rabbits. For such a gentle soul, he certainly has an appetite for the wild.

We went into our rose routine—first digging holes, preparing the soil, trimming off any damaged roots, spreading those roots about naturally. It was a long day, from nine in the morning until six P.M. Most of the roses were now hybrid teas, which I prefer—tall and tidy and beautiful. But I also added a floribunda, flowers in a cluster, which I had seen in Clover's garden. Ivory Fashion is a lovely ivory white with a flush of yellow in the center, and looks as velvety as a gardenia. My garden, I thought, was complete. I had captured the crown, Madame Hardy, and she was surrounded by a court of thirty-one other roses.

About April I start poking around, "mothering" as Tom calls it. I visit each rose and make a note in my garden book as to whether the bush is strong, doubtful, or perhaps gone forever. It's much easier for me to keep track of my roses than my perennials. I wonder if it's because I care more. I've already done the pruning in March but you can't really tell then, although I often suspect. And each year I lose two or three roses to winter. The first spring I couldn't *believe* Savannah, a lovely peach rose from Georgia, had left me. I felt it a personal insult, my hospitality failed. The first loss is the worst. Another year it was Fragrant Cloud. If I care about the rose, I replace it, if not I try another. I'm even becoming ruthless. American Heritage, a noble name but a rose of mixed color and style, at least for me, has had three years to prove itself. This year it must go—probably into Louise's garden.

My spring list doesn't really prove anything except that I'm impatient, longing to get back into my rose garden. A doubtful bush in April usually produces a glorious rose in June. I still refer back to the *American Rose Society Guide*, the little handbook I carried constantly with me in the beginning. It gives a list of roses from A to Z, Accent through Zwerglonig, their classification such as hybrid tea or grandiflora, and their colors and ratings. A perfect score, of course, is ten. Madame Hardy and Queen Elizabeth have made it to nine, and I think that is as high as we will ever go. But I don't raise my roses for their scores, or to make bountiful arrangements. My roses are more than that. They gave me a lift when I needed it most, and they're my friends, my summer pals. When life really bears down, I go into the garden to work. Physical toil, I find, eases emotional pain.

And I like delving into the past of my roses, knowing their ancestry. Families, in the rose world, can be most provocative. Cousins consort, keep company with each other, parents mate with offspring, intermarriage breeds beauty. *No* one is in the closet. It's one big happy family. Peace, the most popular rose, for instance, has as many regal offspring as Queen Victoria once had all over Europe.

More than pedigrees, it's the continuation of a family line that fascinates me. I like knowing that a child of Crimson Glory is rosy Charlotte Armstrong, and Charlotte's child is Helen Traubel, paler than her mother but just as buxom; that Seashell is a grandchild of Tropicana. It helps me understand my roses, their strengths, an occasional weakness, or why a pink bud unfurls into a yellow rose. Or is it, I wonder, because I care so much for the continuation of a family, human or hybrid tea? Or because I can't read my own family tree, one page worth, written in Swedish? I can decipher that my maternal great-grandmother was Sara Pettersdotter, but that's about it. My own background certainly isn't as clearly defined as my roses, or as far as I can figure, as emotional.

When I first read about Peace, a big yellow hybrid tea with pink ribbons, I actually cried. It first flowered for its French breeder, Francis Meilland, in 1942, just as the German army of occupation was moving across France. Monsieur Meilland realized this rose was special and smuggled some budwood to the American consul as if he were evacuating a precious child, or hiding a family jewel. For three years he had no idea what had happened. But when France was freed, Monsieur Meilland learned that the consul had managed to get the budwood to the United States where it was propagated. When the delegates met in San Francisco to frame the constitution of the United Nations, this rose graced every table. It was then named Peace. Someone could write a Broadway musical about this rose.

I learned about Peace from Peter Malins who was the chief rosarian of the Cranford Rose Garden at the Brooklyn Botanic Garden. I've never met Mr. Malins, I dream of seeing his garden someday, and his *Peter Malins' Rose Book* is by far the most informative, as well as witty and knowledgeable rose book I own. I devour it the way other women read cookbooks. And although he writes that Oregold, a hybrid tea, yellow as butter, puts out "grotesquely large flowers," I love *my* Oregold. Almost as much as he loves Madame Hardy.

Madame Hardy *is* quite a rose, and in June it is a full round bush of light green completely covered with small flat white roses, tightly petaled, looking like layers of a Victorian petticoat. June is its debut as well as its demise, but its one monthly performance is a moment of glory. I've discovered, however, that Madame Hardy needs her own stage. She takes up too much room in my bowknot, stretching her arms wildly, even after she has bloomed. And so next March I'm going to transplant her, giving her another place in the sun, all on her own. Some roses, like some women, simply need more space.

I realize I was sometimes too hasty in my planting. I was just so eager to have a rose garden. At first Miss All-American Beauty seemed blowzy, too full, a rouged chorus girl out of line. Now I realize I shouldn't have planted her next to Royal Highness, pale, pink and elegant. But I no longer look at my rose garden as a whole. It's now one to one.

## *Chapter Seventeen*

June mornings I wake early, and even before breakfast I put on my Wellingtons, the black rubber boots I bought from an ironmonger in the small village of Chagford, England, the same village where Evelyn Waugh wrote *Brideshead Revisited*. These boots are probably the closest step I'll ever take to being like an English gardener, and I'm crazy about them, make me think I know what I'm doing. A. A. Milne's Christopher Robin wears them too. The day I walked to that Devon village to buy them the hedgerows were twice my height and laced with wild lilies. My Wellingtons remind me of all that.

And so we walk to the garden, the grass moist with dew, the scent of wild honeysuckle pungent. An occasional pheasant will strut by, and there are always rabbits. When they hear my approach, they freeze, motionless, like the small granite rabbit from Vermont that I have placed in the garden. Another accessory I once tried was planting parsley by roses as I read it was meant to help bring out their scent. I was never convinced, and now I have, spaced between the rosebushes, *fraises des bois*, the small wild strawberries which Clover gave me from her rose garden.

First there is inspection. Sweet Afton is always waiting, while others hide their heads. I hustle them a bit, give encouragement. "Apollo, where are you? Confidence, will you ever grow up?" Then I indulge. I may only cut one rose for Tom's breakfast, but more often I am tempted by five or six. Sometimes I put them in a basket with other flowers of June—the plush pink peonies, the lacy lavender of Anthony Waterer, the fey, delicate columbine. More often I put them one by one in small containers—old perfume bottles, a small brandy snifter, a silver shot glass Tom received as an usher's present long ago, tiny china pitchers, a baby's christening cup. Then I line them all up on the white kitchen counter as if they were children dressed for a birthday party.

I place them around the house. Some I sit between the

crowded photographs of our children on a corner table in the living room. One I might put on the pine mantelpiece next to an old walnut tea box. Usually it's Don Juan because his currant-red petals look well with wood. Placing these roses around is my early morning tattoo, starts *my* day right. I even like to see, after a few days, the fallen pink petals on my apple green desk in our bedroom.

After that trip to England, I planted even more roses. The roses of England would inspire anyone. Imagine a white country cottage, its face fringed with wisteria and roses. Once home I planted mine against the high stone wall that is one of the boundaries of my herb garden, the small garden growing in the open U of our house. I planted Helen Traubel, as majestic as the opera singer she was named after, and Mrs. John Laing, unknown to me but a lovely dusty pink. In between, as I thought the girls would like it, I started Don Juan, a climbing rose. He has grown so tall that he now reaches over the wall of the herb garden, peeking at my lavender and thyme.

There is a chipmunk, living in that same stone wall, who is wild about Don Juan. Everyday he nibbles, leaving evidence of his rosy feast. At first I was outraged. Even thought about a trap. There is a kindly one called Havahart which you can buy at most hardware stores. But as this red rose is prolific, I've decided to share with nature's children, especially this particularly greedy one. Although I must admit, a gourmet.

Chipmunks are the least of my worries when it comes to roses. Beetles are much more of a disaster. Nor do I have to carry a rose around as did Empress Josephine, famous, among other things, for her garden at Malmaison in France. She would sniff, and cup a rose to her nose, hoping to conceal the fact that her teeth were hardly as perfect as her rose. I grow roses only because they please me, comfort me if necessary, give a certain joy, companionship. I probably should make potpourri as every summer I have at least a wheelbarrow of petals. But that's work and roses are work enough. Yet it is such a treat to walk around in the afternoon, seeing what's happened to my roses during the day. And if I lose one and visit a local nursery to replace it, I feel the way most women do when they visit Tiffany's. More than a rosarian, I guess I'm a rosaholic. Age, I've discovered, if you work at it, receives its reward. And starting a rose garden was mine.

I feed my roses three times a season, the last by the middle of August, using 5–10–5 (5 percent nitrogen, 10 percent phosphorus, 5 percent potash). One of Clover's tricks, as she always has a garden party in September, is to give them a swig of Magic Glo, liquid fertilizer which dissolves quickly, but lasts long enough to give a good show of roses.

Whenever there isn't rain, I water, as roses need at least an inch of water a week. This means hosing low, one by one, a long chore, always in the morning. Sometimes if I'm particularly busy, I use an overhead spray, but the leaves must be dry by evening or they invite disease.

And there is certainly disease. When I see that first leaf with black spot I feel the same way I did when our children had measles—dismay. David, a friend I started in roses by giving him a rose certificate at Christmas, boasts that his roses are as clean as a babe, but then his look as if they have on overcoats of dust. I prefer to spray and do so every ten days in the late afternoon. I hate it. But if you're going to have roses, you must. I alternate the formula, both given to me by Liz.

| | | |
|---|---|---|
| ½ teaspoon Benolate | | 1 teaspoon Phaltan or Funginex |
| 1 tablespoon Isotox | *or* | 2 tablespoons Sevin |
| 1 gallon $H_2O$ | | 1 gallon $H_2O$ |

Even with spraying, July is a discouraging month, the Japanese beetles invade. By now I know they prefer a white diet, so good-bye Pascali, Honor, even Pristine, at least until September. I prepare by hanging traps filled with beetle bait, supposedly a female Japanese beetle sex lure, but even sex isn't enough. I go out every day and crush the beetles between my fingers. It may seem medieval, but it makes me feel better. Sometimes I just drop them into a can of gasoline. I turn brutal for my roses.

August is a slower month, a recovery month, and by September there is a renaissance, an awakening of my roses. And they have always been around for our family weddings. For Todd and Diana in September, for Louise and Scott in October. Roses may be an extravagance, in time, energy, and money, but they are certainly a personal affair.

I've even discovered a way to keep Madame Hardy all year round. I could use a cup of her delicate petals in an apple pie, but our apples don't arrive until September. However our raspberries overlap Madame Hardy by about a week in June. Every day I make a batch of jam, and in every other jar I sprinkle a few of her white petals. Months later, in the middle of winter, spread on a piece of Diana's homemade bread for afternoon tea, these petals look like little white hearts in a field of raspberries.

A day of jubilation in June 1982—the lunch on the lawn at Thornhill after the christening of our first grandchild, Albert. In the background, a covey of close friends. *From left to right*: Louise Leser, Bettina McNulty (who was married at Thornhill), and David Ober, our godson.

Some of our sheep looking at reasonable facsimiles of themselves, the trompe l'oeil sheep painted on the barn by my friend Janet Hughes.

The rose garden off season, piled with straw as a winter overcoat. In June it becomes a bowknot of color and scent.

Here's Albert sniffing in the pleasures of my roses, wearing my apron and straw hat.

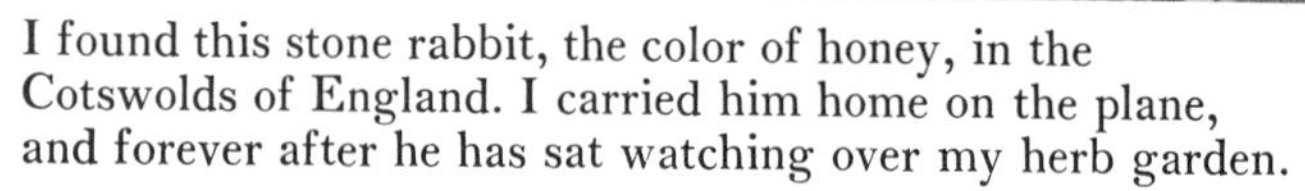

I found this stone rabbit, the color of honey, in the Cotswolds of England. I carried him home on the plane, and forever after he has sat watching over my herb garden.

Getting ready for a winter Sunday lunch at Thornhill. Tom is cooking away in the kitchen, but I'm not worried. I *know* the oyster stew is succulent and ready to serve. I made it yesterday. LEFT: A close-up section of our stenciled dining-room floor. Our daughter Louise and I stenciled the pineapple, a colonial symbol of hospitality and fertility, in every corner. I think it was soon after our day of stenciling that Louise became pregnant with Albert!

Tea is always easy, an impromptu way to entertain. My collection of teacups and pots are always there, and the kitchen clock, once in the Cotton Exchange in New Orleans, ticks away while we sip and sort out the day.

Thornhill with the new wing to the left, and a relatively new grandchild, Albert, leaning on the white fence that has been there for thirty years, put up by Tom and my father when we first moved to the country. Albert is holding *his* little Nantucket Lightship basket.

A year-old Edith, our first granddaughter, sitting on a hay bale rolled like a giant shredded-wheat biscuit. These biscuits weigh about eight hundred pounds, Edith somewhat less.

# *Chapter* Eighteen

DIANA, the maker of delicious teatime bread, as well as of our son Todd's constant happiness, is our daughter-in-law. Our one and only. And when she and Todd were married a few years ago in Sewickley, Pennsylvania, the roses of Thornhill went along with us to the wedding weekend. We all went together, "on location," for a family fete.

That September the curtain rose again on my rose garden. In a large cooler I layered those hardly awake, but those I knew would unfold with color for an evening performance, the dinner we were giving the night before the wedding. And in plastic bags I placed bough after bough of our boxwood.

Diana was determined that our party would not be in the local country club, like everyone else's. I agreed with her. Celebrations should have their own flair, a flavor to remember. But little did I realize she would come up with a forgotten boathouse! And it was charming, this long-windowed Victorian boathouse on a small private lake where once there were sailing picnics in childhood-size dinghies, and in the winter, skating parties by the light of the moon.

We swept away the cobwebs of neglect, cleaned and cleaned, and Grant, Diana's father, painted the interior white. We imported chairs and tables, food and music, even Ned, our friend who flew in from Maryland to help us decorate. By dinner time each round table was centered by a huge wreath of boxwood, filled with a full pie of the blossoms of Thornhill roses. And Beth somehow made eighty-seven place cards, drawing on each a different bouquet of flowers. It was indeed a labor of love, but this was a celebration we had been waiting for, for a long time.

Ever since, as a matter of fact, Diana was sixteen years old. That was when she first came home from school with Beth. She didn't even know Todd—an older man away at college. But I knew. Every time she came to Thornhill I told myself this was the girl I wanted our son to marry. Mothers have a way of dreaming. And it happened. Without any help from me. Well, hardly. I vaguely remember promising Todd a honeymoon in Scotland if he just didn't let Diana get away. The bribe wasn't really necessary, and now I who had been Mrs. Hardie to Diana for years was her husband's mother.

I like it. I like it a lot. And we've had good times together. Their first house in Vermont was a yellow clapboard cottage that looked like a buttercup in the snow. Then they rented one smack in the middle of an apple orchard. In the springtime when you looked out the bedroom window you thought you were above the clouds, white blossoms billowing everywhere. Now they live, while they look, they say, "for another Thornhill," in an old brick house that is the color of day lilies in July. And in every room there is a small token of Thornhill—some chairs, a needlework sampler, a painting or two. But all with a new life. Who else would have thought of putting that Empire sofa in the kitchen?

Together Diana and I found a claw-foot bathtub of regal proportions which she painted lilac—a color which prompted, I think, their first domestic disagreement. And I helped her decide where to put the swing on the porch, what hedge to plant that would be a windshield for the vegetable garden but not "block out the sunsets." And she taught me how to make a basket from wild grapevines. But while mine looked like a sprawling spider's web that couldn't bend, her huge baskets, woven of grapevines, willow, and wild dogwood, are like country sculptures. She once carried one to Thornhill. I thought it so well done that I walked it around to some shops. And now she is in business.

In an even older frame house, their office, Todd and Diana work together on their all-natural chewing gum, their creation, their product, sweetened with Vermont maple syrup and honey. It is called "HARDIE'S TRUE GUM," and the drawing on the gum package shows children running across a field, inspired by Winslow Homer's *Snap the Whip*. In the background are the mountains of Vermont. Especially one called Camel's Hump, the mountain where Diana and Todd became engaged. *They*, it seems, didn't need Scotland at all!

Beth visits them often. A teacher of the young, her last post was in nearby New York State in a boarding school where the students start in the fourth grade, and now she is taking a sabbatical, which, I think, at a certain stage in one's life, is a very good decision. Strong and fragile, wise and wondering, Beth will find her way. Wherever the wind takes her. And when it takes her back to Thornhill, her room is ready, looking exactly as it did when she first came home from that first holiday from college. In school she had a certain stage presence which *must* have helped her as a teacher. I think she should go into children's television. She's thinking of children's books, maybe publishing, perhaps children's museums. In time, somehow, she wants to go into another, different world of children.

And Louise is a mother. Albert and Edith. The gift of all gifts. Grandchildren. With four children of our own, I always thought we'd be given a goodly supply. In a way I was counting on it. A houseful. Then when Tommy died, grandchildren seemed even more urgent. I remember feeling cheated—losing Tommy, losing his children.

I was counting my chickens before they hatched. But it wasn't easy to be an orphan when all around you your pals are showing photographs and telling anecdotes about their grand progeny. I was certainly old enough.

I knew just what we were going to do at Thornhill. These imaginary grandchildren and I. With the boys I'll plant a butter-bean tepee, mixing some climbing morning glories in to make it pretty. That's where we'll hide. Maybe from the girls. Every once in a while.

With the girls I'll gather wild violets and daisies for summer crowns, make dolls from hollyhocks and lilies. We'll press pansies and buttercups and primroses. Then we'll make flowered wreaths on a rainy day. When it's clear we'll sleep *outside* and look at the moon and the sparkle of fireflies.

I've had a few dress rehearsals. Whenever the spirits moved them, Reid and Bess, when they were about nine, would walk over the hill to see me. Now that they are older, probably about twelve, their visits aren't as frequent. But the last time they came they arrived with shiny little paper stars pasted on their ear lobes like grownup earrings. We sat under the apple tree and had high tea, laced with milk, spread our bread with raspberry jam and Diana and Todd's honey.

The trunk in the library is, I suspect, the real attraction. It is a commemorative piece, painted on the top with Lord Nelson's flagship, and "H.M.S. *Victory*, 1803." It is filled with toys I couldn't bear to give away. Once the girls have had their jam and tea, thank you very much, they plunge into the depths of the trunk. They explore, examine, console the llama with only one ear, line up the wooden Swedish horses painted in red with flowered saddles. Then they pack them all up again, as tidy as their manners, and are off over the hill.

# *Chapter Eighteen*

Katey, my college roommate and a grandmother of long standing, says grandhood is "joy mixed with terror." Especially when you hold the first baby the first time. She also told me about the grandchild, sitting in the dressing room while her grandmother tried on a new dress, who asked, "Grandma, who let the air out of your arms?" I'm prepared to answer all questions. Maybe the second time around I'll be quicker.

Tom claims I've been practicing for years. When he says this I wonder if he realizes the great longing some women have for grandchildren. The desire, so natural, to fill out, once again, the family. I've never understood some women who say they're too young to be grandmothers. Too old perhaps, but never too young. Maybe my husband does know me better than I realize. I *do* have that trunk, a salt-box dollhouse, a brigade of tiny tin soldiers, a shelf full of books and puzzles, all those teddy bears, and Fiona Barley, my English doll—all waiting patiently.

When Louise told us she was pregnant, I cried happy tears. This was my hope, and one of the reasons, I'm sure, that I wanted to keep Thornhill going strong. I wanted grandchildren to be able to come home to a farm—Thornhill Farm. And tell me, if you can, a better way to retwig the empty nest.

About the seventh month, we had a serious conversation about names. Not names of the baby, but what the baby was to call *us*. I told Louise about a friend who, when asked this same question by her son, told him she wanted her grandchildren to call her "Perfect." Now there are two little children who do just that. And it is very appealing to hear those young voices calling for their grandmother in the grocery store.

I opted, pure and simple, for "Grandmother." Maybe it is because I never had a grandmother. There were the tributaries, certainly, some aunts, some uncles, but never that river with its strong current of love—that flow of affection when you haven't seen each other for at least a week. Never a grandmother to tell me to stand up straight, never a grandmother to ask me to tea. Grandchildren are a treat, a lovely indulgence that allows you to start over again in half time.

I'm even fond of that saccharine Thanksgiving song about "over the river and through the woods to Grandmother's house we go." Sloppy indeed, but I sing it with gusto. And as I had waited so long, or so I thought, I wanted the label to be correct, if not the packaging. Tom, the future grandfather, said he didn't quite see himself married to a "Grandmother." The vanity of men, how it often surprises me. And I wonder why age seems to bother them more than women. My husband, who looks *years* younger, decided he wanted to be called "Cap'n."

"*That*," I told him, "will be impossible to pronounce." But he didn't listen. He had his rights, he also had his reason. Among his favorite books are C. S. Forester's stories of Horatio Hornblower, that courageous captain of the seas, books he is saving for his grandchildren to read. And to his grandchildren Tom wants to be, pure and simple, a brave captain. Everybody likes a title. There was a moment, but only a moment, when I considered trying out "Duchess" for myself. Why not! Influencing grandchildren to call you by a certain name is one of your few chances for new glory. "Grandmother" was glory enough for me, but those children often have the last word.

Albert was Albert from the very beginning, named after my father. It pleases me, especially since my father, now no longer alive, knew he had a great-grandson named after him. And Albert was baptized in Saint John's Church, where his parents were married, by his grandfather Jim, wearing his great-grandfather Harry's christening gown. After the service there was a lunch on the lawn at Thornhill.

And the lawn was sown with memories. There was that christening long ago—Tommy running around in his white suit and bare feet. And Thornhill's first wedding with Bettina and Henry, but no lawn to speak of at all. There they were passing around christening champagne to honor little Albert, almost royal in a long white gown heavy with lace, the dress his mother wore as well. What if the buttons didn't quite fasten, for one lovely June afternoon Thornhill was filled with the past, the present, and the future. I couldn't have asked for anything more. No, I couldn't ask for anything more.

I have, however, asked a lot of Albert since then. Mostly what to call me. Once it was evident that he was old enough to recognize us, remember us, I tried the Berlitz Method by repeating my chosen name—"Grandmother, grand - mother, GRAND - MOTHER." It didn't work. Then I tried a shortened version. "How about Granny?" And all I would get would be "Deeeeeeee." Now if there is one thing I do not want is to be called by my first name by our first grandchild. Then Albert figured it out all by himself and started calling me "Momma Dee." I love it. It sounds sort of Italian and wonderful, as if I had just finished stamping the grapes of the autumn harvest. And for Tom, Albert has translated "Cap'n" into "CapCap."

When Edith was born twenty-two months later, I saw even more of our grandson. I went to Wilmington, Delaware, to help out. I was so excited that I, as I later learned, deposited money at my bank to my Social Security number rather than my checking account, and withdrew money, quite by accident, from my Growth Fund. Perhaps a timely mistake. Edith and Albert, after all, *are* my growth stocks for years to come.

Edith, known as "Baby E" to Albert, is a calm, comforting baby, while Albert is a joy and a terror, just as Katey predicted. And now he is two and a half, and we're walk-around pals. When I'm at his house and we meet neighbors, Albert slaps his small hand against my knee in acknowledgment, points up at me, and says to his friends, "Momma Dee!" I like being introduced by a grandson. And when we're on the farm, seeing Thornhill through his eyes is the most exciting world.

Thank heavens he's curious. We peek down small holes trying to see the chipmunks, wait hopelessly for them to say hello.

We walk in the woods listening to owls nested in old stumps. He sniffs my roses, then smiles at me, knowing already how to please his grandmother. We sit by the vegetable garden, eating the most tender leaves of early spinach. And when he was a little more than a year he tried to put the fallen leaves back on the white oak tree that Tommy planted. He wanted to make it whole again. Now Albert is part of that whole.

He can also be impossible and exhausting. But all it takes is a long afternoon nap for both of us. Then we're off to conquer the world again. And who could resist a blue-eyed blond, walking into your bedroom with an empty orange-colored bacon carton worn on his head as a hat, as jaunty and as stylish as the cap worn by the young man with a fife in Manet's painting?

He's a mimic, a clown. When Tom does his back exercises on the living room floor, Albert is right next to him, pulling up his small knees to his chest—and grunting. And they spend a lot of time reading together.

Albert also likes snakes. Which is fortunate when you live on a farm, especially in the spring. But I didn't learn this at Thornhill. I discovered it when I took Albert for his first visit to the Baltimore Zoo. He looked high at the giraffes, down deep at the commune of prairie dogs, and he was stunned by the elephants. Can you imagine seeing an elephant for the very first time! Then we went into the reptile house and while I shuddered, he exploded with joy. Boys, after all, will be boys.

We discussed our visit on the way home. At least I did a lot of talking. So much so that at a red light I bumped into the car in front of us. Out leapt a woman, ranting and roaring. While I was terrified, it didn't seem to bother Albert at all. But then Albert had just seen a lion, a real live lion. And that trip to the zoo cost me $125.

Mamoo was right. She always enjoyed her grandchildren's visits on a one-to-one basis. I never understood. I thought she should have fun with the whole bunch. Now I realize her wisdom. It's very pleasant sitting on the front steps at Thornhill blowing soap bubbles with your grandson, watching the small, round iridescent planets landing on the boxwood bushes. Then when it gets dark, lighting one sparkler—I keep a supply for instant magic—seeing it glitter against the night. Then we all go to bed. Sometimes at eight.

Furnishing Albert and Edith is making Thornhill young again. Upstairs a small bedroom has been newly papered with lavender and white stripes, and around the top is a border of mice doing the minuet with garlands of flowers. There's a short Victorian sleigh bed that had to be hoisted through the second floor window because it couldn't curve around the old front stairway. And this room is Edith's room, although she isn't quite a year old, a room poised for a granddaughter.

Then there's the highchair in the kitchen, another Victorian relic, where Albert sits like a king watching over his grandmother's realm, now *his* kingdom. In the living room is an Albert-size chair that started life with his great-great-grandfather, the first Thomas Hardie. Albert is often greedy about *his* chair, and fortunately Edith is too young to invade his small throne. It's almost time, I think, to find a miniature tea table. Once Albert gives up apple juice.

Most of the house, however, looks the same as it did when our own children were young. The living room furniture is more grown-up perhaps, there's more chintz, more fancy ideas, but it is still the Thornhill of thirty years ago. A recent addition designed by our neighbor Walter Ramberg is our present bedroom, and goes out from the library, but it seems a separate modern state, without disturbing the old rhythms of the old house. And the only new activity is in the basement.

Without even knowing his warp from his weft, Tom came home with a loom as casually as most men bring home the even-

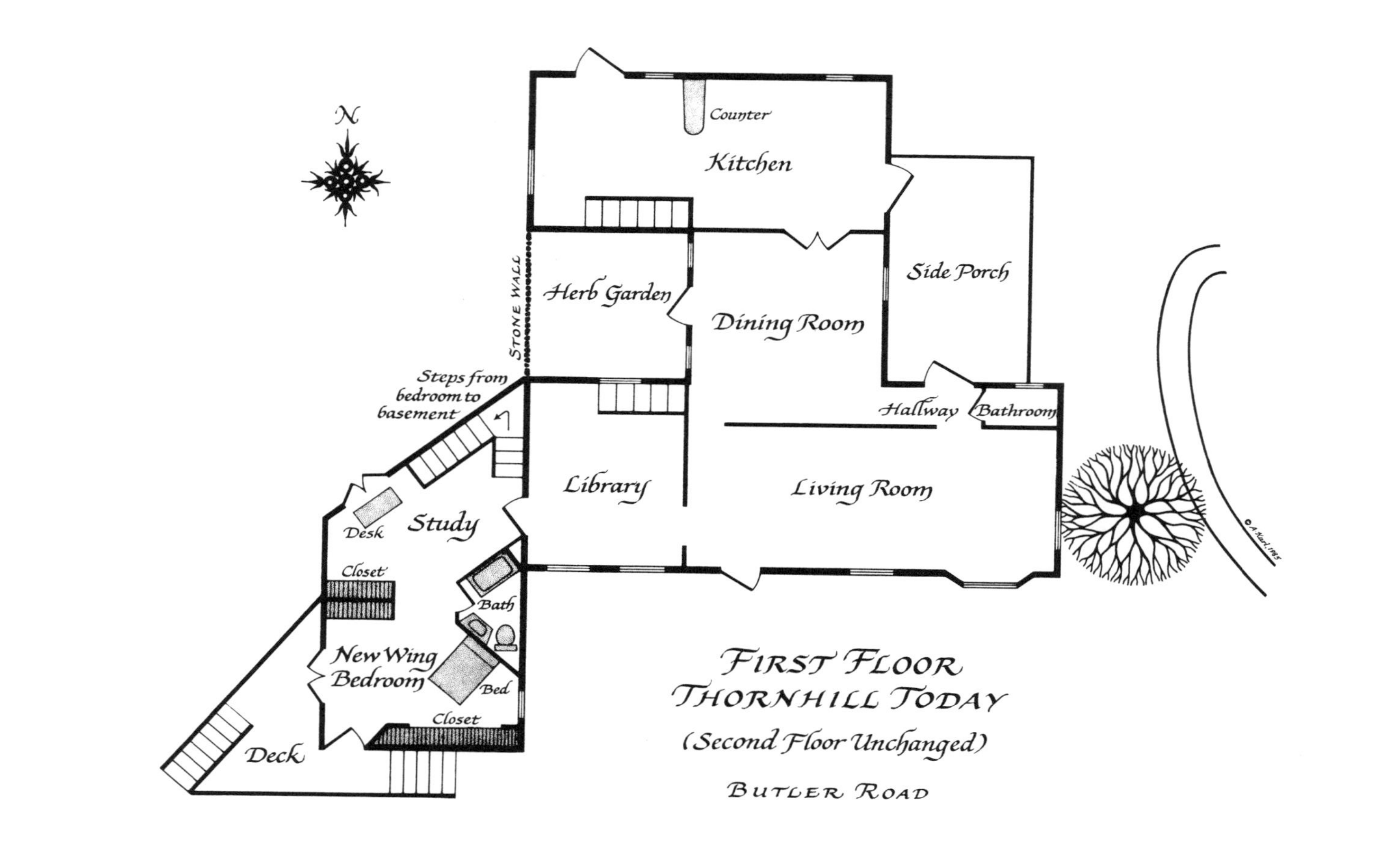
N
Counter
Kitchen
Side Porch
Herb Garden
Dining Room
Stone Wall
Steps from bedroom to basement
Hallway
Bathroom
Library
Living Room
Desk
Study
Closet
Bath
New Wing Bedroom
Bed
Closet
Deck
© A. Karl, 1985
First Floor
Thornhill Today
(Second Floor Unchanged)
Butler Road

ing paper. He wanted to do something "different," he wanted to weave. And what was always his office, he now calls the "Loom Room."

Louise was his teacher, a weaver of glorious cotton rag rugs. She hasn't made as many since the arrival of Albert and Edith, but Tom thinks he is continuing her trade. He flips the shuttle back and forth across the loom, very pleased with himself. His first production was meant to be woollen scarves for our children, but somehow they stretched into small rugs. He was thrilled. Now he's into cotton rugs and all over Thornhill there are small rainbows on the floor, woven by Tom.

The countryside still surrounds the house without interruption. It hasn't changed. The corn is as high, but the harvested hay bales, once square, are now rolled like giant shredded wheat biscuits. And bluebirds have come to share our land.

A few Februarys ago I put up two rectangular gray birdhouses high on metal poles and for the last two years we've had full occupancy in our tiny tenant houses of Thornhill. This is especially rewarding because the mild-mannered bluebird, a bird found only in North America, almost vanished, their nests invaded, their eggs punctured by the English sparrow and the aggressive starling. Now the bluebird is on the rise again, in part thanks to a neighbor Catharine Ballich who has settled almost 300 bluebird houses in our countryside. The small hole of the box can't be entered by starlings, the small floor plan is meant to discourage sparrows while the metal post is too slippery for climbing raccoons.

Their song is the most lyrical. And in late March the male bluebird starts establishing his territory, looks the field over, chooses a house. He sings with vibrant tones, hoping to entice his lady love. Once accepted, it is the female who makes the nest in April. I feel very close to these birds. I too moved into Thornhill in April, came to a house found solely by Tom, made more appealing by his concern for our children's lives. He knew

Thornhill first, but it is I, the mate seduced by his song, who has been feathering the nest ever since.

I've seen four bluebirds flying, like a Navy squadron, from our pear tree to the chestnut, the latest arrivals at Thornhill perching on the limbs of the oldest, for these two trees have been here long before we ever appeared. And they continue to give us gifts. Like the apple trees, legacies from the past.

The occasional year that I have missed the first spring bloom of the pear tree, white blossoms like a huge bridal bouquet, I've been desolate. I felt as if I were late for a family reunion. It may seem strange to miss the costuming of a tree that much, but it's all part of the cycle of Thornhill.

The chestnut spreads, the pear tree stretches. But in the fall the boughs of the pear tree cascade down, heavy with shiny green clusters of leaves, practically handing us its fruit. Harvesting the chestnuts is more difficult, the burrs housing the chestnuts spiky as baby porcupines. Both trees are so generous, yet so different. The pear, an import from France, seems more refined, while the rough chestnut is our American primitive.

When our children were younger, these trees were their eating clubs, how they entertained themselves and their friends after school. Shining the chestnuts against corduroy pants until they looked as polished as their Sunday shoes took a good part of an afternoon. And they carried pears, as well as apples, to their teachers.

When there's such an abundance, it's easier to share the wealth. And we still make pear pies. Although the taste is more textured, many think it is apple. But we know it's pear, and that's part of the pleasure, the surprise for guests. And now it's Albert who is shining chestnuts.

My gardens, obviously, give me great joy. And it's flattering. Flattering when the flowers I've planted fan out into a spectrum of color. I especially like to stand at one end of the perennial garden and look at its changing profile, its angles of green. It's by far the best view, this profile garden.

First are the jonquils and tulips, then the pink of June with peonies and roses against the deep blue of Japanese iris. In July I look through orange lilies at stalks of yellow yarrow. In August it is a potpourri of color like an an old-fashioned patchwork quilt, a mélange of veronica, coreopsis, and phlox of all shades. Then the garden slides into September with the reds of dahlias. This garden which started with two resident rosebushes has reached out on either side, stretched its wings, just as we have.

The house itself has matured. After all it is now 141 years old. And I know we have cared for it more, these thirty years, than any previous occupants, except the Quakers who built it. They built with hope, we continue with hope. As it was important to them, it has become important to us. It has become our life.

I was handed a package, thirty years ago, that I didn't really want to accept. But as in an arranged marriage, it is often after the wedding that you fall in love. We have made mistakes, but this is a forgiving house, a faithful house, always seeming to give us another chance, another spring.

I thought it presumptuous in those early years to give a small Quaker house a name, but giving a name to a house far off the road, high on a hill, is, I've discovered, easy identification. And in the country as the crow flies, addresses are often useless. Sometime the house name is better known than the owners. I've even received mail addressed to Mrs. Thornhill. And after all these years we have put up our first sign at the end of the road. In block letters, painted by Bill Pearson, our former fire chief, now maker of birdhouses, it says simply THORNHILL FARM.

By living at Thornhill we gave, or tried to give our children roots. Roots which they now wear loosely, living in other states, looking perhaps, as Todd says, for their own Thornhill. Maybe it's the aftereffects that make it all worth while, knowing that they *know* and remember, how the country smells after the first mown hay of summer, the early mist rising over the valley, the sounds of morning, and of night.

Looking back I wonder if it was I who needed Thornhill the most, although I certainly didn't realize it at first. It has, I'm sure, shaped me more than I have shaped it, giving me some kind of character, a strength and a background. Maybe it was I who needed a childhood house. And for thirty years I have been of Thornhill. It is the one place I always want to come home to, no matter where I've been. It is my passion and my pride.

In its unassuming settled way, it has sheltered all of us, shared our joys, helped hide our sometime sadnesses. And it is where we have all grown up. Without Thornhill our life, our family would have had a different rhythm. And we, I hope, have given the house reason. With grandchildren Thornhill is going into another generation, a second childhood. I couldn't ask for anything more. A new world, new discoveries, new wonders. "Come Albert, come look at this frog!"

# RECIPE INDEX